Selected Stories of
Mazo de la Roche

He had appeared in St. Loo a month before with a gun and two dogs, Boris and Nell, that never left his heels. He hired as a guide Léon Gosselin, the best chasseur in St. Loo, with the exception of Remi Leduc, landlord of "Le Chien Noir". These two hunted the country for many miles around but never remained away long. They would re-appear in the village when least expected and Léon intimated that it was for the sake of Cécile Racette that his patron sought civilization so frequently. That was the cause of Nazaire's bitterness.

Baptème! How he hated Magrath with his insolent smile and his big white teeth! For what had he come to St. Loo to bring coyness into the honest eyes of Cécile and jealousy into the heart

Printed and bound in Canada

CANADIAN SHORT STORY LIBRARY

Glenn Clever: General Editor

Lorraine McMullen
Donald Stephens
Peter Stich
Clara Thomas

© University of Ottawa Press, 1979.
ISBN-2-7603-4340-5

Selected Stories of
Mazo de la Roche

Edited and with an Introduction
by
Douglas Daymond

UNIVERSITY OF OTTAWA PRESS
Ottawa, Canada
1979

TABLE OF CONTENTS

Foreword

Remembering Mazo

In a Mississauga garden, at Clarkson, Ontario, next to a property where I grew up, "Woodlot", there was recently discovered and rescued from bulldozers, a diamond-shaped shale slab. On it was a brass plaque which read: "Bunty, 13½; Sam, 16½; Tam, 17. The virtues of man without his vices."

As I read about this, what a train of memories emerged! For I cannot think of the name "Bunty", the little black Scottie dog, without seeing the mistress who was ever beside him: the tall, gaunt auburn-haired woman, Mazo de la Roche. In her small brown screened-in summer cottage she was our neighbour for several months of every year, through the years 1926-32. Every morning she would walk through our woods on a path that led to the Clarkson store and post office — a milk pail in her hand and Bunty by her side. Always she would stop to talk to my mother, gathering mushrooms; or to my father, tending his rose bed or delphiniums. Sometimes she talked to me, the gawky teenager. I was definitely in awe of her as a coming Canadian novelist — and as a woman at that. Great!

At that time I was a young school girl with ambitions to be a writer myself. Mazo knew I was writing poetry, for my mother very likely was showing it to her. I had had published a happy little verse which began, I think, like this:

> Let me be common again
> And have common care
> For the way I walk down the street
> Run down a stair

What I was playing with was the subtlety of the English language — that difference between the phrase "the common man" (the everyday man) and "the common woman" (she's just common). To my surprise Mazo questioned the use of that phrase, "O to be common again". She took it in its strict Victorian sense; whereas I was already a twentieth century miss and savoured the non-pejorative "common man" and its reverbations with "Commonweal", "Commonwealth", and "hold in common."

I think I was too shy to question Mazo to her face. She was after all an important writer whose first novel, *Possession,* promised much for our literature. Moreover she was taking a kindly interest in my poetical attempts. She confessed that she also liked to write poetry and had indeed done so as a girl. But I could see that her orientation was, if not Victorian, then indeed Georgian. And certainly in her prose it was the work of Dickens and Hardy that had offered her the strongest inspiration. I also rejoiced in these novelists and though I was more drawn to Shaw (with his heretical ideas concerning language and the alphabet) and to James Joyce whose *Ulysses* was banned in Canada, (but which eventually I smuggled into the country from Paris, wrapped in my woollen underwear.) As well, the new women novelists, prose writers in England — Katherine Mansfield, Virginia Woolf, Dorothy Richardson, and the Parisian Gertrude Stein were beginning to fascinate me.

I could not talk about these to Mazo. Perhaps because I was too inhibited and self-conscious, perhaps because, although she seemed young and vibrant — tall, thin, nervous but with a tawny "Renny-the-Fox" gleam in her brown eyes — Mazo de la Roche was at the end of her forties when she began making her mark as a novelist. True, she deceived us about her age, and about her name (plain "Maisie Roche" at Newmarket school) but that did not trouble us. Was not her cousin, Caroline Clement, with whom she lived, a cousin also of Samuel Clemens (Mark Twain)? And I was deeply moved by Mazo's first publication, *Possession*. Already, as a devotee of Frederick Philip Grove and Martha Ostenso, I felt that realism was the necessary ingredient for developing a Canadian Literature. Mazo, I believed, had the power within her to write the great Canadian novel which would forego sentimental romance and would be concerned with the way ordinary people really lived, worked, loved, and hated. I too was feeling a growing sympathy for the native people, the berry pickers who lived on the fringes of white society in Ontario's thriving fruitland. And Mazo's picture of their misery was not wholly lost in her next and prizewinning novel, *Jalna*. True, it dealt with Ontario's recent past, its settlements of English landed gentry who (like my father's relatives at Cooksville, the Parkers) became gentlemen farmers, orchardists, horse lovers. It was fair enough, I thought, that Mazo's personal knowledge of such people in the New Market and Lake Simcoe area was 'meat' for a Canadian novel.

But Mazo and Caroline were financially insecure. Their childhood and girlhood were subject to many changes of milieu: from Newmarket to Toronto to Galt and back to several different areas of Toronto. Her father was an uncertain breadwinner who eventually disappeared, leaving his languid gentlewoman of a wife at the mercy of relatives. The two girls must have sought surcease, as the Bronte sisters did, in the world of a fantasy. They wrote and acted out plays. By the time of their adulthood it was clear that Mazo could only be well and stable if she was writing. Caroline determined to help her by training as a secretary and getting a job at the Ontario Parliament buildings in Toronto. All summer one would see her, early morning, walking through our woods to the Clarkson railway station and the Commuters' train. Every evening she returned to the supper prepared by Mazo. And after the meal they would sit on their screened-in verandah, listening to the whip-poor-will and to "today's chapter" which Mazo read aloud for Caroline's critical ear.

And what a contrast they were! Mazo lanky, awkward, striding like a man; Caroline petite and delicate as Dresden china, with silver-blonde hair and pale blue eyes. Her accent, we felt, was a bit affected. By that we meant, "limitation English." But we saw the relationship of the two women as most rewarding. It seemed a wonderful way for a woman writer to follow her career in those days of no Canada Council, no developed CBC. We participated, my young friends and I, in the frantic excitement that was generated in our household when Mazo confided to my mother, Florence Livesay, that she was at the top of the list for receiving the $10,000 *Atlantic Monthly* novel award. Mazo was so nervous about it that she and Caroline disappeared into a Toronto apartment while they waited it out.

What did that prize mean? An end to poverty, a chance to travel, freedom to write as one pleased ... or was that to be? Alas, I remember how the publishers then harried Mazo. They did not want her to write of the down-and-outs, the characters she knew that reminded her of Dickens, those disinherited whom she had described in *Possession* and *Delight*. No, she must stay with 'the good thing', popular acclaim for *Jalna,* popular demand for more and more about the Whiteoaks family.

And so it was. Mazo was seduced into writing for a living; and quite a luxurious living it became. Yet all the while, I am sure, she was yearning to be known for her other-than-Jalna writing: *Portrait of a Dog* ("Bunty"), her novels about children — which she began to write after she had adopted two! She did manage to swing back with the novel *Growth of a Man,* based on the early struggles of her cousin, H. R. MacMillan. It was scarcely noticed and has never been reprinted. She often spoke of her love for the short story form and we noted that unlike Ethel Wilson, who began writing short stories but was told she must make them into novels, Mazo saw the broader prospect first. Hardy and Dickens remained her heroes. It is thus interesting to see what the present much needed collection of short stories reveals about this remarkable Canadian woman.

Dorothy LIVESAY

Summer, 1979
St. John's College, Winnipeg.

Introduction

Although Mazo de la Roche (1879-1961) was among Canada's most popular and prolific writers in the first half of this century, the extent and variety of her contribution to Canadian literature have not been widely acknowledged in contemporary criticism. A sensitive and imaginative writer with an aptitude for creating vital characters, a wide range of settings, lively dialogue and dramatic incident, she produced a substantial and significant body of work which achieved international recognition and admiration. Although her first book, *Explorers of the Dawn* (1922), a collection of inter-related stories, did not appear until she was more than forty years old, she wrote a surprising number of works in a variety of genres including twenty-three novels, more than fifty short stories, a history, three biographical works, and several plays and tales for children.

During her lifetime, the chronicles of Jalna, the most successful family chronicle in Canadian literature, sold more than nine million copies in one hundred and ninety-three English editions and ninety-two foreign editions. The success of these novels made her one of the most popular and widely-read novelists in the history of Canadian literature; it also overshadowed much of the remainder of her writing,[1] in particular, her numerous short stories. These stories provide ample evidence that her imagination was not restricted to the world of the Whiteoak family but rather that her talent consistently, and often very effectively, expressed itself outside that world. They reveal, moreover, essential characteristics of all her writing and suggest that her accomplishment should not be judged and cannot be properly understood solely in terms of the Jalna novels.

De la Roche's career as a writer began in 1902 when she published "The Thief of St. Loo", the first of a series of six loosely related short stories set in St. Loo, an imaginary French-Canadian village. When she first achieved widespread recognition with *Jalna* (1927), she had already published more than a dozen stories, several

---

[1] Among those novels which have been overshadowed are *Possession* (1923), *Lark Ascending* (1932), *Growth of a Man* (1938), *The Two Saplings* (1942) and *A Boy In The House* (1952).

of which were collected into *Explorers of the Dawn*.[2] From 1927 until the time of her death she wrote more than three dozen stories including two later collections, *The Sacred Bullock and Other Stories* (1938) and *A Boy in the House and Other Stories* (1952). Individual stories appeared in a variety of Canadian, American and English publications: *Munsey's Magazine, The Canadian Magazine, Harper's Bazaar, The Atlantic Monthly, Maclean's Magazine* and *The London Mercury*.

Together with Martha Ostenso, Robert Stead, Frederick Philip Grove, Raymond Knister and Morley Callaghan, de la Roche contributed to the development of realism in Canadian fiction during the early decades of this century. In her short stories as well as in novels such as *Possession* (1923)[3] and *Delight* (1926), she challenged prevailing fashions in Canadian writing and her work was almost immediately identified with "the new realism."[4] In 1927, the year that *Jalna* was awarded the ten thousand dollar first prize in the Atlantic-Little Brown fiction contest, Lorne Pierce wrote that she had "risen to pre-eminence"[5] among her contemporaries, and *The Canadian Forum* acknowledged that she had been unjustly ignored:

> Once again a Canadian novelist has had to await recognition abroad in order to win appreciation at home.... It must be discouraging for an author, conscious of her own purposes, to find herself carelessly classed with the novel-smiths, who turns out easy and imitative tales calculated to attract readers of popular fiction and to win a quick return in royalties. That was largely the fate of Miss de la Roche until *Jalna* opened the eyes of the average Canadian to the fact that she possesses distinctive qualities as a writer.[6]

In the years that followed *Jalna,* de la Roche was regarded by many as a leader in the evolution of Canadian fiction:

> The flurry caused by a new book of hers comes from people who though they may neither enjoy nor approve her work, yet feel that what

---

[2] Since many of de la Roche's manuscripts are not dated and provide inadequate information about place of publication, the exact number of short stories which were published during this period and thereafter is not entirely clear. Her cousin and lifelong companion and secretary, Caroline Clement, believed that all de la Roche's stories were published; however, a close study of various periodical indexes and correspondence with several journals and magazines suggests that this is unlikely.

[3] V. B. RHODENIZER, *A Handbook of Canadian Literature* (Ottawa: Graphic Publishers, 1930), p. 106. Rhodenizer described *Possession* as "an excellent realistic Canadian novel."

[4] J. D. LOGAN and D. G. FRENCH, *Highways of Canadian Literature* (Toronto: McClelland, 1934), p. 312.

[5] Lorne PIERCE, *An Outline of Canadian Literature* (Toronto: Ryerson Press, 1927), p. 44.

[6] J. F. WHITE, "Mazo de la Roche," *The Canadian Forum*, VII (May, 1927), pp. 227-228.

she may be doing next is a thing of definite importance to Canadian literature.... While there is Mazo de la Roche, there is hope.[7]

De la Roche's stories most often represent a mixture of realism with romance, sentimentalism and melodrama. Frequently she combines realistic settings with strong characterization in which figures tend to expand into symbolic or psychological archetypes. The combination of these elements in her most successful stories exploits the impact of realism and the suggestive power of romance and strengthens the presentation of her most characteristic themes — instinct, repression, freedom and love.

In her short stories as in all her writing de la Roche reveals a substantial faith in instinct and a willingness to challenge the narrow code of conduct associated with Victorian morality and the Puritan conscience. At the same time, she seldom ignores the need for order and the importance of traditional morality. Strongly attracted to unrestrained indivduals who challenge convention and barren respectability in search for greater freedom and fulfillment, de la Roche also recognizes the destructive effects of uncontrolled individualism, the need for continuity and the value of "the persistence of the past into the future."[8] Many of her stories reveal some form of dialectic between individual freedom, instinct and spontaneity on the one hand and tradition, intellect and convention on the other hand. Figures who express the vital energy of nature are frequently juxtaposed to repressed and repressive individuals who cling to the official culture. The results of this opposition are often disruptive, violent and occasionally tragic, and de la Roche frequently focuses on man's capacity for selflessness, endurance and love as positive alternatives to the excesses created by the conflit between repressive convention and restrained individualism.

The stories in this collection are arranged in order of publication and provide an historical survey that reflects de la Roche's scope and development as a writer of short stories. They reveal significant features characteristic of almost all of her writing: humor, irony and gothicism. Following the pattern evident in the novels, many stories contain autobiographical elements suggesting the translation of private experience into fiction. The stories differ in tone and subject matter, but all bear the marks of a versatile and irrepressible storyteller. They range from a didactic tale of sin and repentance, a study of the emigrant experience in Canada and a symbolic

    [7] J. MOORE, "Canadian Writers of To-day," *The Canadian Forum*, XII (July, 1932), p. 380.
    [8] Mazo DE LA ROCHE, *Quebec: Historic Seaport* (London: Macmillan, 1946), p. 108.

dramatization of Christ-like love, to a gothic tale of revenge, an account of the clash of Old World and New World cultures and an ironic narrative of bitter family conflict reminiscent of the Whiteoak novels.

"The Son of a Miser" (1903) and "The Spirit of the Dance" (1910) are part of the series of six St. Loo stories written shortly after de la Roche began experimenting at the turn of the century with the short story form. In these stories, an imaginary village in Quebec is developed into a world with clearly defined landmarks and a precisely delineated social structure. De la Roche gives no explanation for her decision to use the French-Canadian setting in her autobiography,[9] but, in the years surrounding the turn of the century, fictional sketches of French-Canadian life with characters using dialect frequently appeared in Canadian magazines, and writers such as William Mc-Lennan, Edward William Thomson, and Duncan Campbell Scott published collections of stories set in French Canada.

The St. Loo stories are unequal in conception and execution and cannot be regarded as parts of a single narrative. Nevertheless, they offer early evidence of the gothic qualities apparent in many de la Roche stories and reveal her earliest treatment of the confrontation between energetic individualism and social convention. In "The Son of a Miser" (1903), Noel Caron threatens the traditional values of St. Loo represented by the priest who favours rational behavior, obedience, hard work and conformity to the official morality of the church. After years of poverty and repression enforced by his miserly father, Noel inherits sudden wealth and embarks on a career of reckless spending and extravagant living which offends the community and alienates the woman he loves. Eventually Noel repents, abandons his "wickedness" and accepts the priest's injunction "to gain respect by honest work." Despite the echoes of the parable of the prodigal son, Noel's quest for a more vital and free life is presented sympathetically, and the juxtaposition of "the thin gray Christ" and "a wild cherry tree" in the story's final paragraph seems intentionally ironic.

De la Roche's sympathy for the vital and instinctive elements in human nature pervades "The Spirit of the Dance" (1910), a gothic tale of fatal possession by the artistic imagination. Here, Louis de Valleau, a talented violinist, struggles against the well-intentioned but ultimately destructive efforts of his housekeeper and the local doctor to save him from himself. They identify his deteriorating health with the music of his Stradivarius, music which stirs a res-

---

[9] Mazo DE LA ROCHE, *Ringing the Changes* (London: Macmillan, 1957), p. 95.

ponsive spirit of joy and dance in his daughter Gabrielle. The inspiration for de Valleau's playing and his daughter's dancing is closely associated with nature, symbolized again by a tree, and the conclusion of the story suggests that imaginative energy and the artistic instinct are, like the vital forces of nature, both creative and destructive and cannot be suppressed.

The tension between individual freedom and traditional morality is also the source of dramatic conflict in several later stories including "A Word for Coffey" (1926). This story, presented as a first person account, describes the gradual deterioration and eventual suicide of Bill Coffey, a once vigorous and lively seadog suddenly confined within an atmosphere permeated by the Old Testament doctrines of judgment and punishment. Tormented by vivid and terrifying visions of life after death, Coffey loses his "triumphant look" and becomes the pathetic victim of guilt and fear.

The tension generated by conflicting points of view and patterns of behavior are explored again in two quite different stories of the clash of cultures — "Canadian Ida and English Nell" (1911) and "Quartet" (1930). In the former, a story which provided the general outline for *Delight* (1926), Nell, an English working girl, emigrates to Canada in search of her husband only to discover that he has married a Canadian with the expectation of sharing in the wealth she may inherit. By exploiting his guilt and their shared homesickness and disenchantment with the cold and joyless Canadian environment, Nell is reunited with her husband and her homeland. The story provides an interesting view of life in a turn of the century village and foreshadows de la Roche's treatment of the emigration theme in several of her later works.[10]

"Quartet" (1930), a story similar in its general outlines to the novel *Lark Ascending* (1932), also examines the clash of cultures. It describes a visit by David Behrens, a quiet stockbroker from Massachusetts, to the villa of Gaetano Rombarra of Naples. In a room filled with antique furniture and permeated by the atmosphere of the Old World, Behrens meets Rombarra's wife Alice, a woman whom Behrens had once loved. While Rombarra, unable to understand English, watches, Alice complains of his stupidity, denounces his immorality and expresses bitter discontent with her new life. The scene is tense as the layer of superficial cordiality among the characters threatens to dissolve, and Behrens struggles to understand his own confused emotions. Disenchanted and disturbed by the scarcely

---

[10] See *Delight* (1926), *Lark Ascending* (1932), *The Return of the Emigrant* (1929) and *The Building of Jalna* (1944).

suppressed hatred and suffering he witnesses, Behrens withdraws with a new awareness of something decadent and potentially violent lurking behind the apparent beauty, vitality and sophistication he has previously identified with the Old World.

"Quartet" is one of several stories written after 1929 reflecting de la Roche's imaginative responses to the Old World. In the winter of 1929 she embarked on her first transatlantic crossing and celebrated her fiftieth birthday in Taormina, Sicily. During the next ten years, she made her home in England and travelled extensively in Europe. Many of the stories written during this period use English or European settings. "Old Reynard in Springtime", an example of de la Roche's conversion of a personal experience into fiction, is a first-person account of a fox-hunt set in the Malvern region of England where de la Roche settled in 1934. The hunt is treated as a ritual with a long tradition, and the fox's dramatic struggle for survival is seen as a contest in which the true adversary is Fate. The fox is clever, strong, graceful and "wholly self-contained," and the first-person narrator sympathizes with his desperate struggle for survival and keenly desires his escape. On the other hand, she shares something of the detached and resigned outlook expressed by the old man with whom she watches the hunt. Ultimately this stoic acceptance of life as tragic is balanced by a sensitive emotional response to the beauty of the world.

Few of de la Roche's stories entirely ignore either the beauty of the world or the pain associated with human experience and human weakness. "Portrait of a Wife" (1928), "The Cure" (1928) and "The Celebration" suggest a bleak view of mankind's greed, selfishness and envy. Each story deals with a failure of love and the often bitter desire for vengeance which so frequently results from such a failure. "The Cure", the story chosen by Raymond Knister for his landmark collection, *Canadian Short Stories* (1928), portrays the pathetic efforts of an alcoholic to resist his nephews' attempts to displace him as the head of the family business. "The Celebration" dramatizes the gradual disintegration into recrimination and hatred which follows when one member of a family achieves sudden wealth. The selfish and divisive wrangling in this story is ironically counter-pointed to the awareness of the peaceful quiet of the funeral parlour below the Evans family's apartment. "Portrait of a Wife" is a macabre tale of an artist hired by a dying woman who wishes to present her estranged and faithless husband with an image of herself so horrifying in its reflection of hatred and despair that he will be destroyed with remorse. This gothic tale of revenge from beyond the grave also offers some interesting and perhaps autobiographical commentary on an artistic imagination whose strength lies in depicting "cruelty and melancholy".

In contrast to these accounts of malice, envy, revenge and selfishness, "Good Friday" (1927) acknowledges man's need for freedom and affirms his capacity for sacrificial love in a world which is often violent, unpredictable and indifferent to the fate of the individual. Bull Evans' Christ-like compassion for his son and Jenny's patience and fidelity contrast sharply with the scenes suggesting man's essential loneliness and his capacity for violence and injustice. Here, freedom is defined not in terms of personal fulfillment but as a surrender to love.

Love is a prominent theme in several of these stories including those which focus on animals, either domestic or wild. The love of and interest in animals are prominent features of much of de la Roche's writing,[11] and animals are used repeatedly in plotting, characterization and as a source of imagery. Although de la Roche is inclined to sentimentalize and anthropomorphize her animals, her recognition of a Darwinistic struggle for survival underlies much of her work. She also emphasizes the role of instinct in animal behavior and the contrasts between animals and men, contrasts which frequently suggest a preference for the world of nature. Above all, her stories of animals focus attention on qualities and characteristics de la Roche valued wherever she found them — generosity, bravery, beauty, spontaneity and loyalty.

"Come Fly With Me" (1944) dramatizes the experience of two swallows during a Canadian summer. Much of the effectiveness of this story is the result of several rich passages of natural description and the careful contrasts between images of nature and images of civilization. At the centre of the narrative is an acknowledgement of the freedom, beauty and vital energy of the natural world and the elemental and amoral forces which govern it. Instinct guides the swallows and is identified with the rhythmic balance between creation and destruction which characterizes the natural world.

Some of de la Roche's most successful short stories appeared in *The Sacred Bullock And Other Stories* (1939), a collection which has been described as one of the five respectable books of short stories published in Canada between 1920 and 1940.[12] Varying widely

[11] Desmond PACEY, "Introduction" to *A Book of Canadian Stories* (Toronto: Ryerson, 1947), pp. XXVI-XXVII. Pacey believed that de la Roche's animal stories surpassed the work of any of the followers of Charles G. D. Roberts.

[12] Desmond PACEY, "Fiction 1920-1940," in C. F. KLINCK, ed., *Literary History of Canada* (Toronto: University of Toronto Press, 1966), pp. 674-675.

in tone and complexity, the stories from that collection deal with animals and the interaction between animals and humans. Once again the primitive impulses underlying both animal and human behavior are a major concern. Two stories from that collection, "Ninth Life" (1937) and "The Sacred Bullock" (1938), are particularly effective. "Ninth Life" describes a cat's ordeal as she struggles to reach her home after being abandoned by her owners. During the journey, her various encounters with men and animals focus attention on the laws of nature and man's blindness to the powerful instincts governing the animal world. These preoccupations are more forcefully developed in "The Sacred Bullock."

"The Sacred Bullock" is among de la Roche's most intricate and consciously symbolic stories. Carefully structured and tightly controlled, it invokes ritualistic and mythical associations as it moves with increasing intensity and terrifying predictability to its tragic conclusion. "The Sacred Bullock" provides further evidence of de la Roche's distrust of the repressive aspects of western civilization and her conviction that spontaneous and irrational energies must be acknowledged and allowed some creative release if they are not to result in violence and destruction. The pagan ritual, which is associated with youth, spontaneous joy, music, dance and the celebration of vitality and fertility, contrasts sharply here with the cloistered and barren existence of the monks who once inhabited the ruins where the key scenes of the story are enacted. Davey's instinctive love for Glennys contrasts with her fearful and faltering response. She is capable of the maternal affection which she shows to the lamb, but the more primitive aspects of Davey's love fill her with terror. She gives him gifts, works for him and experiences deep emotion in his presence, but she rejects his invitations to a more intimate relationship. Although she caresses the bullock and admires his beauty and vitality, she cannot accept the principle he represents. Davey, like the white bullock, is a victim of the fear of the irrational and instinctive and of the repression and self-destructive violence to which such fears lead. Originally published in 1938, "The Sacred Bullock" quite appropriately expresses an ominous version of the fate of western civilization.

The stories collected here reveal de la Roche's preoccupation with instinctive forces, her sense of the unpredictable nature of human experience and her ironic awareness of the disproportion between man's naive efforts to design his life and the fitful desires, rival ambitions and haphazard events that so often combine to frustrate those efforts. She acknowledges the uncertain, chaotic and potentially tragic nature of much of our experience yet manages to affirm individual freedom and self-sacrifice and to celebrate energetically the potential variety, richness and beauty of man and nature. Few of her stories ignore suffering and man's capacity for greed, ignorance, hatred and selfishness. On the other hand, few fail to offer a sensitive appreciation for the natural world and an admiration for man's capacity for endurance and love. This selection suggests the range and variety of Mazo de la Roche's stories and offers a clearer perception of her unique blend of imaginative energy and sensitive awareness. These stories provide interesting variations on themes, characters and dramatic situations representative of all her writing, and they contribute to a clearer perception and a fuller appreciation of her contribution to Canadian literature and, in particular, the Canadian short story.

The Son of a Miser

How Noel Caron, of St. Loo,
Proved that he Was no Pinchpenny

I.

Noel sat in his own house alone for the first time. It was very still. Outside, the world lay muffled in a fresh fall of snow. Inside, the pine knot smoldered stealthily, as if reluctant to break the hush. Noel sat by the fire in his father's chair, trying to get used to things.

First, there was the chair itself — he must get used to it. He looked at his own boy's hands lying on its worn arms, and it seemed to him that they must wither and turn gray from the association. He thought of those other hands that had rested there so many years; perhaps for to-night, this first night, he would feel more at ease somewhere else.

In the middle of the room there were four chairs turned together, facing, as for some purpose. Their position seemed a menace to the boy, as if they had consciously withdrawn from him. He strode over noisily — how his footsteps echoed! — and displaced them, carrying one to the fireside for use. There were some droppings of wax on its seat. Noel scratched them off with his finger-nail and let them fall to the fire, where they sputtered a moment and went out. He sat down and stretched his feet toward the warmth.

Where did he leave off? Oh, yes, the chair — *eh bien,* he would get used to that very soon. Then there was the house, which was his; and the mill and its profits, which belonged to him — to him, Noel Caron, who had never had two sous to rub together! Noel Caron, son of a miser — ah, that was what hurt — a family of misers, the worst-hated people in St. Loo! How they had pinched, and saved, and worried every coin! And now they were gone, and it all belonged to him!

A new phase of life had been presented to him; the right to say: "This is mine — I will do that." He looked about the bare room, and longed for some way to prove his power.

Because he had been loyal and had uttered no complaints, people thought that he would follow in his father's steps. Only yesterday, he had heard M. Avern, the *ovocat,* whisper to Dr. Girard:

"*Alors,* I suppose this young one will do like the rest — squeeze every sou before he parts with it, add his share to the pile, then die and leave it to the next, as old Caron to-day!"

The doctor had added fervently:

"Heaven pity the girl young Noel marries, if he is to be like that also! They say he has a fancy for Tetrault's Laure."

Then, as *monsieur le curé* was standing in the doorway that night, he had turned earnestly and said:

"Be wise, my son, and lay not up for yourself treasure on earth, where it profits nothing, but in heaven, where the saints will guard it for you!"

He could have struck the kind *curé. Sacré!* Did they think him a fool? He kicked at the pine knot, and it flickered faintly. If they only knew how he loathed this life of grasping! Had not he sat with his father in the dark for the cost of a candle? Had not his second slice of bread been grudged him, when his boy's appetite craved meat? Had he not been denied the things that boys most prize — snowshoes, skates, good clothes? And later, had he not done the work of two at the mill for nothing? And they thought he liked it! All but Laure — she knew, she knew!

He would show them how to spend, even he, Noel Caron, son of old Caron, the miller, whom the boys called Pinchpenny! He wondered how much that leather bag contained. More than once he had lain in bed and watched his father count its contents stealthily, making little towers of battered coins and moving them about with his bony fingers, as in some covert game. Well, it was his turn to play the game now, and the stakes would be high, *pardieu!*

By the light of a candle he raised a loose board in the flooring and withdrew his father's hoard. He emptied it on the table — musty coppers, tarnished silver, and moldy gold, his heritage lay heaped before him. To the boy, it was full of stupendous possibilities. As he stared at it, the slight lines about his mouth appeared more distinct, he looked older.

He must count it carefully — yes, but first more light. One candle for Noel Caron? Not much! In the dresser there were four. He placed them together in a cup, and set them burning. Now more wood on the fire! He brought his arms full from the shed, an heaped it on the hearth. A small flask of brandy used during his father's sickness caught his eye. He poured it into a glass, and, placing it on the table with guilty elation, sat down to count.

For hours there was no sound but the handling of money. The room grew hot; the frost began to melt on the pane; Noel stretched himself and took a gulp of the brandy. There were one thousand dollars.

Blisters came out on that side of the table nearest the fire; the cameo head was quite spoiled; Noel pulled off his coat and swallowed half the brandy that remained in the glass. There were three thousand dollars.

The fire had crumbled into downy ashes; little puddles of water dripped from the window-sill; Noel finished the brandy and rose unsteadily. There were five thousand and eighty dollars in all.

"Five thousand and eighty!" he laughed. "I'll show them how to spend! I'll let the brakes go loose! The *curé* shall be sorry that he spoke!" He felt his way along the wall. "Five thousand dollars — how it gets dark! — five thousand — what was it? Ah, diamonds for Laure's hair — how they'll shine! They'll not call me Pinchpenny then. I'll have a tall silk hat — and Laure — I'll have her, too!" He fell across the bed face downward.

Three hours later the curtain of frost was drawn once more across the window pane, and the white daylight, filtering through it, fell on Noel, asleep, and on his fortune, scattered over the table and the floor.

II.

Din, din, din, din! went the hammer. Adolphe, in the mill, was picking the stones. Din, din, din, din! So white were his hands and his hair and his coat from the meal, and so gray were they from specks of stone, and so intent was he upon his work, that he might have been a stone man just coming to life, or a live man just turning to stone.

When his new master called him, he did not hear. Noel came and touched him on the arm.

"At work as usual, I see, Adolphe," he said somewhat diffidently, because of their new relations. They had been fellow-workmen, fellow-slaves; now it was master to man.

Adolphe nodded non-committally.

"Do you think," went on Noel, "that you could make the work go without me, just for once, this morning, 'Dolphe? I have important things to do."

The hammer stopped, and Adolphe drew one gray forefinger meditatively across his lips.

"I shall try," he grunted.

"You'll not forget the pea-meal for Ma'am' Trudeau, nor the corn for Jo Duval?"

"I will do as you say."

"That's good," said Noel, gaining confidence. "You can do yourself no harm by pleasing me!" Then, in a burst of elation, he dropped a half dollar, over Adolphe's shoulder to his knees. "Here, take that, *mon vieux,* and drink the health of the new miller!" And as he reached the door he flung back: "You'll find he's no Pinchpenny, him!"

Adolphe delicately poised the coin on the tips of his thumb and two first fingers, and addressed it thus:

"He says, 'Good,' does he? And me also, I say, 'Good.' If he keeps on like this, I shall own a mill myself, one day." And he turned to stone again.

Noel strode through the crunching snow to the house of Brazeau, the horsedealer. Brazeau was a shrewd fat man.

"*Bon jour,* miller," he said with his sleek smile. "I hope it goes well with you since the departure of your lamented father."

"You had no love for my father," said Noel, with a curt gesture of dismissal. "I am here concerning a horse. Have you still that tall black mare you brought from Montreal?"

"*Mais oui,* miller," chuckled Brazeau with raised eyebrows. "I have had hope to sell her to M. Landry, but still —"

"How does she sell, then?"

"An even hundred, miller."

Noel laughed shortly, as at some inward joke.

"Lead her around," he said, smiling. "I'm getting rid of my treasure on earth."

But not till the honest Brazeau saw the money with his own fat eyes would he clinch the bargain; then one hundred dollars in musty coins changed hands, and the black mare, shimmering like satin, was transferred to her new master.

"How is she named, Brazeau?"

"La Joie."

"La Joie! That's good. A pretty name," laughed Noel, and he rode away.

"It was a waste of money," mused Brazeau, following him with his eyes. "But it is excellent for the trade!"

III.

As he drew nearer to the home of Laure, Noel became more joyously excited. He sang softly to himself:

> *C'est la belle Françoise, lon, gai,*
> *C'est la belle Françoise,*
> *Qui veut s'y marier, ma luron, lurette,*
> *Qui veut s'y marier, ma luron, luré —*

and swayed his body to the tune. He pulled off his cap and rode bareheaded. He kissed the mare's pricked ears.

"Ah, my little, little love," he whispered to her, "do you know where we go? We go for Laure, the angel Laure! She'll sit on your back, *ma belle,* with me! We'll let the bridle loose, La Joie, and gallop fifty thousand miles through paradise!"

A handful of snow caught his ear. The horse shied. He turned in the saddle and saw Julie Ouellette laughing as she swept her doorstep.

"Where goes the little miller?" she cried. "How we are brave and gay! Ah, Noel" — clasping her hands — "you look like a *grand seigneur,* only more handsome! I wish I had your fine red lips!"

He urged the mare suddenly toward her.

"You may, Julie! You may!" he cried impulsively.

She ran to her doorway screaming. When she reached it she called back:

"Tell me in truth, Noel, where go you?"

He pointed with his whip to the cottage of the Tetraults. Julie thrust out her lips scornfully.

"That girl? She is fat, like a sack of your own meal!" She swept viciously.

"She is jealous," Noel said to himself. "Jealous for me!" His eyes danced. *"Au revoir,* Julie!" he cried. "If you see diamonds on the sack of meal, be not surprised!" Then: "Julie, your hair is very red, like old Pelletier's nose!" And he galloped away in a whirl of snow to the house of Laure.

Without dismounting, he tapped with his whip on the door. Laure opened it. She caught her breath for a moment as she faced the frosty air. She caught it again, more sharply, when she beheld Noel on horseback. His eyes smiled expectantly at her.

"Noel, explain!"

"Come closer, then — here, to my stirrup!"

She ran to his side, hugging herself because of the cold. He drew off his mitt and touched her cheek with his fingers; but he delayed the joyous moment.

"Explain!" she said again.

"Laure, the eyes of La Joie are black, is it not so?"

"Mais oui, they are black. What then?"

"Laure, they are all pale compared with yours."

"Fie, Noel!"

"Laure, the frost is white, is it not so?"

"Ma foi, oui."

"Laure, I can see a bit of your neck, and it's white like the frost."

She caught her dress at the throat and broke out angrily:

"What a fine fool is this! He speaks in riddles of black and white, when I would have him talk sense! For shame! Your father was buried yesterday. Have you forgotten that?"

He sprang to the ground beside her.

"Tiens, my Laure, you do not understand. He is gone, I know. He was very old. What was his is mine. They call us misers here. I want to make them lie! I'm going to spend my father's money fast, fast — and on you, Laure! We'll buy bangles for your wrists, and diamonds for your ears, and white kid shoes! I go to sow the wind

that the *curé* speaks about! I paid a hundred dollars for La Joie an hour ago!"

It was as if he had struck her. She put her hands against his breast and thrust him off.

"Ingrate! You come to me to help you in your wickedness? You think I have a desire to throw your father's savings in the dirt?"

"I do it but to right myself."

"I am to be made a doll, then, in order that St. Loo shall lie? Don't speak to me!"

"Thousand devils! You refuse?"

"I refuse, and I refuse, and I refuse!"

"*Bien!* There is one who will not refuse!"

"Go to her, then! Ah, Noel, you break me the heart!"

She threw her apron over her head and ran sobbing into the house.

IV.

A group of men stood talking before the post-office: the *curé*, Brazeau, the horse-dealer, and Tetrault, the father of Laure. Brazeau had just told of the purchase of La Joie by Noel Caron.

"One hundred dollars for a horse!" said Tetrault. "It is infamous!"

The *curé* also was amazed, and somewhat puzzled. He questioned Brazeau closely. For what purpose had Noel bought the mare?

"He said something about a treasure on earth, *m'sieu'*," said Brazeau importantly, "but I could get no more. He has a close mouth, that boy!"

As they stood thus in earnest conversation, they were suddenly disturbed by the shrill cheering of children and the yelp of dogs. Brazeau was the first to discover the cause.

"*Voilà, m'sieu'*," he chuckled, "here he comes himself at full gallop!"

La Joie, at first sight, seemed to be running away; but if so, it gave her rider small concern, and she who sat before him cared still less. Noel's cap was gone, and Julie's red hair was blown across his face.

The *curé* ran forward and raised his hand.

"Stop!" he ordered.

They passed so close to him that he was spattered with snow from the mare's hoofs.

"La Joie has the bit in her teeth!" yelled Noel. "I'm getting my money's worth, Brazeau! The treasure on earth —"

His voice was lost in the wind, and in a moment more they had vanished behind a bend of the road. Brazeau and Tetrault turned to the *curé* with gaping mouths. The priest's face was set and stern.

"My children," he said, "I forbid any of you who are in trade to sell anything to Noel Caron above the value of one dollar. Let every one be told. You did wrong to sell him that horse, Brazeau. He has flung my counsel in my teeth. He must be punished. Tetrault, forbid your girl to speak to him. Let her show her disapproval by her silence!"

There was dull anger and disappointment in the eyes of Tetrault. He had had hopes concerning Noel and Laure.

V.

As the good *curé* had commanded, so it was done. When Noel went to the shop of Martel, the tailor, to order a suit, he was refused.

"I have nothing against you, miller," said Martel, "but *m'sieu' le curé* has forbidden it expressly. 'Nothing above the value of one dollar to Noel Caron,' he says. I am sorry, but I cannot make a suit for one dollar."

Noel looked not ill-pleased.

"Eh bien," he said, "I shall buy in St. Michel. Without doubt, I shall be well suited there. But you lose a good customer, Martel!"

Three days later he appeared in St. Loo wearing a long black coat, a tall silk hat — *chapeau de castor* — and yellow gloves. Simultaneously, Julie Ouellette flaunted a scarlet cloak. Noel's thoughts had been of Laure when he purchased it, and the scarlet, with Julie's red hair, was a veritable curse in color. As for Laure, she wept fresh tears at each new folly, and prayed in secret for him; but when they met, her eyes avoided his.

Noel gave up working in the mill, and devoted himself assiduously to the spending of his money. Not only did he deck himself with incongruous finery, but he heaped it on his friends, the Gosselin brothers. It was a sight to be remembered when, one saints' day, the three walked arm in arm about the village dressed alike in coonskin coats and tall silk hats.

Each succeeding week young Caron became more reckless. His house was the scene of wild carousing. Once, for a wager, he mounted La Joie at midnight and galloped to the highest peak of the Pointe des Rochers, blindfold.

On the following Sunday Julie Ouellette appeared at mass with diamonds in her ears. The *curé* observed a stir among the women of the church, and he soon perceived that the girl's finery was the cause. He fixed her with his eye and beckoned sternly. She came forward, flushed and trembling.

"Julie Ouellette," he commanded, pointing an accusing finger at the jewels, "take off those cursed baubles from your ears, and put them out of sight!"

She obeyed, weeping.

"Now kneel where you are, and remain so. Pray for your sins!"

He turned once more to the altar.

That was the last that was seen of Julie's diamonds.

So the spring came, and as the snow melted, so melted the contents of the leather bag. The money that had been hoarded in deprivation, in penury, in despicable meanness, was recklessly wasted in luxury, in wild living, in misplaced generosities.

The climax came when Noel and Henri Gosselin went to Montreal. They were absent a month. No one knew what occurred there, but Henri was brought home sick, and two days after their arrival Noel sold La Joie to Brazeau for fifty dollars. Later, it became known that he could not settle his accounts at the Black Dog, the village hotel. The habitants of St. Loo laughed in their sleeves. They waited with self-righteous smiles to see the end. And Noel faced the fact that a spendthrift, when his money is gone, receives no more commendation than a miser.

He stood in his doorway one night, facing this fact and the blackness outside. Yesterday the ground had been white, but a warm rain had fallen all day, and to-night all that remained of the snow lay in a few soiled and sunken heaps in sheltered spots. Here yesterday and gone to-day — "like my money!"

From where he stood he could see the yellow blur of a light in the mill. Adolphe was at work picking the stones for the next day's grinding. The tap of the hammer came insistently through the open door — din, din, din, din! It grated on Noel's ears with its song of ceaseless industry. What a poor fellow was 'Dolphe! Always slavishly at work. And for what? Had he any ambitions, Noel wondered? He made up his mind to call him in on his way home and talk to him. He felt lonely to-night; and he used to like Adolphe, when he was a boy — six months ago.

Presently the light went out, the key turned in the mill door, and Adolphe's gray figure melted into the fog.

"*Hé*, Adolphe! *Holà!*" called Noel.

Adolphe came slowly; he stood in the strip of light that fell from the door, looking up in silent inquiry.

"I never see you now, Adolphe, you work so hard. Will you come in?"

"Me? Oh, I am not enough clean! My feet are mud, my coat is meal. They say you have bought velvet chairs."

Noel gripped the man's arm and dragged him in.

"Yes, they say, and they say, and they say too much in St. Loo!" He pushed Adolphe into a chair. "It takes little enough to make them talk!"

"Little enough!" repeated Adolphe. "Do you call this little?" He looked about the room, whose gaudy pictures matched ill with its rain-stained walls.

"I call it so little," said Noel, "that I would like to wake up some day and find it gone. I can't think in this room, 'Dolphe. I used to dream dreams here — such foolish things — but *dieu,* I'd like to dream them all again!" There was silence for a moment, then he asked suddenly: "Have you dreams sometimes, Adolphe?"

"*Mais oui,* I have dreams." He laughed his dry laugh. "I was coming to that. One of my dreams concerns you. It is that I wish to buy the mill."

"To buy the mill? You?"

So this was why he worked so hard!

"It is that. I have six hundred dollars to give you, in cash. I will pay the rest off as I can, if you will permit me. Of what value is the mill to you? Its little profits are as nothing. It would mean much to me."

"If this man knew," thought Noel, "that I have only seven dollars in the world and owe it ten times over!" He said: "Without doubt, then, *mon beau,* there is some other dream behind all this? Give me her name. Is it Minette Pruneau, or the fat-cheeked Anne?"

"It is neither of these," said Adolphe solemnly. "Guess again."

"The milliner? But no, she goes with Honoré Roy. I have it, then — the Widow Potvin and her cow!"

"It is none of these," said Adolphe serenely. "It is Tetrault's Laure. She is a pious girl, and her father owns five cows."

Noel put his hand suddenly before his eyes, as if he found the light too strong.

"Bien — of course," he said slowly. "I had not thought. It is all arranged? And Laure?" His voice broke.

Adolphe turned up his palms deprecatingly.

"Not yet," he said. "I have not spoken. There will be no difficulties. It will be time when I have bought the mill."

"Ah, yes," said Noel. "It will be time — then."

A silence fell between them; then Adolphe, vaguely conscious of a subtle change in the other's attitude toward him, rose to go. Noel lighted him to the door without speaking.

"You will think of what I have said, miller?" the man ventured, as he reached the bottom step. "You know me. When I say I pay, I pay. I will work these to the bone to do it." He held up his ten gray fingers, already bent with work.

Noel nodded dispassionately. He had not heard what he said.

He waited till he heard the suck of Adolphe's sabots in the muddy road. Then he closed the door and bolted it. His face was tense like that of a child who strives to keep from violent crying. He sat down by the table and buried his head in his arms.

VI.

In the church of St. Bazile the people were on their knees. The sonorous voice of *monsieur le curé* intoned the sacred mass. A breath of incense floated down the aisle. The hearts of all were lifted, for this was Easter Day.

In the front seat knelt Laure, her eyes fixed on the lighted altar, her thoughts fixed on that which was forbidden. She was recalling other Sundays when she used to steal a sidelong glance across the church and see his dark head bent and his dark eyes seeking hers. Now he knelt there no more.

The church door opened, and a step came up the aisle. She heard a sharp intaking of breath throughout the church; then he passed close beside her and stopped at the chancel steps.

He wore his threadbare jersey and worn suit of six months before, which, because he had so developed since that time, would barely meet across his wellset frame. His long limbs protruded from their garments most uncouthly. He carried in one hand a leather bag, and in his arms his coonskin coat, his otter cap, his tall silk hat, and his silver-mounted riding crop. These things he laid on the chancel steps and knelt beside them, his eyes intently on the *curé's* face. The priest came to him.

"My son!"

Noel spoke then in a clear voice.

"Father, forgive me! I have been a beast! I waste my father's money — I insult the Holy Church — I laugh — I drink and gamble — I make myself more filthy than the brutes — for what? Because that the people of St. Loo have called me miser! At first I only think to spend a little, but they stare and talk, and then the drink gets in my head, and *voilà,* I go loose! But last night I waken up. I determine to confess before everybody. I want just one chance — to begin again! My money is gone; I have but these things here, my coat, my hat, my jewelry, in this bag — take them from me — they are a curse! I am Noel Caron, the miller!"

His face glowed in the ardor of his renunciation. She who knelt in the front seat thought he had never looked so fine.

"My child," said the *curé* tenderly, "you have been evil, it is true, but you have a long life in which to gain respect by honest work. Yours is a strong body, and it holds a strong nature. Work hard, for it is honest toil that tames that which is brute in man. You are forgiven. And if there are some among us who have urged you to do wrong, let them to their knees now, for their sin is no slight one."

He turned then to the altar.

It was with a free heart that Noel stepped out into the warm spring air. He sniffed it as a dog does. He was glad he had confessed on Easter day. He, too, had risen.

Where his road turned down a steep hill to the town, there was a little wayside Calvary. The reddening branches of a wild cherry-tree drooped above the head of the thin gray Christ. Here he found Laure kneeling with her rosary. He stood by silently until she rose. Her eyes met his. He took the hand that held the rosary in both of his.

"*M'sieu' le curé* has absolved me," he said softly. "The good saints have forgiven me. What of Ste. Laure?"

"She has forgiven, too!"

[1903]

The Spirit of the Dance

With a great sigh of relief, Doctor Girard lifted the latch of the Seigneur's gate and passed into the quiet shade of the laurels, and the grateful coolness of the grass path which led to the Seigneur's front door. The door stood open, and somewhere, from the dimness beyond, Madame Berthe emerged at the sound of the knocker. At sight of the doctor, she began to talk volubly as she advanced.

"Ah, Monsieur Girard! How glad I am that you are come at last! Monsieur de Valleau is greatly exhausted — the result of this terrible attack, you understand — the eyes staring — the chin sunk — and he shivers — *mon Dieu!* like this —" and her plump sides shook in futile imitation.

Doctor Girard removed his broad straw hat and fanned his heated and bewildered face.

"But, *nom de Dieu,* madame," he objected, "it is incredible! When I left monsieur this morning, he was vastly improved, the pulse tranquil, the brow cool — it is incredible — incredible."

He repeated the word several times mechanically as though to conceal behind it some half-formed thought. Then tentatively, he raised his eyes to the face of the housekeeper with the kind keenness peculiar to men in his profession.

"Madame Berthe," he said, speaking softly, as he always did to women, "what did Monsieur de Valleau do that induced this second attack?"

The quiet insistence of his tone produced in her a sort of agitated calm. Her breast heaved, but her voice reflected the calmness of his.

"Is it necessary, professionally, monsieur, that you know?"

"Very necessary, indeed."

"For the good of Monsieur de Valleau?"

"For his good."

Madame Berthe raised her arched brows appealingly; the doctor bent his bristling gray ones in final decision. "For his good."

"Très bien!" she broke out. "I will play the spy! My tongue shall repeat what my eyes had no right to see. But if it benefit Monsieur Louis, for what does my honour count? You understand! And to speak — what relief! I feel sometimes Monsieur Girard that I must burst with the secret if I retain it longer!"

The doctor nodded sympathetically and she went on:

"You ask, monsieur, what the Seigneur has done to induce this relapse. I answer — nothing. He is powerless, I believe, to combat the cause of these sicknesses. And the whole cause, Monsieur Girard, is the Stradivarius violin! It calls to him with a thousand tongues, each one more false than the tongue of a woman - - *hein?* You laugh? But we are false, monsieur. Once with that brown harlot on his arm he is become as a straw, blown about by every gale of melody. After the ecstasy, there is the price to pay in his poor throbbing head and broken nerves — *voilà!* I send for Doctor Girard! As for Mademoiselle Gabrielle, she only encourages him in his madness, and she — my faith — with four Saints' names!"

She paused to take breath. Doctor Girard, seizing the opportunity, led her with gentle pressure into the dim parlour, and, placing an arm-chair for her, he seated himself opposite with an air of determination.

"Now," he said, "behind all these metaphors, there is something more than a bagatelle. Seated so, we can discuss the matter with more composure, and you will be able, my dear lady, to lay the entire case before me with your accustomed precision and admirable discernment."

Madame Berthe relaxed for a moment into an appreciative smile; then, with a wave of her plump hands brushed an imaginary veil from between them, and began:

"Voilà! the whole story!"

"I have lived in this house, as perhaps you know, for more than forty years. I arrived from Old France a year before the birth of Monsieur Louis, the present seigneur, and consequently, two years prior to the death of my dear lady, his mother. Since that time he has been as a son to me, always gentle, always considerate, and yet, on occasion, of a mulish stubbornness. When he desires anything, one may as well give in with a good grace, for he will have his way in the end, of a surety.

"As a child, he was like a little bird, so full of music, hearing voices where others were deaf. For example, the great poplar that shadows the house — you have observed it?"

"One of the stateliest of its kind, madame."

"*Eh bien!* He would lie on the grass by the hour with his little face turned upward toward its trembling leaves. 'Don't you hear it Tante Berthe?' he would call, 'That's the Spirit of the Poplar whispering to me!' And me, monsieur, I heard nothing save the leaves rustling in that aggravating way that poplars have, but pouf! I made pretense to hear it also — to please my little Louis.

"*Alors,* when he was fourteen, the old seigneur presented him with a violin all inlaid with pearl. That was the beginning. Before a month, he could play anything with assurance from the songs of Old France to the boatman's chant of Canada. But for the dance music, he was superb! Incomparable! You know Remi Leduc, monsieur, who keeps the tavern?"

"He is a rascal, madame."

"Without doubt. But you admit that he fiddles well? *Alors,* I have seen Monsieur Louis and Remi, as boys, at a country dance, making music that put the devil in one's heels — and such a picture they made — young Remi with his wicked black curls and bold eyes and my dear lad so slim and pensive and all lost in the melody. But to return! Finally Monsieur Lambert, Louis' tutor, declared it a waste of time for the boy to drudge over Latin and mathematics with so great a talent unrefined and the old Seigneur was persuaded to send him to Montreal to make a study of the violin. So Monsieur Lambert conveyed him thither — the worst day's work of his life. For five years we saw him only during short visits. Then, when he was twenty the old Seigneur sent for him. He was growing feeble and he wanted his boy at his side. *Mais* — do you think that Monsieur Louis remained here in content? No, it was nothing but Rome, Rome, Rome! It seemed that a great master of the violin taught there and nothing would do but he must have lessons of him, and, *en passant,* I believe, to see a little of the world. Now had it been dear Paris — but *Rome!*" Madame Berthe's dimpled fingers waved contempt.

"However, Rome it was, and music it was, till there was no living in peace with him! For me, I liked his playing less than before — all the *esprit,* the gaiety had gone out of it. It made one think of Ember days, and cold night winds and the poplar tree. Finally, monsieur, the music came between the father and son. There was no longer the same camaraderie. They would sit almost silent at their meals, the old Seigneur worried and depressed; Monsieur Louis dreamy and preoccupied. In spite of myself, I was in sympathy with the boy. It is the woman's way, *n'est-ce pas?*

"And, *en effet,* there was small pleasure in a little village, for a young gentleman of his attainments. Then, one spring morning, quite unexpectedly, the old Seigneur died in this same arm-chair. *Mon Dieu!* After the first hour of grief, I could see the resolve in my boy's eyes, shining in spite of himself. One night, a month later, he led me to the hall window, which gives on the south. 'Tante Berthe,' he whispered in my ear, 'don't you hear the Spirit of the Poplar Tree? It's calling me — 'Louis de Valleau, come to Rome!' And oh, Tante Berthe, I must heed the call and go!'

"It was his way of breaking the news to me; and of what avail was it that I should demur? *Après tout,* he was a de Valleau and I his house-keeper. So, almost before I realised it, our adieux were made, and I was left to face the solitary years."

She fell silent and the unheeded tears ran down her cheeks. Doctor Girard looked out at the poplar, whose trunk, an arm's length from the window, showed sternly against the green of the laurels. When he had given the house-keeper time to recover her composure he turned to her and said gently:

"We all know, madame, how the Seigneur went to Rome, and how you bore those years of loneliness without complaint."

"Thank you, monsieur. It was almost seven years till his return, but he wrote faithfully. It goes without saying what pride I had in his success.

"*Alors,* he wrote one day that a beautiful and gifted Italian lady had given him a rare old Stradivarius violin of great value. Monsieur," with a slight shrug, "everyone knows that he married her, and that four years later, he came home, broken in health and spirit, with the Petite Gabrielle in his arms, all that was left to him of Rome and that unhappy union. Tell me, what do they say in the village concerning her?"

"That at the best, she is worse than dead to him; that, at the worst, he is better here than there."

"Ah, they know much, monsieur, but not the worst, which is —" Madame Berthe leaned toward him with an air of mystery and whispered — "that she was no great lady but *une danseuse,* who won her bread by her agility and so pirouetted into the heart of my boy. Would such as she be faithful even to a de Valleau? *Mon Dieu,* no! But he is loyal to her — quixotically so — to the extent of sending her every *sou* that can be spared. *Spared!* Heaven forgive him! He does his best to starve us that the economies may be sent to her at Rome!"

"These economies, then," asked the doctor, "is it that they affect the health of Monsieur de Valleau to such an alarming extent or —

but I see, madame, that the half of your disclosures have not been made. Pray proceed."

"Ah, doctor, the Seigneur would rather die than that I should inform you of this? But in what a dilemma am I? Shall I allow him to die when you perhaps can save him? Doctors, too, like priests, remember nothing that is best forgotten, *hé? Eh bien,* there are two things from which you must save the Seigneur, himself — and the Stradivarius violin."

Doctor Girard nodded, his patient dark face immobile. Madame Berthe proceeded.

"Music, in its place, monsieur, is a joyful thing. Am I not a Frenchwoman? The promenade — the costumes — a tang of the sea in the air — the military band — oh! *très agréable! Mais* — music in the dead of night, a piercing bizarre wailing of one violin — is it agreeable, monsieur? Does it soothe the senses? As for the dancing of Mademoiselle Gabrielle, *I* call it *indecent.* And without doubt, it is that which kills the Seigneur by inches.

"It was in this manner that I became cognisant of it. In November last I was a martyr to neuralgia of the teeth. *Eh bien!* One night about the hour of twelve I raised myself from my couch in despair. I am crazed with pain. Will nothing relieve me? Suddenly, I remind myself of the ginger tea. I determine to make a cup with just a suspicion of whisky *blanc.*

"I light my candle and grope my way toward the pantry. Then, as I open the stairway door, I am paralysed with horror by an unearthly sound of music. During a moment I try to convince myself that it is but the howling of the wind for it is a stormy night. But no, as I strain my ears I become certain that it proceeds from the chamber of Monsieur le Seigneur. It is the violin! And, blessed Mother! Such music! It was like the cry of a soul lost at sea — it was as the creak of the guillotine — still more it resembled the dance of the dead leaves in November and the bare branches of the poplar scraping on the eaves.

"But there is not much of the dance in me. I stumble down the stairway to the Seigneur's door. I press my eye to the keyhole. My knees tremble as with the ague.

"The chamber is half-lit by a shifty moonlight. There is one bright patch directly before the door. Suddenly I become aware of the sound of quick breathing. I press my eye still closer. Then in the moonlight I see mademoiselle in her night-robe. She darts forward, she crouches, she spins like one possessed. Her lightness, her grace, her tricks of the hands and head are those of the trained dancer.

"I can no more remove my eye from the keyhole than I can remove it from its socket. I remain there I know not how long; then the music ceases and I see no more of mademoiselle. The voice of the Seigneur comes then, very weak and broken. He is saying — 'Draw the blind, my child, and then to thy bed. Promise me that you will forget this night.'

"I hear the child say, 'Yes, papa' — the sound of a kiss — then, in a moment, she is in the hall.

"Once the door is safely closed, I clutch her by the arms and drag her to the pantry. She makes no sound. She is dazed by my attack.

" 'Little evil one!' I scream, shaking her — in truth I am beside myself — 'Explain!' I scream, 'explain!' "

The house-keeper voice rose to a high pitch and Doctor Girard made a warning gesture.

"Ah, forgive me if I appear foolishly wrought up, monsieur, but these occurrences have preyed on me for nearly a year! For the rest, there is little to tell. I questioned Mademoiselle Gabrielle closely. She is a truthful child although like no de Valleau I have ever seen. She said, looking me in the eyes: 'My papa called me and I ran to him in my nightrobe. When I entered his room he was playing the Strad. Without resting his bow, he nodded and smiled at me and said — *"Dance!"* I cross myself, Tante Berthe, it is the truth. I knew the way at once."

" 'Had this ever occurred before?' I demanded. Yes, twice, she replied; once a long, long time ago, and once in the summer. Did I not remember, when her papa was ill? *Hélas!* I had cause to remember!"

"And the next day?" interrogated Monsieur Girard.

"My toothache was departed."

"And Monsieur de Valleau?"

"Enervated beyond speech, and irritable, *mon Dieu!* like a caged lion!"

"And Mademoiselle Gabrielle?"

"As though nothing had happened — gay, singing through the house, gambolling with some young kittens, and imploring me to make a *pâté* for her supper."

"How often has this occurred since?"

"Once again in the early spring and during the last month, three times."

"You have seen nothing?"

"Absolutely. At times I awake in the night starting with perspiration, listening involuntarily for the sound of music. It is but a fancy. Only by the extreme exhaustion of the Seigneur on the following day can I draw any conclusions concerning the night before. I am convinced that my dear Seigneur is powerless to resist this evil, and, as for mademoiselle, who can blame her? She is as the good God made her. The dance is in her blood. Does the bird know why he sings? It is the Stradivarius alone which is responsible. While it is in the Seigneur's chamber may the Saints pray for him! *Voilà tout.*"

With this pious invocation Madame Berthe laid her palms together with some complacency. It was not often that she had so good a listener or a narrative so thrilling.

Doctor Girard rose without comment.

"I neglect my patient," he said abruptly. "If you pardon me, madame —"

He bowed at the door and turning, ascended the steep stairway. At the turning his spare figure was lost in the upper dimness.

*

In the chamber of Monsieur de Valleau, it was so dim indeed, that a moment passed before the doctor could discern the face and hands of his patient showing pale against the carving of his high-backed chair. Then he advanced.

"Ah, a pleasant morning to you, monsieur! Shall I open your shutters a bit? I can make nothing tangible out of you in this gloom."

"Yes — and nothing very tangible in the sunshine either. I am growing to be such stuff as dreams are made of, doctor."

The voice came with penetrating clearness, vibrant as the tone of a 'cello. Doctor Girard unlatched the shutters, admitting a pathway of sunshine light. Then, being seated, he laid his fingers lightly on the Seigneur's wrist.

"H'm! As I expected — extreme lassitude, following a period of intense excitement. It is inevitable."

He raised his eyes to the Seigneur's face with frank scrutiny. The Seigneur's own eyes, long-lashed, with something of the delicacy of a woman's, narrowed a little, then he smiled faintly.

"Whom am I to thank for the insinuation in your tone, Monsieur le Docteur? Is it that you imagine I have been drinking?"

It was not the habit of the little doctor to beat about the bush. He came to the point now with trenchant directness.

"Not alcohol, monsieur, assuredly not. But there are other excesses as evil in their effects." He nodded toward where the Stradivarius lay in its rosewood case. "Music for example! Sometimes people become crazed over that. I have been observing you carefully, monseigneur, and I think that is at the root of your trouble. I may as well say I am positive this is the case." Catching a gleam of anger in the Seigneur's eyes, he added, with a slight shrug: "You see, I am your medical adviser, otherwise, to me, you were above suspicion. But that which I suspect — I *know*."

Louis de Valleau made as though to rise, then, with a certain weariness of movement, habitual to him, and now accentuated by his physical depression, he threw himself back in his chair and faced the doctor.

"Ah, Girard," he said, with one of his sudden smiles. "You have me at last, old humbug! It goes without saying that you are right. It's the music madness that is killing me — the madness of music — and motion — the music of motion" — he passed his hand confusedly across his eyes — "Ah, faith! I'm a poor sort of fellow. I shall go on a little longer, while the spark holds out to burn and then — at last — I shall step off into the night, and so — *bon soir!*" He made a light gesture of the fingers as one who casts away a cigarette, at the same time watching the elder man, somewhat boyishly, to observe the effect of his words.

Doctor Girard scratched his grizzled chin in thought for a moment, then he raised his inquiring gaze to the Seigneur's face and asked slowly: "And when you step off into the night, Louis le Débonnaire, will Mademoiselle Gabrielle accompany you, or will she remain behind perchance to reap the harvest you have sown?"

*

An hour later, Madame Berthe, in attendance in the hall below perceived the little doctor marching soberly down the stairs with the Stradivarius violin held awkwardly before him. As he reached the bottom step he extended the instrument to madame, who took it by the neck gingerly, and for a moment they contemplated its urbane polished surface in silence. Then madame, breaking into tears, laid her head in the black lace cap, quite simply on the homely breast of Doctor Girard.

With a tenderness in which there was a hint of exasperation, he patted her plump shoulder, grumbling: "Madame, for the love of Heaven, contain yourself! Tut! tut! For what are you crying? God bless me what a woman!"

The pats became almost fierce, and Madame Berthe was induced to raise her head and straighten her cap, which was drooping dejectedly over one eye.

"I am an old fool!" she cried. "But it seems too good to believe! Tell me, doctor, did Monsieur de Valleau surrender it willingly? Shall I dare approach him?"

"Of a certainty. You will find him quite penitent and very docile. Be cheerful in his presence, make a deal of him — you women know the way. Above all, see that he eats plenty of nourishing food. It is of the utmost importance. Some good Burgundy a cutlet to breakfast, French chocolate, broiled chickens, grapes — in short, let him live well. We cannot produce a materialist, madame, from a diet of music and pills!"

He knew more of the house keeper's economies that she was aware. As he stood on the threshold, he added in a whisper: "And if he demands the violin, send for me, send for me."

The doctor's spare figure had barely disappeared behind the laurels, when Gabrielle emerged from them. She was in white and her curling brown hair hung closely about her face. The warmth of an honest wrath showed in her olive cheeks. Her eyes, smaller and more almond-shaped than her father's, had in their depths a latent reckless-ness that went well with the poise of her small finely formed head.

"Tante Berthe!" she burst out, "are you in love with Doctor Girard? Tell me — I demand to know! For I saw you in his arms one moment ago — with my own eyes! Tante Berthe, I think you are a very wicked old woman, I do indeed! As for Doctor Girard — grr-r!"

She towered fiercely over poor Madame Berthe, who had sunk in a confused heap on the door-sill, and now, rocking herself to and fro, inquired pathetically: "What has come over me this day?"

"Tell me, were you making love, *ma* tante?" reiterated the child. "It is no use to deny. I caught you in the act. Last fête day I saw Henri Gosselin and Marie Roy making love. It was the very same — her head on his shoulder, her hat over one eye, as your cap to-day — oh, it was unspeakably the same!"

The picture of herself thus conjured up touched Madame's ever keen sense of humour. She began to laugh hysterically.

"Oh, naughty child!" she gasped, embracing Gabrielle, "for what was I born! I leave my beloved France and come to these wilds to nurse your dear grandmamma. I bring up your poor papa. I am a mother to you although you are like no de Valleau I have ever seen. Finally, in my old age, I am accused of making love to a bourgeois Canadian doctor! *C'est fini,* let me crawl away to die!"

Gabrielle was conscience-stricken. She pressed her cheek to that of the house-keeper and slipped her arms about her neck whispering: "Forgive me, *ma tante,* it is I who am wicked, me, with four Saints' names. I will eat mutton broth to my dinner — I will embroider my sampler for an hour — I will even wear my hair in plaits without complaint! Do you love me now?"

"Là, là, chérie! Attends donc! And I shall tell thee why thy foolish old nurse laid her head on the shoulder of Doctor Girard. It was that she might shed tears of thankfullness because she believes that he will be able perhaps to make thy dear papa quite well again."

She led Gabrielle to the oak-beamed parlour then and told her what had taken place and how they must be heedful to keep the Seigneur always cheerful and that it was to be her little part to bring him flowers, to read to him; that she must be a little mother to him in place of a daughter, and she must kiss him on both cheeks, but never, never, speak of the evil Stradivarius. Monsieur Girard depended on her.

Gabrielle's cheeks flushed as she listened and her eyes widened in contemplation of her new responsibility. Heretofore, she had been refused admittance to the Seigneur's room during his illness; now she would be allowed to lavish all her love on him and that would make him well without fail. She hugged Tante Berthe rapturously and then demanded:

"But if I nurse my father what will be your part?"

"Ah, that is the heart-break, *ma petite!* Monsieur Girard says it is imperative that thy papa have the best of food, the most expensive wine, peaches, chocolate, young fowls and cutlets — where is the money for these? That is what vexes me. You see, our little garden here produces none of them; indeed, we shall have to send to Quebec, I fear. I have almost no money, and I dare not harass thy papa when he is so ill. Where, then, can we obtain it?"

"Tante Berthe, I know, by the way your lip twists, that you have some plan. Is it to ask Monsieur le curé?"

The house-keeper smiled uneasily.

"No, not that. Thy papa would prefer to die — I am certain. But there is a way — it is true. I have been thinking of it — it seems unavoidable — to sell the violin."

Gabrielle reddened to the neck. She left her seat and went to where the Stradivarius lay on a marble table. She drew her fingers caressingly across the strings and said slowly with a little catch in her voice: "It would be like stealing — like stealing."

"Fi donc!" exclaimed Madame Berthe hurriedly. "What things you say, child! When the good papa is quite well again, he can buy it back. I will make that stipulation on the bargain."

The truth was that she had determined not to give the Stradivarius house-room for another night. Might not some ghostly bow draw from its strings the prelude to another midnight dance? Come what might, she would save Louis de Valleau and his child from themselves.

"Ah, but no one would buy it," said Gabrielle, hopefully.

"I have thought of that also," said Madame Berthe. "It shall be Remi Leduc, the landlord of *Le Chien Noir*. He broke his fiddle yesterday over the head of Jean Baptiste Ratte because he *would* beat time on the floor with his hob-nailed boots. *Eh bien!* Remi shall buy the violin and when thy dear papa is quite himself again, we shall buy it back, my pet — *n'est-ce pas?"*

Gabrielle nodded; she dared not trust herself to speak. She was struggling to grasp the extent of the void which the loss of the Strad would make in her eventless life. It had been as one of the family. Its silvery notes had called her with the yearning of a mother's voice. When a little child she had gazed at her own reflection in its deep red-brown surface as in a mother's eyes. A hot tear splashed on it, and with her finger she traced the moisture on the polished wood. It took the form of a cross. She was thrilled by the thought it was marked thus with the sacred sign for a sacrifice.

The remainder of the afternoon she went about dreamily, scarcely speaking, and once, when her father drew her to his side and kissed her, she burst into tears, and implored him to say that he loved her and was entirely pleased with her. When the tea hour came, she carried her salad and brown bread to the porch and ate it from the doorstep, and grew comforted in watching how the sunlight left the lowlier things, bit by bit, till at last only the topmost branch of the poplar tree was gold.

Inside, Madame Berthe consumed many cups of strong tea preparatory to her encounter with the landlord of *Le Chien Noir,* with whom she meant to drive a thrifty bargain. At twilight she emerged, wearing an air of great cheerfulness and her winter cloak, which only partially concealed the form of the Stradivarius beneath her arm.

She would have embraced Gabrielle, but the child turned her face away, so she contented herself with kissing a bit of white neck that showed between the curls.

When the gate clicked Gabrielle, watching through her hair, saw the ample bonnet of Tante Berthe bobbing above the hedge as she trudged down the road. How hot she must be in that heavy cloak! Gabrielle felt sorry now that she had not kissed her, and, after a moment's reflection, she ran to the gate to wave a kiss and call an *au revoir*. Madame Berthe halted and returned the salute as well as she could, being so much incommoded.

There was no difficulty in persuading the landlord of *Le Chien Noir* to purchase the Seigneur's violin. Already, he was lamenting his stupidity in breaking his own beloved fiddle over the bullet head of Jean Baptiste Ratte. The poker would have been equally effective and infinitely harder to break! So he paid the ten pounds which Madame Berthe demanded, so cheerfully, that the good soul felt a pang of regret that she had not made it twenty. In this manner, the Stradivarius, which had been the idol of a Roman antiquary became the pride of a little inn-keeper of Quebec, and its mellow-throated strings were tuned to lowlier themes.

Thus supplied with ample means to indulge her housewifely instincts, Madame Berthe purchased seasonable delicacies to tempt the appetite of Louis de Valleau, who dutifully ate his *pâtés,* his Burgundy, his mellow peaches, his clam *purée,* without inquiry as to their probable source.

As the days passed without reference to the Strad from her father, Gabrielle's courage rose and she began to be very happy in her post of nurse and little mother to him.

They spent their days together, and when twilight fell they would draw their chairs close to the window to catch the last light on the page she was reading.

One evening she read "La Feuille." It was in late September, but the breeze that ruffled her brown hair, was balmy. As she reached the words:

> *"Je vais où va toute chose,*
> *Où va la feuille de rose*
> *Et la feuille de laurier."*

— the Seigneur's white fingers covered the page and he drew her closer to him.

"Shut the book sweetheart," he said, "shut the book and let us sit quiet for a while together."

So Gabrielle stretched her arm across his knees and laid her head against his breast with her face upturned to his; and the Seigneur looking down at her, praised the tinting in her cheeks and hair and said her mouth was like her mother's.

The thought of her seemed to increase his sadness, and presently he suggested that they take a turn in the air on the balcony beyond the bedchamber. So they paced up and down with his arm about her neck. The peacefulness of the night was falling, and from the garden's obscurity the sweet odour of the white stocks came up to them.

When the Seigneur tired, they leaned their arms on the balustrade watching how the lights came out, one by one, in the village below. The Seigneur discovered a yellowing branch on the poplar tree and said that autumn was come at last, but Gabrielle insisted that it was but the work of some destructive worm. He did not answer and she heard him repeat to himself:

> "I go where all things go,
> Where goes the leaf of the rose
> And the leaf of the laurel tree."

Gabrielle, slipping her hand into his, whispered, "Father, will you not come in now? The dew is falling." He smiled at her and obeyed. At the door she whispered again: "Father!"

"Yes, sweetheart."

"Father, I do not intend to read these verses about the fallen leaf again, because they make you sad."

*

When Gabrielle awoke that night the moonlight was on her face, and she believed for a moment it was that which had aroused her. Then she saw her father standing at her bedside. In contrast to the sombreness of his long maroon dressing robe, the clear-cut purity of his lineaments was such that she fancied him a part of her dream. He touched her again.

"Wake up, *ma petite!* Father needs thee."

She raised herself to her knees and laid her hands on his breast. "For what, *mon père?* Art you ill?"

He bent over her and answered in a half-playful manner, as though to reassure her: *"Mais, non.* Not ill. But my heart cries out for the old Strad — to hear it singing on my breast — ah, little one, I am not to be denied this time! You see the music is here," touching his forehead "and it must get out at the fingers or — confusion — confusion — madness — no, I don't mean that, not that — but bring the Strad to my room without delay — I won't be denied, Gabrielle."

"But, papa," she gasped in terror, "the Strad — the Strad — it is not — oh, *mon Dieu* — it is gone — a long way — Tante Berthe —"

"I know you must pass her door — but go on tiptoe. Have care on the staircase, the third step creaks — remember. Oh! we shall not disturb madame!"

He gave one of his old gestures, stood in the doorway a moment, smiling at her, and was gone.

Gabrielle pressed her fingers to her eyes and formed herself to face the task which lay before her, to regain the Stradivarius at any cost to take the music from her father's head — his poor bewildered head — lest he should go mad with the music always singing in his brain. She crept to the chair where her clothes lay folded.

"Blessed Sainte Gabrielle," she murmured, as she drew them on "help thy child." Then she fell to repeating over and over with a sense of comfort — "Mamma, oh, mamma!" She had never said that before.

Her frock on, she stole, scarcely breathing to the staircase. The third step creaked loudly. She had forgotten to avoid it. There was a moment of painful listening in which it seemed to the child that her whole being became as an ear, that she could hear with her fingers and her forehead. But the midnight silence was broken only by the ticking of the great old clock in the hall below. She ventured the remaining steps.

With timid fingers she drew the bolts on the front door and stepped out into the moonlight. She had never been alone in the outdoor night before, and the familiar scene in the unfamiliar aspect brought a clutch of dread to her throat. The chirp of the crickets which in the morning was so merry, seemed at this hour to have a sombre note. "They never sleep," she thought, wonderingly.

On the grass path there was no need to tiptoe. The full moon hung low and luminous in the sky and every grass spear glistened with its weight of dew.

"The fairies are at work," she thought now, "spinning the cobweb for the morning."

Something alive started from the grass at her feet and she fled back to the friendly shelter of the stone porch.

"Gabrielle Catherine Anne Marie," she panted, "little coward, wicked little coward — and you with four saints' names!"

She began then to repeat her bedtime prayer aloud, and, thus armed, she passed safely over the grass path, through the vine-covered gate and on to the road. How long and white in the moonlight! She ran quickly and, after a little, she left off saying her prayer and repeated again: "Mamma! mamma!"

At the foot of the hill which led to the church there was a little roadside Calvary. She knelt to cross herself and started to see a small bird fly from its shelter. The road was rough and once she fell, but even as she cried a little in self-pity, she saw the bright lights of *Le Chien Noir,* and was cheered. At the doorstep she summoned her courage and knocked with her knuckles. The music within ceased and the landlord flung wide the door. His burly figure filled the opening; the Strad was tucked under one arm. At sight of the girl his handsome florid face gaped in mute astonishment; his very curls seemed to stand more upright.

But Gabrielle had no time for explanations. She stretched out her hands toward the violin imperatively.

"For to-night — just this once — Monsieur *le* Seigneur demands it — my papa, you know!"

"Bapteme! Ma'm'selle, are you gone mad?"

"No — oh, no! Not me — but my papa — if he does not get his violin — he is very ill, and the music is all in his head, you see —"

"A thousand pardons, ma'm'selle! If I had the intelligence of a pig I should have understood at once. You will permit that I carry it to the gate. *N'est-ce pas?* The hillside makes a lonely walk for so young a demoiselle." Gabrielle shook her head.

"But no, M'sieu Leduc. I prefer much to go alone. I shall run all the way and the Strad is very light."

"Mon Dieu! You should see me run! An antelope, Ma'm'selle Gabrielle." He looked at her intently, observing how she was growing something more than a child. Gabrielle impatiently took possession of the violin with — "No, no, I shall run faster." Then, looking wistfully up at him she added: "You will keep it secret — my coming?"

"As the grave, Ma'm'selle. What a mystery for Saint Loo! I am discoursing sweet music on the Strad — I am called, summoned to the door — I perceive a vision in white — the violin is wrenched from my grasp — the vision disappears — *pouf!* like that! I am alone. *Quelle grande mystère!* Also, mysteries are good for the trade."

The last was to himself, for Gabrielle having gained possession of the Strad, ran off without ceremony, and was now but a white shadow up the road. As for fear, she felt none, with the slim brown body of the violin pressed against her breast. When she passed the little Calvary this time, she looked the other way and made no sign.

At last she felt the cool moist turf of the path beneath her feet and latched the gate behind her. Close beside her father's open window, its branches almost entering the room, stood the poplar, very still and slender, wearing an air as of meditation.

She entered and passed swiftly up the stairway. In her own room she slipped off her clothes to her nightgown. Then, barefooted, with quickening pulses she turned the handle of the Seigneur's door. He was sitting in his high-backed chair drumming softly with his fingers on the carved arms. He reached eagerly for the violin. Gabrielle brought it and, leaning against his chair, watched his skilled fingers turn the keys to the desired pitch.

"Was I gone long, papa?"

"Gone long? Oh, no — but a moment. Thou art a dear little one — *diable!* When had I it tuned so low? And the E string — it is execrable — ragged, ragged, like madame's fringe! Ah, hear that, Gabrielle! reedy, sweet, is it not? Up to concert pitch to-night, my love! Faith, I have neglected thee! But now — you hear that, Gabrielle? In marvelous form!"

He drew his bow and delicate cadences filled the air. Gabrielle went to the window and knelt there, cooling her hot brow and neck. A light breeze had sprung up and through the quivering leaves of the poplar the stars glowed and peered at her.

She was very tired, her legs trembled; she wished that to-morrow might be like all other days. She would forget about to-night then. Or course Tante Berthe would be furious. Very likely she would only get lentil soup for dinner. But what did that signify, when her father was made happy? For herself, she was glad also to have the Strad at home again. It stood for all the fanciful imagery of her childhood. Its strings were the genii which called from their haunts the little people of her own dream world.

Now, to her listening lazily, the music came as a whisper through the marshlands, just enough to stir the rushes. She could see them gently swaying, she could hear the waters lapping; then it gained a note in volume and she heard the fairies coming. Coming running down the hillsides, climbing up the swaying rushes. She could hear their whirring wings and their joyous laughter tinkling. Then a cloud fell, and the marsh god in his twining purple draperies rose and hovered o'er the marshlands dancing in the fitful moonlight — "These are the thoughts," pondered Gabrielle "that Tante Berthe says come from the Evil One!"

She tried to put them from her and turned her face to the room. But try as she would, she could not quite free herself from them. She saw her father through the haze of the marshes and he seemed a part of the dream. She was not tired now, but cool and rested.

A fresh gust of wind blew the white window curtains into the room, twisting and untwisting, bellying like sails. Gabrielle rose.

She looked her father in the eyes. He smiled at her. This was a night when the Italian mother was dominant.

She raised her arms and stretched them to their fullest length. The sleeves of her gown fell away from them and her flexuous young body hung for a moment in suspense. Then the fire of the dance leaped in her veins and she threw herself with graceful force from posture to posture, her white limbs bathed in moonlight. Then as the music grew wilder, she became only a part of the harmonious whole, like the waving poplar and the singing violin. Her light movements were as unstudied as those of a bird that swings on a wind-blown bough, and as abandoned. At times she was almost hidden in the shadow — only a pale something that rose and sank and softly whirled, and again she sought the patch of moonlight and happy laughter bubbled from her lips; her robe made a fluttering sound.

Louis de Valleau's white fingers flashed along the strings, his great eyes glowed. He was pouring out his soul through the Stradivarius and she — she had never danced so well before. It was a supreme moment. They both realised it, and as their eyes met once, they exchanged glances of admiration and delight as the dance proceeded.

One moment more and the music softened dreamily; the dance grew more harmoniously sustained; then — little by little — the melody trailed off into a tranquil chord scarce audible. The breeze fell, leaving the curtains limp and white against the window, where the poplar tree stood motionless with an expectant air. Gabrielle sank to her knees exhausted. It was ashes after fire.

She crept to her father's chair and, laying her arms across his knees, looked up into his face. The Strad, silent now, was still held lovingly beneath his pointed chin, but the soul of Monsieur *le* Seigneur had gone out into the night.

[1910]

Canadian Ida and English Nell

The small, eager face of the girl peering through the rain-splashed window of the railway carriage and her tense grip on her little belongings showed her an unaccustomed traveler, though her weary eyes and wrinkled dress suggested that the journey had been long. When the brakeman, swinging down the aisle, pronounced with stentorian precision, "Acford! Acfor-r-d W-est!" she rose with nervous haste, and, clutching her bundles a little closer, hurried to the door, where she clung, swaying, while the other passengers craned their necks to see the traveler who was so keen to be at her journey's end.

Her dress showed her to be English, a working girl one would say; but she carried her small dark head with more spirit than most of these, and a Welsh mother had given her a pair of fine blue eyes.

With a final jolt the train drew up, and in a moment more the girl had stumbled down the wet steps and was on the station platform. She threw back her head and drew a deep breath of joy, for at last! at last! she breathed the very air that Albert breathed.

Very muggy air it was on this November morning, and heavily freighted with the smell of the tanneries, to which Acford owed its being. But to the girl it was as wine and brought a flush to her cheek, for this was Canada, this was Acford, and yonder was a freight car being loaded with hides which Albert himself might have handled! She sniffed joyously and did not feel the rain that drenched her hair.

A yellow 'bus stood at the platform's edge, and the driver, lounging on a wheel, eyed her sarcastically.

"A fine morning it is for star-gazing," he said.

"I see a 'ole ship o' stars," answered the girl.

The man considered this a moment but could make nothing of it, so he asked:

"Are you the new girl for the Acford House?"

"Is that where Albert boards — Albert Masters? If it is, w'y, I'm for there all right!" She laughed, happily.

"Albert Masters?" repeated the driver. "Ah, one of them little Cockney fellers! Sure! He boards there, or did. What's he to you?"

"Oh — a friend," she said, still smiling. "And I think I'll get in if you don't mind. I'm awful wet."

"And I'm awful dry," said the man, "so that's a good reason for both of us to hike for the Acford."

He mounted his seat and by loosening the door strap made it possible for her to enter and occupy one of the moist leather seats, where scattered crumbs of cake told tales of an infant passenger.

The 'bus pitched fearfully and the seat was so slippery that one of her bundles was constantly on the floor, and she was obliged to brace her feet on the opposite seat to maintain her own balance.

She had glimpses of yellow frame shops, with now and then a new brick building, but the street was deserted. "My word," she thought, "after London, this is like a cemingtary!" Then, with a thrill came the thought of Albert and his joy at seeing her. Surely he could not be vexed with her for following him. It had been a long, long year; she had earned the passage money herself, and ten pounds to the good to set up housekeeping, and his savings added to that!

"Gone to sleep in there?" asked the driver, pushing his head in at the door. "We're here, because we're here, because we're here —."

"And I'm better here than there," laughed the girl, clambering out. "Wot's the price?"

"Nixie, when you've got a pair of eyes like them," he answered. "You tell Albert I said that. I ain't afraid of any Cockney!"

The Acford House had a deep stone porch, leading to a low hallway, pleasant with the smell of ale. The sound of men's laughter came through a shutter-like door.

The 'bus driver tapped on this and called, "Bill!"

The door swung open and a young man appeared, shirt-sleeved, with a cigar between his teeth.

"Say, Billy," said the driver, "this young lady wants to see Albert Masters. He boards here, don't he?"

"Not now," replied Bill, "but he'll be in for a nip at noon, sure. What's he to you?"

His eyes were bold and the teeth that gripped the cigar very white, so the girl dropped her lids and said, demurely.

"Oh, a forty-second cousin, if you like."

Billy laughed and took her traveling bag.

"Well, you just come up to the ladies' parlor with me and I'll pinch Albert for you all right."

He led the way upstairs. The 'bus driver looked yearningly after them, then slowly disappeared into the bar.

Bill gave her a seat by the window and balanced himself on the edge of a table opposite as though for a chat, but from below came the ceaseless banging of a bell and cries of "Bill! Bill!" Then a scuffling sound and some one yelling, "Chuck him out!"

Bill flung angrily downstairs, the girl looking after him for a moment with shy admiration, before she settled herself contentedly in the chair to watch for Albert.

It was a quarter to twelve by the clock on the mantelpiece. In fifteen minutes more the tannery would close for the dinner hour. She rubbed a clear space on the misty pane and looked out. On the opposite corner of the street was a tailor shop. She could see the tailor sitting cross-legged, stitching placidly. No youthful bliss awaited him in fifteen minutes! In a window across the way a baker's wares were temptingly displayed — rows of shiny buns and jam tarts. She was very hungry, but — what a meal when Albert came!

At five minutes to twelve a whistle blew shrilly, and a flock of little children, the smallest of the school, scampered down the street, hurrying home out of the wet. "Dear little things!" thought the girl. Perhaps some day she and Albert would send a little kid to school.

A great bell clanged and, with a start, she perceived that the hands of the clock pointed to twelve. She ran to the mirror to tuck some stray locks beneath her hat. How sallow her face looked after the seasickness, and how blue below the eyes! Her little white hat, too, was soiled and mussed. She rubbed her cheeks to give them a color, and twitched a fold of the pink silk handkerchief about her throat into view.

The front door banged. Softly she crept half way down the stairs and leaned over the rail. A dozen men had entered and were pushing toward the bar. The smell of hides rose from them. Albert was not among them. The last one, a yellow-mustached Scot, saw her, and caught at her skirt with, "Coom along an' hae a drap, my lass!" But she shrank back.

Again the door banged. Three Englishmen, mere boys, passed in chanting a London music-hall song. It was coarse, but it brought the tears to her eyes. Would Albert never come?

As the bar filled the noise increased, and other men entering saw her and some called to her.

Again the door opened and closed, more gently this time, and a man entered alone. She knew the step before the thickset figure appeared. She leaned toward him and held out her arms.

"Albert! Oh, Albert!"

He stopped with a jerk of the head as though struck, then he saw her and his face went white.

"Gawd Orlmighty, 'elp me!" he gasped. "Nell!"

She reached down and caught his face between her hands and kissed him.

"W'y, Albert," she whispered, "ain't you glad to see me?"

He freed himself and pointed fiercely up the stairs.

'Out o' sight," he said, hoarsely; "get up there quick or they'll see you!"

With a fearful look at the bar door he ran stealthily up the steps behind her, and the girl, stumbling ahead of him, sobbed now in dread. He closed the parlor door behind them, locked it, then turned to face her with an accusing frown.

He had round, childish eyes, with a slight cast in one, and wide-spaced teeth which gave his smile an almost infantile look of candor, but they were set now in a desperate effort at self-control.

"Well," he growled, "you 'ave made a bally mess o' things! You 'ave."

"Oh, Albert," she wailed, "I thought you wanted me! You said the money was the only hindrance — and I earned it all myself — honest, too — and I've ten pound left for furnishing — and —. Oh, Albert, don't you love me no more?"

"Blarst the money!" he said. "Wot the 'ell do I care for your ten pound? And you promised to obey me, and now you comes over 'ere, as chipper as you please, arter me a-tellin' you perticlar to stop 'ome! You're a nice, dootiful wife, now, ain't yer?"

As he called her wife his face softened. He came and put his arms about her trembling form.

"Aw, Nellie," he said hoarsely, "I'm in a 'orrible fix and I orta be arskin' your forgiveness instead of runnin' on yer. Don't you cry, ducky! I do love yer, but — but —. I s'y, Nell, daon't you look at me thet w'y. I cawn't tell you —." His voice broke and he hid his face on her shoulder.

"Go on, Albert," she said gently. "I'll try an' bear it."

"Oh, it's orful!" he moaned. "I didn't go for to do it — but she just chivied me inter it an' — an' — I married 'er six months ago!"

He raised his eyes to look into hers, but the sight of her white agony made him hide them again.

"Oh, Gawd!" he whined, "I wish I'd never seen 'er ugly red 'ead, I do!"

"Red 'ead," she repeated dully. "I cawn't 'ardly believe it. Wot did you s'y 'er nime was?"

"Ida."

"Canadian?"

"Yus. And a baggage she are, too."

Of a sudden Nell pushed him from her.

"Oh, you — you — brute," she cried fiercely, "an' me eatin' my 'eart out in old London for you!"

"That's orl very well *in* old London." He wagged his head resentfully. "But it's another story *'ere!* Wot wiv the bloomin' climate, an' the stink of the vats allus in a feller's nose, an' 'is 'eart cryin' out for 'ome, 'e ain't responsible for wot 'e does! — An' — an' I thought I'd find a w'y out of it, I did!"

Nell threw up her chin defiantly.

"She ain't your legal wife, any'ow."

But Albert shook his head dolefully.

"You daon't understand a little bit, old girl. W'y, if I tried to cut loose, she'd 'ave the lor o' me, an' I'd get a term for bigamy, an' you'd be disgriced. Oh, I couldn't bear ter 'ave *you* disgriced in this bloomin' country! But a thought *'as* come to me." He took her in his arms again and rubbed his cheek on hers. "Lord! I'd clean forgot wot a little beauty you was, Nellie!" (No need to rub her cheeks for color now, and her eyes — how blazing!) "I allus loved a black-haired lass — well, I was sayin' as 'ow it come to me that if you'd tell you were my *cousin——*."

She laughed bitterly.

"Yes. I told the 'bus man that — for a joke!"

"You did? Good! Now, we shall s'y, old girl, that you're my little cousin, wot 'eard there were a kitchen girl wanted 'ere. You can easily get the job an' earn good money. I'll see you every day, an' then, some-ow, we'll find a w'y out of this fix. But just keep dark for the present, won't yer? I cawn't stand a row."

"You coward!"

"Call me orl the nimes you will, Nell. It's yer right to do it. But I cawn't bear to see you disgriced. Aw, Nellie!"

Two tears rolled down his cheeks.

Then the poor girl, being very tender for him, promised, with a sinking heart, not to disclose their real relationship until Albert should "find a w'y."

So it came that the eager passenger of the Westbound train found herself at her journey's end more lonely than when she had been in old London dreaming of a little home with Albert in far Acford.

II

Albert made all the arrangements for his sad-eyed little cousin, even to the wage, the largeness of which amazed Nell, though, with Cockney shrewdness, she concealed her surprise. She was handed over to the cook, Mrs. Sye, a Surrey woman, whose husband, Old Tommy, was the porter and of much less importance than she. There were two other maids, both Canadians: Edith, the dining-room girl, who had once, for a night, been on the stage in vaudeville, and who ever since had worn the most beautiful boots and rolled her eyes amazingly; the other was the chambermaid, little brown-eyed Annie, who, Nell soon discovered, loved the shirt-sleeved young man, Bill.

They were all very kind to her, and Old Tommy stood so long questioning her, with a bucket of water in each hand, that his wife had to order him about his business.

There came a great rush at dinner time. Nell was set to fill dishes with cabbage, stewed tomatoes, and potatoes, the three for each order. At first she was much confused between the cook's excited face and Edith's rushing out, calling:

"One on beef, rare! — Two on pork! — Beef, on a side! — Soup and fish for a traveler!"

But she tried to imitate Annie's coolness, and served so well that when it was all over Mrs. Sye, mopping her face, said that it took an English girl to get onto the racket without any fuss, whereupon Edith and Annie gave their heads a toss.

When they had eaten their own meal — in spite of her trouble the soup tasted good — great stacks of dishes must be washed; and that over, she was set to scrub the dining-room, and later she had an hour in her bedroom, but not alone. She was to share a room with Edith and Annie, and they lounged on their bed, watching her unpack and teasing each other about Bill and a boarder named Sandy.

They told her about Ida, whose place she was to fill.

"The way she ran after your cousin Albert was a fright," said Annie. "Every noon hour, no matter how we was driven in the kitchen, she must mop the upstairs hall, so as to meet him. She used to carry hot water to his room for his shave, too. Didn't she, Ede?"

"Sure," affirmed Edith, who was easing her feet after two hours of the beautiful boots. "And often, when I had the tables set, she'd slide into the dining-room and lay a serviette at his plate. The tannery boarders ain't allowed serviettes, you know, Miss Masters."

At the name Nell dropped her head lower over a drawer she was filling. Then Annie changed the subject.

"Look here, Ede," she said sternly. "Bill says that if you don't quit shutting the dining-room door when he's eating he'll complain to the boss. How do you s'pose he can mind the bar through a shut door?"

The discussion thus started lasted till Mrs. Sye called up the back-stairs:

"Come along, girls, do! There's five early teas on!" Which sent them all scurrying to the kitchen.

At last the day was over. Nell, crouching on the foot of her narrow iron bed, watched Edith and Annie dress for an evening party. She had never seen hair so wonderfully done, and how fresh they seemed and full of spirits, while her whole body ached; but oh, it was nothing to the ache in her heart!

When they had gone, and she was left in the solitude she craved, she made her few preparations for the night and crept to the friendly shelter of the sheets, and there the dry sobs shook her as she raged against Ida, and, after a while, her pillow grew wet as she moaned his name.

Another day came, and many others like it. Nell worked so hard that she won the approval of the whole kitchen. The hard work was her only solace — the hard work and the short meetings with Albert, snatched at noon, or beside the great range at night, while she nursed Birdie, the cook's little child, in her tired arms. She thought that perhaps the sight of her with a child would touch him.

With the same object in view she gave him her first month's wage to keep for her.

Young Albert pocketed the money, well satisfied, and urged her to bide her time in silence till he should be able to "find a w'y."

She had a fear that some day Ida would come to the hotel to see her. Ida did come. She happened to be dressing a doll for little Birdie when she became conscious that the girl's chatter in the dining-room was augmented by a new voice, laughing immoderately. At the same moment Annie appeared through the swing-door.

"Say, Nellie," she began eagerly, "Ida's in here and she's coming out directly to see you. She wants us girls to ——."

With a white face Nell pushed the clinging child from her and, with an imploring look at Annie, fled up the stairs to her own room.

Annie came running after her, and, kneeling beside the bed where Nellie had thrown herself, she put her arms about her warmly and whispered:

"Oh, Nellie, I believe you're just heartbroken over some man — that makes you act so queer. I'm fond of Bill, you know, and sometimes he's awful mean to me!"

But before the month was out Annie's friendship had given place to jealousy, and her round cheeks had grown a trifle paler, for Bill, being "awful mean to her," had turned his fickle eyes on Nell. At first his attentions were but casual, such as untying her apron-strings when he came to the kitchen to fill his sugar basin; but after a little they became more marked. He would fetch her a glass of porter when she swept, and once, of a Jewish peddler, he bought her a blue silk tie.

And when Annie saw this her round eyes grew so wistful that Nell resolved to put an end to his familiarity.

Next morning, armed with this resolution and a mop, she was washing the oilcloth-covered floor of the reading-room when Bill entered, cigar between his teeth, and set down a foaming glass of lager on the table near her.

Without raising her eyes she plied the mop with redoubled vigor.

"What's the matter with you, Nell?" he asked in surprise. "Got a grouch this morning?"

"No, but I don't want any of your beer," she retorted, swishing the mop perilously near his patent-leather boots.

Bill moved a little closer.

"Now you just splash one drop of that dirty mess on my boots and you're going to get into trouble, see?"

Nell's blue eyes were mischievous. With a deft turn of her wrist she sent a spray of soapy water over the immaculate shoes, and was preparing another, when Bill, uttering a growl of pretended rage, sprang across the watery space that divided them and caught her in his arms.

She would have struck him, but at that moment Albert appeared in the doorway, his jaw hanging in mute astonishment. She fixed her eyes on him and waited.

Bill took his cigar from between his teeth, grinned down at her for a moment, then kissed her on the mouth. Still Albert did not strike him.

Bill, following her gaze, saw Albert, and, with a wink at him, released her, then rattled down the stairs in response to the ever-ringing bell of insistent thirst.

Albert came so close to her that she could feel his breath on her face, but the blow she longed for did not fall. Instead —

"Nell," with a nervous little laugh, "if Bill Goldham was to marry you it would be a damned good thing for both on us, old girl."

She gave him a long, long look, then, without a word, she raised her pail and mop and carried them to the kitchen.

That night, for the first time since she had come to Acford, her pillow was not wet with tears.

The end of January came, that time of hopeless and enduring cold. The very stench of the tanneries was frozen out. Dearly would Nell have liked to creep into bed with the two others, for warmth, but dared not because of Annie.

"One would think you two girls was starved," complained Mrs. Sye, "you look so pasty, and never a word to throw to a dog, either of you!"

"Women is kittle kattle," said Old Tommy from his corner, "an' no one knows it better nor me. Two wives I've 'ad and beant afeared on any woman; but I grant ye they're fair mysterious, an' if a man body but 'ad the time, they'd make a pretty bit o' study."

"If men bodies would study their Bibles more and women less, it 'd be a far better world," said Mrs. Sye, thumping her dough.

They were all in the kitchen together. Annie and Edith polishing silver, Nell at the ironing board, Mrs. Sye baking scones for tea, and her husband in the corner nursing little Birdie.

Tommy opened his mouth for a scathing reply, but gaped in silence as the swingdoor flew open and Ida, red-haired and radiant, appeared in the aperture.

"Lord, what a heat!" she laughed, showing her even, white teeth. "I'm glad I'm out of this in my own home, with a little parlor cook-stove, and just us two to do for!"

Her eyes fell on Nell and to her she came rather awkwardly, holding out her hand.

"Seems a pity we couldn't be friends," she said. "And you Albert's only relation in this country."

Nell straightened herself, still clutching her iron.

"Don't you offer your friendship to me ——." Her voice quivered. "Don't you dare do it!"

"Come now, girls. No nasty words!" interposed the cook.

"Let 'em 'ave at it, mother," said Old Tommy chuckling.

"This ain't no street fight!" Nell flashed at him. "I ain't goin' to pull anybody's 'air. But don't you let 'er offer me 'er friendship, that's all!"

"*I* wouldn't be *seen* scrapping with the likes of *her!*" cried Ida, also addressing Old Tommy. "But I must say it's a hard way to be treated, just when I'm off to my own cousin's funeral." She seated herself, with an injured air, and raised her hands to her large black hat. *"Is my hat on straight, girls?"*

"Sure!" said Edith, adding soothingly, "It's a regular beauty, and so genteel!"

Mrs. Sye asked: "Which cousin is that, Ida? Lottie?"

"No, Irene. The one learning dressmaking at Bayside. It was double pomonia. They're having the large hearse down from Milford. My married sister and I are going to drive over in McLean's cutter and stop the night. I thought I'd just drop in and tell you, expecting, of course, to find *everyone* agreeable." With an air of melancholy she adjusted a gold bangle on her plump wrist. (Oh, the scorn in Nell's blue eyes, and the way she spat on her hissing iron and wished that it were Ida!)

Mrs. Sye brought her a cup of tea and a scone, which she nibbled with little fingers curled.

"Where will Albert get his tea?" asked Annie.

"Oh, there's potatoes to fry and apple sauce," Ida replied carelessly. "For breakfast he'll just have to forage. I may be back by noon to-morrow." Then she added, in a mincing tone, while drawing on her long gloves, "I think it is extremely probable that I shall return to-morrow."

"Fool!" Nellie shot after her as her nodding plumes departed. "To show off to me!"

The ironing was done now; the ironingboard stood upright in its corner; with scarlet cheeks the little ironer stole past Birdie and her dolls, up the back-stairs, and threw herself face downward on her bed.

All her bitterness toward Albert had melted since Ida's visit. How could a poor boy hold out against such a red-haired tyrant? She had forced him to marry her, and now by force she held him. Well, wit had overcome force before now, and when the wit was fed by love ——. Oh, God, give him back to me!

She feigned sleep and heard Mrs. Sye bid the girls let her lie as the work was light that night. Noiselessly she slipped to her feet and removed her working dress. She would not cheapen Albert by her rags! She bathed and put on fresh white undergarments and her blue Sunday frock. Her thick black hair she coiled in many smooth braids and on them perched her little white hat. Then, with her purse in the pocket of her long gray coat, and with never a look behind, English Nell fared forth to claim her own.

III

The great green door snapped behind her, her nostrils curled to draw in the crisp Canadian air. Her step was light. Now the little town, which had always seemed so alien to her, spread itself in friendliness. Evening already poised with violet wings above the roofs, but every upward-curling spire of smoke was pink.

Oil lamps burned in some of the windows, and where the blinds were up she saw the little bobbing heads of children. The mothers were preparing the evening meal. Her man, too — her man — oh, he should have his supper!

She stopped at the shop where, inside, frozen halves of beef hung from the ceiling, and there were displayed deep platters heaped with sausages. She bought three pounds of these and a chunk of cheese.

Again outside she almost ran, and she loved the way the cold bit her cheeks. Over the railway track, behind some dwarfed apple trees, stood Albert's house, a rough-cast cottage.

The front door was locked, but the back door yielded, whining on its hinges. The room was dark and very cold. A cat, that had been crouching on the stove hearth, scurried noiselessly into a corner. She closed the door and stood motionless a moment, alone, in Albert's house — and *hers!*

Cautiously she shuffled across the floor and touched the table, where she laid her parcels. She lifted the stove lid and discovered a few embers flickering like a forlorn hope. When stirred by the poker a tiny flame shot up and gave her from the gloom the main objects of the poor room. A scarlet shawl dangling from a nail showed in the light like blood.

Nell lighted the oil lamp with a wisp of burning paper and set about her preparations without delay, for she knew that in a few minutes the great town bell would strike the hour that freed the factory hands, and made every man a master in his home.

The thought fired her. She had learned much of cleanliness and neatness from Annie, and now she flew so fast from table to stove, and from stove to cupboard, that the cat, which had crept back in feline curiosity, eyed her in wonder, and mewed to sniff the sausages.

Love can make a kitchen glow. The lamp was trimmed — the table scrubbed — the pot of potatoes began to boil; and the sausages, smeared with drippings, fumed in the oven. The blinds had been drawn, and somehow the red shawl had come to the floor, where the cat found it and made a bed.

The lamplight glistened now on a table spread for two; mounds of buttered toast and slabs of cheese; and two chairs, hobnobbing with an expectant air.

A step crunched on the frozen path, some one kicked the snow from his feet before entering. The town bell must have rung unheeded in her hurry — Lord, how her heart beat! She hid her head in the cupboard.

Albert entered.

For a second there was silence as he blinked in the light, then he demanded with sarcasm:

"Well, an' wot's the matter wiv *you,* Missis Orstrich?"

No answer.

"Might I arsk wot brung *you* 'ome so bright an' hearly, I dunno?"

Silence.

"So, you've turned narsty again, 'ave yer?" And he added, in a complaining voice:

"If you 'ad *some* men you'd get a good smack on the jor!"

She faced him.

Albert's mouth widened in an astonished, even a frightened, grin. The eye with a cast turned from her as though to wink at some bystander and remark, *"Ain't* she a corker!"

"Nell!" he broke out. "Nellie, old girl, *'ow did you dare?* Lor', but you're a plucky 'un! An' supper for the two on us! Aw, Nellie, you loves me yet, doan't yer?" He closed his arms about her waist. "Give us a good 'un now!"

"Not arf a one," she refused, putting her hand over his mouth. "Wait till we've 'ad supper."

"My eye! I thought you were Ida, sure, an' w'en I *saw* it were *you* ——." He rocked her ecstatically in his arms.

"Wash up a bit now, Albert. Make 'aste, or the saursages will be overdone."

"Saursages!" He cliked his tongue. "I s'y, this *is* a little bit of orl right, Nellie! Whot does *she* give me for supper, can you guess?

'Otted-hup pertaters an' apple saurce! Apple saurce an' *'er saurce,* that's wot *I* get." (He was mumbling through the towel now as he rubbed his rudy face.) "These 'ere Colonials is orl right in their plice, but — they cawn't appreciate a Londoner as another Londoner can, you lay your Davey on that!"

The platter was set before him now, a steaming mound of mashed potatoes, garnished with sausages — not a mean half dozen, mind you, but four-and-twenty fat ones, bubbling with grease as though they would fain burst into song like four-and-twenty black-birds.

Albert's mouth was so full that he could not speak, but he reached across the table now and then to slap her playfully on the wrist, and anon he would shake with silent laughter.

As for Nell, she did not laugh much, but when she smiled a determined-looking dimple dented her left cheek in a way that boded ill for Ida.

When he had done eating she drew him on to talk of Ida, and he said, while feeling luxuriously in his pocket for a "fag":

"She 'as 'er good points, you know, an' one o' them is 'er dear old father. 'E's a well-orf farmer, got a 'undred acres a mile out o' town, an' just two dortars, so I suspect that w'en 'e pops orf, Albert Masters, Hesquire, will become a landed proprietor. An' w'en that 'appy d'y comes — no more tannery for this 'ere bloke!"

Nell smiled, but the dimple looked almost wicked.

The "fag" was between his teeth now, and he stretched out his hand for a match.

"Give us a light, girl, an' come sit on my knee. That were a mighty refined bit o' eatin' you gave me, an' now I wants that kiss."

She gave the cat the platter to lick and then slid to his knee, and held the blazing match to the cigarette. He eyed her keenly while he puffed.

"Wot's come over you to-night, anyw'y? You look so chipper an' somethin' besides — I cawn't tell wot."

"I'm just thinkin' it is like a bit of old times, dearie." Her shoulders shook a little.

Albert snuggled his cheek to hers.

"Now, don't you tyke on, young 'un, *becars* I'm goin' to look arter you in spite of 'er, an' anyw'y, don't let's begin worryin' right on top o' them saursages." He could feel her trembling, and he said to comfort her:

"Aw, do you mind the old 'op-pickin' d'ys in Kent, w'ere we first met? Those were the times! Do y' mind the warm, soft evenin's, an' the nights w'en the pickers dawnced an' sang arf the night through, an' we ——. Aw, Gawd, let's ferget it!"

"No, no! Go on!"

"Will you ever ferget the nights in old London at the music 'alls, drinkin' beer, an' the crowd of us goin' 'ome in the starlight singin' the songs we'd 'eard?"

"They don't do much singin' an' dawncin' in this country, Albert."

"Naow," he sneered. "The song is froze in their 'earts wiv the cold, an' the dawnce dried up in their bones wiv the work. Wot's the use?"

"I remember. Talk some more."

"Then there were the Bank 'Olerd'ys at 'Amstead 'Eath — lord! Do y' mind the menageries an' the cockshies, an' the pianerorgans, an' wasn't I waxy neither w'en I caught you a-dawncin' the mazurker wiv a Jackey?"

"Jackies allus dawnce better'n Tommies, someway."

"That's becars they 'ave the 'ole deck to practice on. Then there were the swing boats, an' the movin' pictures, an' the shootin' at bottles for chocolate an' fags! An' arter is was orl over there was our own little room wiv some 'errings an' a bit o' greens to our supper. An' onct you 'ad a *hyercinth* an' — it bloomed."

His voice had grown pensive. For a moment there was silence in the room, save for a soft rasping of the cat's tongue on the platter.

"It seems to me to-night wot I can smell that hyercinth on your hair, Nell, an' as sure's fate there's a bit on it got inter your eyes — sort o' purple, they are."

She sat up straight and looked him in the eyes.

"Awbert," she said, using the old pet name, "do you mind the time you struck me that blow? And I lay in a swound a long time, an' — an' there was blood ——."

He drew her passionately to him.

"D-don't, Nellie, d-don't! I want to ferget wot a brute beast I've been to you!"

"It were just onct, Awbert, an' you were sorry arterwards!"

"I loved you more than ever! I'll never lay a finger on yer again, s'elp me! But *w'y* do you want to tark abart it, darlin'?"

Suddenly she freed herself from him and rose to her feet.

"Becars, I want you to think of it *just once more.* I'll tell you now wot I 'aven't before — this is our last supper together. I came to-night to s'y farewell, Albert — no, no, it's no use tryin' to 'old me — I'm leavin' for 'ome to-night!"

He had caught her dress and dragged her to him. She held her arms tensely at her sides.

"You're just tormentin' me, Nellie!" he cried. "S'y you are! You cawn't go 'ome wivout *me* — an' I'm tied fast! *Oh, Gawd, these women!* S'y it's only a bluff, girl!"

She hit his shoulder with her clenched hand.

"Wot do you tike me for, anyw'y? Do you fawncy I shall drudge my life out at the hotel, wiv *'er* flauntin' 'er plumes in my fice? Do you think I'll be jeered at by the other servants for my starved looks wiv *'er* a-gettin' fat on *you?* Do you think — Oh! 'ave you no 'eart? — that I'll wet my pillow wiv my tears every night, an' 'er red 'ead w'ere mine should be?" Her voice panted through the hot little room like a live thing struggling to get free. Her hands were on her heart.

"Oh, shime, I say, to the mother that bore you!"

He fell to his knees at her feet and twined his arms about her.

"Aw, Nellie, don't look at me like that! I'm broke! I'm broke! Just give me a chawnce an' I'll desert 'er. I swear it! That's wot I've been wantin' to s'y orl the time, but you drownded me out!"

The sight of his round boy's eyes, wet with tears, moved her to the tenderness always so ready for him. And she knew she was the victor. She said:

"Albert, are you sure that you *want* to leave 'er for always an' come wiv me, for keeps? Are you *sure?"*

"Wot's come over you to mistrust me so?" he sobbed. "Arter orl I've done for you! W'y, I married you on the square, didn't I? I'm glad on it, too," he hastened to add, "an' I'll foller you to the hend o' the hearth, if you'll let me!"

She smiled a bit sadly.

"It's becars you're just a man that it's 'ard for you to understand everythink I feel. But — I love you — cruel well ——. So, we'll begin again, my dearie."

She took him back to her heart then, unreservedly, as the tree takes back the truant bird.

They had not much time in which to make their simple preparation. Albert, all agog now, rushed about the tiny bedroom cramming his belongings in a traveling bag.

And Nell, left to herself, whipped out the rapier of her woman's wit and gave poor Ida her *coup de grâce*. She cleared one end of the white pine table and wrote on it with a charred stick. In fierce black characters she wrote the words — oh! to be there when the cast-off read —

> IDA, CANADIAN IDA,
> I HAVE COME AND
> TOOK MY OWN.
> ENGLISH NELL.

With the eye of an artist she regarded her masterpiece. As she pinned on the jaunty white hat she even broke into a bit of song:

Oh, it's 'ome, 'ome, 'ome!
And it's never more to roam
From our fathers' little sea-girt isle!
Don't you 'ear the billers, roll,
And the stoker shovellin' coal,
And our 'earts beatin' out the miles?
Oh, it's 'ome, 'ome, 'ome ——.

"Hello, Awbert, you ready?"

Albert, closely buttoned in his Sunday togs, waited, bag in hand. And, lest he should give one last regretful look about the room, she quickly turned out the light and pulled him to the open door, where the moon shone down.

"Look, Awbert," she cooed, turning his face up to it, "over your left shoulder — the new moon — wish on it!"

Albert rose to the occasion.

"I wish," he said solemnly, "that we may see the next new moon shine on Britanier's breast!"

They stood gazing up in silence. The cat, which had followed them, rubbed her sides against Nell's skirt and purred loudly.

At last with a sigh they withdrew their gaze and, giving each a hand to Albert's bag, hurried down the white street, stretched like a stainless new path before them, to the station.

When they reached the tracks she stopped him, pressing his arm closely and looked into his face.

"Tell me," she said — "tell truly now, wot was it that made you come wiv me? Wot *one thing touched you?*"

"I think," he hazarded, his brow puckered in thought, "I *think* as it were the saursages."

"No," she insisted, her blue eyes on the stars, "no, it *weren't that,* Awbert. It were rememberin' that *blow!*"

[1911]

A Word for Coffey

I was talking with a seafaring man beside the harbor of St. John. He had been loading kegs of nails on a little schooner, but he must have been his own master, for in the middle of the afternoon he sat down on a keg and told me the story of Bill Coffey.

Coffey was about as bad an old man as I've ever seen. You couldn't look at his face without knowing that he'd lived an awful tough life. He'd a kind of a devilish look like one of them gargoyle faces, and he'd a triumphant look too, as though he was glad of all he'd done and only wished it might have been worse.

He'd been born in Ireland, but he'd knocked all over the world since he was a little feller, and one country was no more to him than another. But I always think that him being born in Ireland accounted for the queer thing he did at the last. For the Irish are a queer race and no mistake. Once they get an idea in their heads they get kind of possessed by it.

Coffey had been a splendid seaman in his day, neat, and smart, and strong as a horse. But if there was trouble on board he was certain to be in it, fighting, mutiny, bloodshed — why, he'd even been on a pirate ship once in his young days. He'd bit the ear off one man, and the thumb half off another, and he'd killed a Portugee, though somehow he'd not swung for it. But I'm telling about his death and not his life. I just wanted to show you what sort of rum old codger he was.

It happened that I sailed with him on his last voyage. I was only about twenty then, but he was getting oldish. We'd sailed from Colón, and as we were coming out of the gulf we were caught on the edge of a hurricane. We were kept mighty busy, and in the midst of it a great comber came along and struck Coffey and sent him flying into the sea. He was up forward at the time. Then a backwash caught him as he landed in the water and sent him back on the ship, this time aft on the starboard deck. When we got to him he was cursing enough to raise your hair, but he didn't seem much hurt.

But some time after, a sort of paralysis took him, and he was done for as far as work was concerned. He'd taken a fancy to me, and he thought he'd like to spend the rest of his days in the house that I called home. That was a boardinghouse kept by my aunt by marriage, a Mrs. McKay. She was Irish, too, and a kinder woman never lived, though she was so religious.

It did make me feel funny to come home after a voyage and find Coffey sitting up at my aunt's table in a clean white necker-cher, looking as respectable as he could with that face. My aunt was a grand cook, and he knew when he was well off. And she was glad to have him, for he kept her best room permanent; and I never let on to her what sort of a life he'd led.

He was able with the help of his sticks to walk at a terrible slow pace to the dock, and there you might see him, unless it was raining cats and dogs, day in and day out, telling queer yarns to anyone that would listen to them, and looking like some battered old hulk cast up on the rocks by a storm.

Tourists liked to take pictures of him, and he'd pose for 'em with one eyebrow cocked and his chin sunk in his neckercher, looking what they called "picturesque"; but if they could have heard the remarks he made about them when they'd gone! He seemed as stuffed full of hate as the hold of a privateer full of loot.

But he was always very civil and respectful to my aunt. She was a fine, clear-skinned woman with a steady gray eye that could give any man look for look, and put him straight in his place, if need be. He took an odd fancy to her only child, little Alfred, a boy of nine. If Alfred had been a bad young one, I could have understood it better. I'd have thought Coffey'd found an apt pupil to train in the ways of wickedness. But Alfred was as religious as his mother, with her big, steady gray eyes, only he was sallow, and delicate from birth.

Sometimes Coffey would bring him along to the dock, and you never saw such a queer pair of companions, Coffey rolling along like an old tub in the trough and Alfred trotting alongside, grasping hold of Coffey's stick, which was carved to represent a sea gull's head with the beak open. He'd sit quiet as a mouse while Coffey spun a yarn, his eyes fixed on the sea with a look that used to make me wonder if he'd live to be a man. But he was a human boy in lots of ways, too, for he was desperate proud of Coffey's liking for him, and I've seen him swagger across his mother's kitchen with his hands in his pockets, fairly crowing, "Mr. Coffey's sigly" — Alfred had adenoids and never could say the letter k — "and I'm sigly. We gets along fine."

When Coffey got down on his seat, it was hard for him to get up again. We used to take him by the arms and heave him into a standing position, young Alfred pushing from behind; and once we got him up on his pins, he'd stand rocking like a bent old oak in the wind till he could get up strength to navigate.

That last year he was with us, I was away all winter on a long voyage, and when I got back I saw a great change in Coffey. It wasn't so much that he'd failed in body as that he'd an anxious, yearning look in the eyes that I'd never seen there before. He'd always had that triumphant look I've spoke of, as though he didn't regret anything he'd ever done.

It soon came out what the change was. The fear of death had taken hold of him. And not only death, but the terror of the here-after. That winter had been a terrible one of cold and fog. He'd hardly had his nose out of doors, and, sitting in the house by the fire with no one but Alfred to talk to, religion had got in its work on him. Alfred was subject to bronchitis, and he was out of school all winter, and I guess the only fun he had was in talking about repentance and hell-fire with Coffey. Though he couldn't go to school, he managed to get to Sunday school, and my aunt told me how the old man would watch for him to come back, with his hairy old face pressed to the pane, glaring up the street for the first sign of that little codger and, when he saw him, shouting to her: "Ship, ahoy, there! Open the door for Alfred!"

And Alfred would be pretty sure to have some new horror to add to the old man's misery, and he'd spin texts off like a regular preacher and expound the lesson of the day with his eyes shining like stars, his mother said, and Coffey shaking in his old carpet slippers.

"Well, I call it a shame," I said, "to scare the poor old sinner in his latter days like this, for it isn't as though anything on earth could save him after the way he's carried on and all."

"Alfred can save him," said my aunt. "And you just see if he doesn't!"

I tried to get Coffey's thoughts into different channels, but it wasn't any use.

I took him down to the dock the first fine spring day, with a grand breeze blowing off Fundy, and the gulls sailing overhead. I fetched up a few cronies he used to like to yarn and cuss with, and I filled up his pipe with my own tobacco, but it wasn't any use. It was Alfred's first day at school since winter, and Coffey kept muttering, to himself more than to us: "It'll be too much for the child.... He ain't fit for it.... I wish he'd just run along out and come down here where he'd get the sea breeze."

And the odd thing was, Alfred did appear before very long, trotting down the wharf on his spindling little legs, and his hair flying in the wind.

"Oh, Mr. Coffey!" he says, leaning against Coffey's shoulder. "I was took bad in school, and teacher had to let me out, and mother said I could come down here to you where I'd get the good air. And all the way I ran I kept saying to myself" — he put his mouth to Coffey's ear and whispered. Coffey's jaw dropped, and he clutched the boy to him, and it seemed as though a sudden tremor ran through him.

After that Alfred was never away from his side. They'd give each other queer, secret looks, and when they were alone — and we left them together mostly then — Alfred was always talking, talking, with his little, shining white face turned up to Coffey's grim old mug, and his two hands spread out on his little thin knees.

One day when there was half a gale blowing, the two had taken shelter behind a pile of bales, and when I came up behind them they didn't hear me but went right on talking. Coffey's gums were showing in a fearful kind of smile, and he was saying: "Ye know well, Alfred, that I've lived a bad life, and now, with the fear of death and eternal punishment on me, I get no wink of slape at all. Ye see I'm afraid to go to slape for fear the life'll just slip out o' me, and me not knowing it, and I'd wake up before the Judgment Seat."

"You must just resign your soul to the Lord, Mr. Coffey," Alfred says.

"Och, that's just what gets me," groaned Coffey, "for He'd have the weasand out of it in a jiffy. Alfred, you must never forget that you're to put in a good word for old Coffey, if the time comes when we stand before the Throne together. You've promised me, mind. And He'd believe you even if you did lay it on a little thick about me goodness, Alfred darlin'."

"I'll put in a word for you, never fear, Mr. Coffey," pipes Alfred, eating gumdrops out of a bag Coffey'd bought him.

Tears were trickling down poor Coffey's cheeks. "Now what would ye say, Alfred, supposin' you an' me — just the two of us — was stood before the Throne this minute — me all shiverin' in me nakedness, an' Him settin' there ferninst us with His long white beard, an' the eyes of Him like two searchlights — what would ye say, Alfred? Ye'd stand up for Coffey, wouldn't ye?"

Alfred took the gumdrop out of his mouth and stared up in the old man's face. He spoke clear and solemn: "I'd — I'd — up an' say to God, 'Be aisy on Coffey, God. He ain't so bad as he looks.'"

"Good — good —" gasps Coffey. "Go on, Alfred. That's the talk. You're a marvel."

"'He ain't so bad as he looks,'" Alfred repeats, still more solemn. "'He's terr'ble pious in all his goin's and comin's. He pays his board on the tick o' the clock. There ain't a whiter soul in our street — 'ceptin' me own. Be aisy on him, Lord.'"

"It's great," gasps Coffey. "Say it again!"

The wind and the waves suddenly set up a great noise and drowned the rest of their talk. I sneaked away feeling very queer.

One night I heard a shuffling noise in the passage outside my door. Someone seemed to be dragging himself along and breathing very heavy. I hopped out of bed and softly opened my door just wide enough to peek out.

There was the old man in his nightshirt in the passage, carrying a candle at such a slant that the grease was dribbling all over his hand. He shuffled along to Alfred's door and went in. I was after him in a minute, keeping very quiet so as not to awaken the other lodgers.

He was standing over Alfred's bed, staring down at the little shrimp and drawing deep sighs as though his heart was heavy as lead.

I laid my hand on his arm. "What's the trouble, Coffey?" I whispered.

"Och, I'm feared," he says, "that the wee lad's goin' to get away on me."

"Get away?" I asked. "Get away where?"

"Out of this world," he says with a terrible groan. "Into the next. He's as wake as a kitten, and this life's too much for him. Look ye, Tom, the day he gives up the ghost I give up the ghost too, for I can't risk facin' the Wrath alone."

Well, there's no use in talking to anyone that's as crazy as that. I led him back to his bed and covered him up like a baby and blew out his candle. Next morning I told my aunt that I thought she ought to get rid of him. He might set the house on fire prowling around at night, or do some mischief to little Alfred. But she said, nonsense, that he doted on the child, and there was a chance he'd leave him his money.

"Oh, that's it, is it?" I said. "Well, if you knew where that money came from, Aunt Mary, you mightn't want Alfred to touch it."

"There's no money," she says, "so dirty that it can't be put to a good use."

The end came about three weeks later. Coffey all this time had been like a man moving in a dream. His eyes had a glazed stare, and he and Alfred were always passing that queer, secret look to and fro between them, like a bad coin they couldn't get rid of.

It was a wild sort of evening in April. The sky was flaming red, and the waves that tumbled up against the pier were as green as those jade stones you see sometimes. The gulls were flying low and crying the loudest I've ever heard. I'd just strolled down after tea to look at the weather, and I was talking to a West Indian sailor, when I saw Coffey and Alfred walking hand in hand, looking in each other's faces and smiling. Well, I thought, where is this thing going to end? And I forgot for a minute what I was saying to the West Indian.... He was facing the harbor, and suddenly his face changed and then he gave a yell.

"What's wrong?" I asked.

"The old man," he said. "He grabs the kid in his arms and jumps into the water."

We both started on a run to the end of the pier. It was a quiet time, and there seemed no one about to help. There was no sign of Coffey or Alfred. I've never been as scared in my life. The things Coffey had said about the boy pleading for him at the Judgment Seat came back like fire in my brain, and I gibbered and shook like an idiot. Thank goodness, two men in a motorboat came along, and I and the West Indian got in, and a second later we saw the two rise not far off, bouncing about in the green waves like toys.

It was the West Indian that leaped out and held them up till we could get all three aboard. Coffey's arms were clasped around Alfred like a vise, and he had on the triumphant grin he'd used to wear when I first knew him. He was as dead as a doornail.

But Alfred was not dead. We had only worked with him a few minutes when he showed signs of life. When he was breathing regular

I took him in my arms, wrapped him in my pea jacket, and ran with him to my aunt's house, only a block away. We got him to bed and sent for the doctor.

Alfred lay on his little bed like a dead child. His mother was sobbing at the foot while she chafed his feet, when the doctor came in. He was a large, noble figure of a man, with a full white beard spread out on his chest, and a shining white forehead above heavy brows and piercing blue eyes. You could almost understand how Alfred came to think he was God, but at the time, following all the other excitement, it gave my aunt and me a terrible turn.

The doctor felt his pulse and lifted his eyelid and looked in his eye. Suddenly both Alfred's eyes flew wide open, and he glared up into the doctor's face. Then he doubled up his skinny little body as though he was galvanized by fear. And then he seemed to gather all the life that was in him for one big effort, and he scrambled to his knees. The blanket we had around him slid off, and there he was, stark naked, with his heart jumping against his ribs like a fish in a net. He folded his two hands as if in prayer, and he began to plead for Coffey as he'd often promised to do before the Judgment Seat.

"Please God — I want to say a word for Coffey — be aisy on him — he's not so bad as he looks — not so bad as he looks — he does be a terr'ble pious old feller — please wash away his sins — like you've washed away mine — and — oh, God, I'm awful cold!"

Of course the doctor didn't know what the child meant, but he was properly startled, for Alfred looked like a little saint, and he gabbled like one possessed. We couldn't do anything with him till the doctor made him certain that Coffey was forgiven and washed whiter than snow.

That rascally old fellow had planned the whole thing some time before, for he'd made a will leaving all his money to my aunt and stating that a suitable monument was to be raised and inscribed to Alfred and him.

Well, we put up a nice headstone to him, though he didn't deserve it, and my aunt was able, because of the money, to give up taking lodgers and live private, except for me, and send Alfred to college for a grand education. He's almost through for the ministry.

[1926]

Good Friday

Looking critically at Bull Evans, it was difficult to believe that anyone could love him, and still more difficult to believe him capable of a great love for another. He had a lowering, heavy, ferocious face, a thick neck, and a body so powerful, so free in its movements, that it seemed made for violence rather than sober work. Even the whirring lawn-mower seemed in his hands a weapon of destruction rather than a simple garden implement. He drove it down the long velvet stretch of the warden's lawn, with a fierce precision that left no unshorn ridges, and sent a grassy spray whirling high above the wheels.

Yet, though it was difficult to think of him as loving and being loved, he was at this moment basking in another's love as he was bathed in April sunshine, and nursing love for another in his heart as the mellowing earth was nursing the spring flowers.

It was Good Friday, and on Easter Sunday he would be a free man. His two year sentence, following a drunken fray in which an officer of the law had been badly injured, was over at last, shortened by several months for good behavior. For some weeks he had been allowed to work in the warden's garden, and it was the next thing to freedom to be there among the budding shrubs, the gay daffodils and hyacinths, and the stretch of blue sky above the lawn. Another day, and he would step from this garden out to real life and Jenny! The thought of Jenny sent a thrill of joy through him.

He thought of his young son, Tom, and of what a big fellow he must be now. A nice, quiet-tempered boy, like his poor dead mother. It was a lucky thing Tom hadn't inherited the wild temper that had twice landed his father in the "pen". The first time had been a six months sentence for assault. That had been years ago when Tom was only five. Bull shivered in the warm sunshine as the recollection of the first month in prison came back to him.... It had taken a long time to live down that prison term. Tom's mother had never lived it down. She had had a different look in her eyes ever after, a look that had roused a dull rage in him, rage at the prison, rage at himself, and rage at her for not being able to get rid of the look. It was as though the prison had thrown a shadow over her from which she had never emerged. It was almost a relief when, two years later, she died from typhoid, and there was just little Tom left.

Now here was Jenny with the shadow of the prison over her. But Jenny was different. Her face smiled out through the shadow: plucky, trusting in him; above all, loving him. A country girl, very respectably brought up, out at service. And the catastrophe had happened just a fortnight before they were to have been married! Not a week of his term in prison had passed without a letter from Jenny. The letter always seemed to bring the very presence of the girl into the prison. Bull wished with a poignant wistfulness, as each one was handed to him, that he could have read it himself. But the chaplain read them to him beautifully, and told Bull that he was lucky to have such a girl, and to try to be worthy of her.

On Monday they would be married.

The sky poured down its sunshine like a caress. The earth seemed to press upward to receive it. It was fine to be out here mowing the warden's lawn instead of working inside the chill, dark workshop where he had spent so many months.... It made him laugh to think of Jenny. The laughter rumbled away in his inside and then sputtered between his lips. He had a sudden desire to throw himself on the young grass and roll.... The bright head of dandelion stared up at him out of the grass. An instant later and the sharp knives had whirred over it. It flew into the air in the midst of the grass spray, and then fell face downward. Bull stopped the mower and picked the little gold head up. It was funny, but he wished he could have stuck it on the stem again. A sheepish grin softened his face as he held the flower on his thick palm. Curse it all, this freedom just around the corner was making a fool of him! But the silly flower had seemed so darned glad to be out of its dark prison into the sunshine. Just like himself.

A shadow fell across the grass beside him. It belonged to Mr. Stacy, the chaplain.

"Good morning, Evans," he said. "So they have given you an outdoor job for a change. I'm very glad of that."

"Yes, sir. I'm goin' out so soon, I'm hardly worth watchin' I guess."

"Oh, yes. I remember. I hope you'll get on very well, Evans. You're going to be married, aren't you? The young lady who wrote to you so faithfully."

Bull grunted, not so much surly as embarrassed.

"Evans, I hope you'll remember some of our talks. You have good stuff in you, I am sure of that. Keep it on top, and, in time, the bad.... If ever I can be of any help to you, don't be afraid to come to me. I'll give you my private address." He took out a card in his slender white fingers in such contrast to Bull's blunt ones, grimy, grey, with the pallor of prison. As the card changed hands, the dandelion which Bull had been trying to conceal, fell to the ground. He pocketed the card, with an incoherent mutter of thanks, and moved on with the mower. But Mr. Stacy moved by his side.

"Because I saw you pick up that flower before you saw me, Evans," he said, in a low voice, "I am going to remind you what a beautiful time of the year this is for you to make a fresh beginning. To-day is Good Friday, the day when One gave his life that we should live. Easter is the time of resurrection, of hope, of a new start for you...."

A kind man, but Bull was glad when he was gone. Such conversations embarrassed him horribly. Religion was all very well in its way. He had listened, very civilly, to a good deal of religious talk in the past two years. He had even tried to find out, when he was in his cell alone, whether he believed in God, but he always got rather rattled when he thought about Him.

He preferred to think about Jenny.

A little filmy cloud that had been drifting across the sun, passed by, and the sunshine was more golden and warmer than ever. A plump little brown bird flew across the lawn carrying a strip of cotton rag, too heavy for it. It fluttered and bobbed, but would not be defeated in its purpose. Then up under the eaves of the warden's house it flew triumphant. Going to build its nest next door to the prison, eh? Another little bird waiting under the eave for it, exclaiming at the size and quality of the rag. Both of them busy by now, lining the nest....

The lawn-mower whirred, the feathery spray of grass flew from the wheels. Bull began to sing very softly a song he had learned from a negro cook, when he had been stoker on a lake boat.

"Oh get you ready, chillun,
Oh get you ready, chillun,
Dere's a great camp meetin'
In de Promis' Lan'."

Nature which had denied him gentle looks, had given him a voice of singular sweetness and beauty. If it had been heard in his youth by a philanthropist with an ear for music, what a different life Bull might have had! But he did not even know it was good. He knew, however, that there was a queer power in it, for women always showed kindness to him when he sang for them. Now the refrain came sweetly muffled from his lips, over and over again. He moved, gently swaying, like one in a dream. The figures of the gardener, of the guard by the gate, of a group of other prisoners just passing from the warden's garden into the prison-yard proper, were like figures in a dream. It was wonderful to be allowed to work out in the garden these last days, almost free. He wouldn't feel so strange, so unaccustomed when he went out with Jenny. Some of the prison smell would blow off him.

As he reached the end of the lawn near the warden's house, he noticed that two prisoners, under the direction of a guard, were wheeling barrows of bricks along the gravelled walk that led to and circled the lily pond. This 'pond' was a bricked-in pool where exotic lily growths were encouraged by the warden. A small fountain played in the middle. Bull had heard that the wall was in need of repair.

He glanced casually at the two prisoners. One was a feeble looking fellow who sagged under the load of bricks. The other was a tall straight youth not yet out of his teens. Bull threw a second look at the boy as he turned the mower to go in the other direction, then a shock of recognition made him stop stock still. His heart missed a beat, then began to pound heavily against his ribs.

The tall youth was his own boy, Tom, wearing the prison garb, slouching steadily along before the guard with the air of an old timer.

It was like a nightmare. It was like the mad dreams he had had when he first came, when his brain had conjured one horror after another to torment him. Could it be Tom? No, it could not be Tom. Such a thing was impossible. He was a good quiet boy who could never get into trouble. He mowed the length of the lawn, then turned back, moving with calculated directness towards the group by the lily pond. Just as he reached the graveled walk he stopped and bent over the mower, apparently tinkering at the knives with his fingers. Under his shaggy brows his gaze rested apprehensively on the taller convict. He was squatting with his back toward Bull. Just then the guard and the other man moved away towards the prison yard, leaving the boy with MacWhinney, the Scotch gardener, who stood looking down at him with the unfailing curiosity he had for each new prisoner.

Bull rose and went over to MacWhinney's side.

"Mower's on the blink," he said, keeping his back to the youth. He had pushed a pebble into the cogs.

"Weel," said MacWhinney, "it's no right to be, for it's almost brand new." Frowning a little he went to examine the machine.

The kneeling boy lifted his face to Bull's. It was Tom's face, pale and sullen, and it went suddenly dark red at the sight of his father. All the blood had gone out of Bull's face. He said, in a choked voice:

"How the hell did you come here?"

"Motor car," muttered Tom. "Jimmy Biggar an' I pinched one and took two girls out. There was an accident and an old lady on the street got hurt."

"Were you pickled?"

"I guess, a little."

"How long are you in for?"

"A year."

MacWhinney called out: "Look here, you men, no gassin'! You get on with your work you new fellow! Bull, there's a stone somewheres in the mower but I can't locate it. Take it back to the yard. It's noon, anyway."

"Mr. MacWhinney," said Bull, "this here boy's my son. Can't I have a word with him, please?"

The gardener, fired by curiosity, came towards them at once. "Weel, I never! It's a strange meeting for ye. I don't know that I ever saw such a meeting in the nine years I've been here. It's quite an occasion. The one just goin' oot, and the ither just comin' in. Weel, weel".... He looked eagerly from Bull's face to that of his son. "Your boy doesn't favor ye, Bull."

"No," said Bull heavily, his soul very sick within him, "he doesn't. Mr. MacWhinney, might I have a word with him alone, please? I just want to have a word with him before I go out."

"I daresay I could fix it up with the deputy to let you have a few minutes conversation with him in his office." He became very important.

"I only want a minute now, before the guard comes back," said Bull, trying to quiet the devil of ferocity that was stirring in him.

"Ah, weel," said MacWhinney, good-naturedly, "have your little chat, and I'll tak' the responsibility. It's an occasion, sartainly. Just a *leetle* chat, now." He backed a few yards away, still keeping his eyes on them.

Bull stood staring into young Tom's face, so innocent with something of the womanish look of his mother. He had to look up at him, Tom was so tall. What a hell of slime he would wade through in the coming year! Never be the same again. If it was joy-riding this time, what would it be next? Safe cracking, hold-ups, perhaps murder. A year of the teachings of that place and Tom would have nothing left to learn. And not only the talk of crime but the other talk — the horrible whispers that would make him toss in his cot all night in a fever of sick imaginings.... Bull glared up at him, wishing with all the might in him, that he could by some magic word or act, spirit the boy over the prison walls, far away to safety. His glare was so ferocious that it roused resentment in the boy. He muttered:

"Well, what can you expect? You're in here yourself, aren't you?"

By the paling of his father's flushed face, he saw that the thrust had reached home. His short upper lip curled in a malicious smile.

Bull might have stood the words, though they cut him to the quick, but the malice in the smile was too much. His arms shot out, and the next moment young Tom was flat on the gravel from as hearty a cuff as father ever gave son.

"Here now! here now! None o'that!" shouted MacWhinney, running over. "We'll attend to the lad without your help, Bull. Mebbe if ye'd done more chastisin' when he was a wee 'un, he wouldn't be needin' it now."

"Mebbe," agreed Bull, heavily.

The guard came trotting up from the gate.

"What's up? a fight?" he asked.

"No, no," said MacWhinney, rubbing his nose, and staring down at Tom; "but number eighty-six has just discovered his young son here, and he's put out about it. He's knocked him down."

Young Tom lay sobbing on the gravel, his nerves, already strung up, completely broken by the shock of the blow. He wanted to lie there and howl, as he had as a five year old, and beg his father to pick him up and take care of him. He wanted his thickset strong father to pick him up and carry him out of the prison yard. He didn't want to be a prisoner. He wanted his father to take him away, to save him, to protect him. He lay, utterly demoralised, the sun beating down on his tear-blurred, blubbering face. Bull's heart was wrung by the appeal in the look.

"I'll report you," said the guard. "This kind of thing ain't allowed. You ought to be ashamed of yourself. If there's any knockin' around, the boy ought to knock you, for bein' such a father. What's he in for, hey?"

"What are ye in for?" asked MacWhinney, giving the boy a prod with his toe.

Bull's eyes flickered, but he held himself in. The moment had not yet come.

"Get up, you young lubber, and answer when you're spoke to," said the guard, and he, too, gave him a prod.

The boy began to gather himself up, his long spindling limbs all angles like a colt's.... That boy, that child, in here for a year! Never, oh never, not while Bull had life and strength to fight for him!

His eyes held Tom's for an electric instant. They said: "Watch me. I'm going to help you. Do what I say."

"Now then," repeated the guard, "What are you in for?"

"Stealin' a auto. There was a smash up."

"What's your term?"

"A year."

"Huh!" He turned to Bull. "I'm goin' to report you, eighty-six, for attackin' a fellow prisoner. And I don't like the look in your eye." He turned petulantly to MacWhinney. "I wonder why Johnson don't come and relieve me. It's past noon. The whistles blew five minutes ago."

But the last words were a gurgle. His arms were pinned to his sides. There was a blinding splash, and he was face downward in the lily pond, tangled in long rubbery stems and slippery undergrowth. His mouth was full of water. He struggled trying to free himself, trying to shout. Another struggle was taking place on the gravel. MacWhinney's face was ridiculous with astonishment. He gave a shrill yell. Then Bull's hand was on his throat. Young Tom pulled his legs from under him. Then Bull threw him in on top of the guard.

"Now," said Bull, "run for your life."

They bounded side by side down the lawn and passed unmolested through the warden's gate.

It was a narrow street, deserted at the noon hour. After the prison wall ended, it ran between lumber yards, crossed a railway track, and ended in an unused wharf on the lake.

"If only we can get to the lumber yards," thought Bull.

They passed two little boys playing marbles on the sidewalk, and safely reached the yards.

The first piles of lumber seemed to open up to receive them. They ran down a long alley formed by successive piles, then wedged themselves through a jagged opening into the next alley. They ran along it, then, as before, found an opening through which they gained the next. Here the lumber was piled so closely that they had to run the length of the alley to find egress from it. Bull's plan was to reach the tracks and board a freight car if possible, and, failing that, make for the lake front, where among old sheds they might lie concealed till dark.

A lazy noontide silence lay over all, broken only by the slow shunting of a distant locomotive. A sweet resinous smell rose from the pine boards around them. Bull's face was dripping with sweat. The struggle with the two men, followed by the sharp run had almost winded him. He stopped leaning against the lumber. Young Tom stopped too, looking at him inquiringly.

"Why are we stopping?" whispered Tom.

"Sh... listen."

The sound of men's voices came from the other side of the pile, and the clink of dinner pails. Some workmen were eating their lunch in there.

"Did you hear anything?" asked one.

"There are some kids playing around," returned another. There was a gulping sound as of tea-drinking, then the first asked:

"Did you say she was a light-complected girl, Bill?"

"Yes," answered Bill, "she was awful light complected. And she'd a kind of snub nose...."

A voice called from far down the vista of lumber piles:

"Hi, there! Have you seen anything of two men? Two prisoners have escaped!"

There was a clatter of tins as the workmen jumped to their feet. They ran in the direction of the guards.

There was silence then, and the sound of the distant engine again was heard.

Bull cautiously moved around the pile to where the workmen had been sitting. Their lunch things were scattered over the ground. Some coats were laid together in a heap. He picked up two of them and handed one to Tom. He pulled off his convict's jacket and dragged the other over his thick shoulders. It was so tight that he looked grotesquely stuffed in it. Tom had slipped into the other.

They emerged on to a rough common matted with last year's grass. Here and there puddles glimmered in the sunshine. They ran, leaping, splashing, the ground seeming to run like a heaving brown sea before them, the roaring of the train bearing ever nearer. Tom reached the shelter of a shed by the track and glared back at his thick-set father laboring after.

"Oh, Dad, run, run, for God's sake!" he implored.

They stood as close to the grinding wheels as they dared, their bodies tense, then a spring from the boy, a scrambling jump from the man, and they were lying face down on the jolting sand-strewn floor of a flat car. The train moved heavily, thunderously on.

Bull lay clutching the fingers of one hand in the other. He had torn and broken his nails in the scramble. He groaned with the pain. He lay still a long time it seemed, not thinking, just trying to breathe, listening to the pounding of his heart against the throbbing of the wheels.

At last Tom touched him on the breast. "Are you all right?" he asked.

Bull opened his eyes. "You bet," he gasped. "You all right?"

"You bet."

Tom cautiously raised himself on his elbows and looked about. They had passed through the suburbs and were now in the open country. On one side of the track rolling meadows of the tenderest green were backed by young woods. The sky was a great blueness. On the other side of the track the lake rippled radiantly to the horizon. Tom wished that they were sailing in a boat. It looked so free out there.

Bull drew his hand from under him and examined the stubby bleeding fingers.

"Gee," said Tom, "you hurt your hand, eh?"

"Yeh!" He rolled over on his back and stared up at the sky, that sky that had looked so benignly down at him only an hour ago, but that now only threatened his freedom with its light. If only it were dark so that they might be hidden!

His face was caked with sweat and sand, and, where his hand had passed over it there was a smear of blood.

His heart was beating steadily now. He could think. Now that the first dash was effected, there was a bare chance that they both might escape. The object he had set his heart on was to take the boy to an old pal of his, named Dodds. He had stood by Dodds once when he had needed it badly. "If ever I can do you a good turn, Bull," he had sworn, "I'll do it."

Once he had got rid of the boy, there was a faint chance that Bull might escape arrest himself. If he got North to the lumber camps perhaps.... It seemed strange that he should be skulking about, trying to avoid capture, when, only an hour ago, he had stood on the brink of freedom. A feeling of bitterness swept over him when he thought of Jenny. Jenny who had been so brave and patient for those two cruel years. If he was caught, his second sentence might be pretty stiff, especially if the gardener and the guard were hurt.

Tom had found three cigarettes and some matches in the pocket of his coat. Each lighted one, and they lay puffing deeply. Their nerves were soothed. Neither spoke again until the last possible puff was extracted from the stub, then Tom asked:

"Anything in your pockets?"

Bull produced a large red handkerchief.

"Better clean your face up, Dad. It looks fierce."

He scrubbed his face vigorously.

After a silence, the boy asked shyly: "Why did you do it, Dad?"

"Do what?"

"Make the break? You'd have been out in another day."

"I wasn't going to have you living among that crew for a year. I was willing to take the risk."

"Say, you're a corker, Dad! Gee, I wish I'd another cigarette."

"Take the other, I don't want it."

"Sure?"

"Sure."

But Tom would make him take one puff, so that he would not feel himself greedy. Bull took it slowly, closing his eyes.

The train rushed past two small stations, the men lying flattened on the floor of the car. At the next it stopped with a sudden jolt. They were between bare fields, at some distance from the station, but Bull, straining his eyes, thought he perceived a stir of excitement. He feared the train was being searched. In any case, they could not risk being carried slowly past the stragglers on the platform.

"Here's where we get off," he said.

They dropped to the gravel that sloped down from the track to a deep ditch. They ran along the ditch bent almost double. The first cover that offered itself was a rough cedar bush. They crawled under a broken rail fence and entered it. Bull was breathing heavily. His face was blotched purple and white. As he had been the unlucky one when they boarded the car, so he was again when they left it. His legs being shorter than Tom's and his frame so much heavier he was no match for him in agility. He had slipped and rolled down the gravelled bank, cutting his head on a stone at the bottom. Now he ran, stumbling often, through the wood, holding the red handkerchief to his bleeding forehead.

It was a desolate bush, scrubby, stunted, marshy, the haunt of many crows which circled, cawing above them. If it had not been for Bull, young Tom's nerve would have left him altogether. He felt like a hunted wild thing. They were tormented by thirst and faint for food.

They walked all afternoon, hoping to come out on a side road which Bull judged would lead them to Dodds'. Twice they lost their way and began to think that the wood was to be a trap for them, but towards sundown they found it and, aching in every muscle they still quickened their pace. They must find Dodds' house before night. They had not gone far when they saw behind them a load of hay, drawn by two horses. They waited for it and Bull said to the driver, an old man:

"Look here, will you give us a lift? We've been cutting wood down yonder, and I got my head hurt when a tree fell. I'm goin' back to my brother-in-law's."

The man looked at them without suspicion or interest. "I don't mind," he said.

They climbed to the top of the load and stretched themselves on the hay. The horses jogged on. They lay looking at each other.

Bull noticed that Tom's ear was red and swollen where he had struck him. He said:

"I wasn't goin' to take any lip from you about me bein' in there first."

"But you were, after all," answered the boy.

"Yes, I was," admitted Bull. He asked after a little:

"Just how old are you, kid?"

"Eighteen last January. How old are you, Dad?"

"Forty-two."

"You must ha' been married pretty young, eh?"

"Yes, pretty young, and your mother was younger still."

Then Mary's face came before him. It floated against the blueness of the sky, now smiling in joy over baby Tom, now shadowed by that first prison term.... Then Jenny's face came. He rolled over in the hay and groaned.

"Head hurt?" asked Tom.

"You bet."

Tom grinned sympathetically, but he was done out. He fell into a heavy sleep. The sun was getting low. Bull half-dozed himself but he started wide awake in feverish alertness the instant the wagon stopped.

They were before a brick farmhouse, standing in a treeless space.

"Guess you'll have to get down now," said the farmer. His little eyes, as he watched them descend, had in them the first gleam of suspicion.

"Where'd you say you're goin'?" he asked.

"To my brother-in-law, Jim Parker. Know him?"

"No, never heard of him. That's a bad lookin' head you got. Sure a tree done that?"

"What have you got to say against it?" asked Bull, staring hard at him.

"Oh, nuthin'." But his eyes followed them gloomily as they trudged on down the road.

At twilight they came to the edge of the hamlet where Dodds had his small business. Bull would not venture into the street until it was too dark for them to be seen clearly. They took refuge in a little grove where the ground was starred by tiny pink flowers, and a spring bubbled into a pool. They threw themselves on the ground and drank. It seemed that they would never get enough of the pure cold water. They washed their faces, Bull bathed his cut head, they bathed their burning and blistered feet. Then they lay on the grass listening to the gurgling of the spring and gazing at the dim red afterglow beyond the tree trunks.

"Gee, this is a pretty place," said Tom. "I don't mind the country when it's like this."

A church bell began to ring.

"Why, say, this ain't Sunday, is it?"

"No," answered Bull. "It's Good Friday."

"Good Friday, eh? But say, why do they call it Good Friday? It's something about hot cross buns, isn't it?"

Bull hesitated, he scratched his head. "Well, no, Tom.... Why, you must ha' heard.... It's the day when they crucified.... When Jesus died, you know." He was terribly embarrassed. He had never uttered a word on the subject of religion in his life before.

"Oh, sure, I've heard something about it. But say, if he was God, what did he let them for, eh? Why didn't he strike them dead or something? You bet I would."

"Well, the chaplain made out that in some kind of a way he wanted to die to save us...."

"Save us from what?"

"Oh — everything."

"And did he?"

"Sure."

"But *why* did he?"

Bull considered soberly.

"I guess for the same reason I wanted to save you. To take the risk for your sake."

Tom was silent for a moment, then he said, solemnly: "And this is Good Friday, too! Gosh, that's funny!"

He looked into Bull's face, and Bull saw that he understood something of the sacrifice that was being made for him. He said:

"How long do you s'pose you'll get if they catch you, Dad?"

Bull tried to grin. "Oh, I dunno. Perhaps five — mebbe more. I thought that if I stood up and told them I done it to get my boy away, they'd let me off light."

Tom broke out: "Oh, you shouldn't have done it, Dad! You shouldn't have done it."

"Well, I haven't been much of a father to you, Tom, but you keep straight from now on, and I'm satisfied."

The last notes of the bell died away! the first grey shadow of the evening fell....

Less than an hour later, Bull was walking towards the railway station of the next village alone. Dodds had been quite willing to give young Tom shelter, to hide him till the affair blew over, then either to keep him on working for him as his nephew, or try to smuggle him across the line, as seemed expedient, but he showed unmistakable eagerness to get rid of Bull. Not that he was ungrateful for what Bull had once done for him, but he was nervous of risking his reputation which he said meant a good deal to him in his business. There wasn't much risk in keeping Tom. He might pass unnoticed anywhere but Bull — he had given an expressive look at Bull's bull-dog head and ferocious face. However, he had given him a hat that could be turned well down, he had given him ten dollars, and got his wife to put up a packet of sandwiches.

Young Tom had nearly broken down when they had parted.

Now Bull was trudging the dark road alone, munching the bread and meat as he went.

There must have been a marshy place about for the frogs were piping without ceasing — a strange, sad kind of sound. Above in the deep velvety spring night a few clear stars shone out. "Just as though they were keeping an eye on me," he thought. His head was a little dizzy but his mind was quiet. His mind indeed had a special kind of clearness. He could look back over his life, seeing it all spread out like a map. He saw his childhood in an orphan asylum; the beatings for those ungovernable fits of temper of his; his hard-worked youth on a farm; his running away to the city; his loves; his marriage; Mary; Jenny.

He looked up at the stars and wondered what it was all about... this Good Friday business for one thing... being saved by sacrifice,

and all that... it was too much for his brain. The night grew so dark
that he felt a strange isolation. He hungered for companionship. If
only Tom were with him. Or Jenny. He pictured himself and Jenny
walking under the great velvety sky together, hand in hand, free to
go where they willed, whispering sweet things to each other. "My
own dear little Jen.".....

"Oh, I love you, I love you. You're the only man for me!"

But he was alone, except for the frogs that piped all about him.
He trudged heavily on, very tired and lonely. To keep himself company he began to sing one of the negro hymns he had learned from
the schooner cook. There was something about those hymns that he
liked, and his beautiful voice, so out of keeping with his ugly face,
was rich in feeling as he sang, very softly:

> "It ain't ma fathah,
> It ain't ma mothah,
> It's me, oh Lawd!
> It ain't ma sistah,
> It ain't ma brothah,
> It's me, oh Lawd—
> Greatly in the need o' prayer."

Over and over he sang it, drawing comfort from it, feeling not
so terribly alone. The dark immensity, after two years of prison walls,
did not seem so overwhelming when he sang.

At last the lights of the village showed in a faint cluster. He
found the railway track and followed it as Dodds had directed. He
pulled his hat still lower as he neared the station. The platform was
deserted. Dodds had told him that he would be just in time to catch
the night train going north. He would go by train to Overton, and
work his way from there up to the lumber camps. With luck he
might still be free.

He smiled grimly when he had, without attracting a second
glance, bought his ticket, and pocketed the silver in change. He sat
in a corner of the station, apparently absorbed in an old newspaper
he had picked up.

The train was a little late but it came thundering in at last. A
man and two women appeared at the last minute and boarded it
with him. He found a seat by himself.

As the train sped through the night, hope leaped within him in
a mighty bound. The passage through the night was so strong, so
swift, he felt that nothing could stop him.

His ticket was collected without question. He tilted his hat forward. It eased the pressure on his cut head, and shielded his face. He sighed deeply, and slept.

He awoke with a start as the train stopped before a station. It was pale dawn outside but the lights still burned within. Two men, one of them in a blue uniform, appeared in the doorway of the car. Their eyes were on him. He knew it was all up....

He was very tired when he re-entered the prison. He did not seem to care much about anything. They took him into the deputy warden's office, and there he saw Jenny sitting on a straight-backed chair. He remembered that he was to have been freed this morning. She had come to meet him. They had told her everything and her face was stained with tears. She was young and pretty. The old deputy had been sympathetic.

"Evans isn't worth a pretty girl like you waiting for," he had said. "You ought to just forget him and get some nice boy your own age."

Jenny turned her anguished eyes on Bull. He looked terrible in the sunlight, torn, dragged, dirty, with blood caked on his forehead. The deputy's gimlet eyes were on him, too.

"You seem to like us here, Bull," he said jocularly. "You've come back, eh?"

Bull paid no attention to him. "Jenny," he said, sadly, but with a certain serenity, "I did it for the kid."

"And what about me?" she wailed, wringing her hands. "And it's Easter time and you would have been free!"

He could not answer, he could only look at her in silent misery.

She turned away from him, but after a moment she came to him and put her hands on his shoulders.

"Oh, I love you, I love you. You're the only man for me!" she breathed. "I'd wait for you if it was for ever."

[1927]

Portrait of a Wife

César Barbet was a young painter of great promise though he had not yet accomplished much in a material way. He had never yet had the good fortune to paint the portrait of a person of wealth or distinction. His subjects had been models or his own friends. His picture of his friend Paul Chassel, his last achievement, had created something like a stir, and he waited, almost breathlessly, for some recognition from the public.

Chassel, himself, did not encourage him.

"The critics," he said, "found the picture interesting. It is unusual. It is alive. But with what a melancholy and disintegrating life! You have captured in it all the bitterness and disillusion of my past. No one looking at it would desire to have his — or more especially her — portrait painted by an artist with a so evident flair for the cruel and mordant."

César's elation drooped a little. There was truth in what his friend said. Of those who had the intention of having their features immortalized, how many would seek out an artist, to describe whose work, the critics had searched for the most macabre words in their vocabulary?

He had succeeded thus brilliantly with Chassel because Chassel had had a melancholy life, and his strength lay in depicting the melancholy, even the horrible.

He went over in his mind the subjects of his best portraits.... Yes, in every one of them was the taint of tragedy. And, unconsciously, his art had been exercised in portraying this rather than beauty. Yet, tragedy was beauty. The woof of the canvas of life was tragedy, and no amount of paint could obliterate it.

Yet in spite of his philosophy, he was depressed. Two weeks passed after the chorus of praise which had greeted his portrait of Chassel, and he had had not one enquiry from a prospective client. He began to wonder if he should be driven to commercial art in order to exist. His sensitive spirit shrank at the very thought of such a possibility.

Then, one morning, the first clear day after several of depressing fog, he was called to the telephone. A low sweet feminine voice enquired:

"Is that Monsieur César Barbet?"

After his answer in the affirmative, which he had tried to make not too eager, the voice went on:

"I wish to interview you in regard to having my portrait done by you. Could you come to my house this morning?"

She gave an address in a fashionable quarter, and César promised to wait on her there inside of the hour.

As he was whirled through the streets in a taxi, his mind was filled with delightful speculations. This sudden change in his fortune seemed almost too good to be true. A woman, young by her voice; beautiful, his florid imagination assured him; rich, or she would not have lived in such a locality! He wished he had had the time to call up his friend Chassel, and crow over him a little. What time had been to spare he had spent in changing into another suit, a well-fitting morning suit of an English cut which showed to advantage his slender supple figure.

He glanced down over himself with satisfaction as he rang the bell of the tall imposing house with its air of detached reserve.

He was at once admitted and shown up an impressive stairway by a servant who knocked at a door at the end of a dim hallway.

Inside the room, he was startled to find the furnishings those of a luxurious bedroom. The blinds were drawn but a clear light like sunlight was diffused by several tall electric lamps. One of these stood by the bed, and there his attention was at once held in an emotion approaching horror.

Propped up beneath the splendour of the silken canopy was a young woman about thirty, apparently in the last stage of some devastating disease. She was swathed in a brilliantly hued dressing-robe which only intensified the deathly pallor of her emaciated face. Her long hair, so richly black and luxuriant that it seemed like some tropic growth which had sapped the last drop of her vitality for its own nourishment, hung in a heavy cloud over her shoulders and the embroidered pillows. Her hands, palms upward, the fingers curled like the petals of dying flowers, lay limply on the bright coverlet. Her grey eyes, lighted, as though from some transcendent emotion from within were fixed on him in burning concentration from the moment he entered the room.

"Monsieur Barbet?" she asked, in the same musical voice that had spoken over the telephone.

He bowed, quite unable to speak.

"Please sit down." She indicated a chair near the bedside with a movement, not of the pallid hand which seemed too feeble ever to stir again, but of the strong brilliantly grey eyes.

"I have been reading the comments of the critics on your portrait of Monsieur Chassel with interest," she went on. "I only wish that I were able to see the picture itself. But as you see, I am tied to my bed."

César murmured words of thanks and commiseration.

"However," the even voice proceeded, "I saw a really excellent reproduction of it, and that, combined with the enthusiasm of the critics, has inspired me to have my own portrait done by you."

"I am indeed honoured," murmured César.

The intensity of her gaze deepened, as though she would search his very soul. "You must have a very unusual mind for so young a man to paint as you do."

"Isn't melancholy, disillusion, a characteristic of youth?" he asked, attempting an ironic smile.

Ah, but not such melancholy, not such disillusion as you put into the face of your portrait of Monsieur Chassel!"

"It is there in the face of Chassel, himself!" cried César.

"That may be! But only one with a genius for the mordant could have so depicted the hollow heartbreak of his life.... I have a friend who knows something of Monsieur Chassel's past. She says you have immortalized it. What is your secret? Ah, I must not ask you that. It lies in your own soul. In the hidden places of your soul, where the light of cold reason never penetrates."

César began to feel more at ease as he talked about himself.

"Madame de Mauriac, I am not at all an extraordinary young man. My life is so normal that I am sure if you knew its events, aside from the excitement of creative art, you would find it intolerably stupid. But while my outward life is serene, I have a strange febrility of imagination which impels me to add a certain extravagance of horror to whatever I paint. I have tried to keep it out of my portraits but I have, as you know, not succeeded, since you were attracted to them by that very quality. It was the same when I was a young child. They bought me pretty drawing-books with pictures in them to copy, but under my hand they became grotesque, horrible. I used to weep at the sight of them, and I would tear them up and bury the fragments rather than that my parents should see them. Then I would be punished for destroying my pretty book."

He had declared that he was not extraordinary but now he glowed in the light of this bizarre confession.

"It is what I should expect," said Madame de Mauriac, her face lighting with an expression of such cruel satisfaction that César involuntarily shuddered. He thought he had never seen so ferocious a mouth. It was the mouth of some small evil animal — a rat, a weasel, at bay.

She smiled.

"You find me repulsive, Monsieur."

"No, no —" he stammered, his face reddening.

"Never mind. It is but natural. You see bitterness and cruelty in my face. Lean closer and look. Tell me, what else do you see?"

He bent and looked into her eyes, heavy with passions brooded on in secret. Seductive, strangely disturbing eyes, the memory of which was always to remain with him.

"I see great pain," he said, slowly, "cruel jealousy, and love turned to hate."

She drew a long, quivering sigh. "Ah, how clever you are!"

For one instant she closed her eyes, as though there were depths in them which she would curtain from a gaze so penetrating. César leaned back in his chair, almost faint from the heavy perfume that rose from her couch, as from a bed of exotic flowers.

After a silence, she said in the voice still so surprisingly full of vitality:

"You will wonder, Monsieur Barbet, why I should wish to preserve on canvas features which are so soon to decay. I will explain. This portrait is to be a legacy. A last gift to a husband, on whom I poured many gifts, not the least of which was the whole store of my love."

"But, Madame —" stammered César.

"I know what you are thinking. What a terrible picture! Unbearable to have in one's home. Horrible to own. That is true....

Well, he may destroy it if he will after one glance. But — if this portrait is as it should be — that one glance will sear his soul." She lifted her lip in the smile that César found so repulsive, and added — "I want him to see what he has done to me."

"Oh, Madame, do you think he deserves to be so hurt?"

Her eyes blazed up at him, but her head did not turn, nor did a finger stir of those wilted flower hands.

"Nothing that might be done to him could possibly repay him for the agony he has caused me. It is because of him that I lie here. He is a murderer. He has killed me."

Her tense and vibrant tones rising from her immobile body were like the bursting into protest of a stone.

"Will you paint my portrait or will you not?" she demanded.

For a moment César hesitated. The thought of this commission was repellent to him. Then his febrile fancy asserted itself. To let himself go with such a subject! To present on canvas, embellished by his own mordant imagination, that face, the very throne of hatred and despair!

He bowed his head, but he could not meet her eyes. It was as though they had conspired to a crime together.

The portrait progressed day by day. Day by day César became more absorbed in his work. He thought of little else. He avoided his friends, excepting Chassel, in whom he had confided the story of the commission, begging him to find out if he could something about Madame de Mauriac and her husband.

Chassel found out she was the daughter of a wealthy banker, and had Polish blood. That de Mauriac, two years younger than she, was of a poor but aristocratic family, and that they had been separated for three years, some said owing to his infidelities, and others because of her unreasoning jealousy and exacting temper. No one knew where de Mauriac was. He had gone off with some other woman it was believed.

Madame de Mauriac talked little during the sittings. Obviously she was too weak for the effort of conversation. Frequently during the rest periods she would close her eyes and ignore him, but sometimes, her brilliant gaze would fasten upon his face, and she would tell with astonishing vigour some incident of her married life, trivial maybe, but always calculated to show de Mauriac in an evil light. She would watch catlike, the effect of her words on César. The expected expressions of sympathy were always ready on his lips but in reality he scarcely heard her. The face on the canvas held him with an hypnotic power. It rose between him and everything he saw. He had horrible dreams at night, and, waking, clammy with sweat, could scarcely wait till morning came when he might go on with his work. Once Madame de Mauriac was too ill to allow of his presence. For two days he wandered about, deeply disturbed. What if she should die, leaving the picture uncompleted?

When he was called to resume the sittings he found her much worse. She looked more dead than alive and scarcely seemed to recognize him. But, when he carried the picture to her bedside, the sight of it put fresh life into her. The smile of satisfaction that curled her lip had something godlike about it.

The fever of his imagination unrestrained, that very fever fanned to intensity, knowing that the picture was not to be exhibited but might be as shocking as his perverse fancy and her pitiless spirit willed, César produced a portrait, unique in its horror.

When the last lines had been drawn about the mouth with its look of animal ferocity, the last luminous stroke accenting the eyes, César stepped back and looked at his work.... He was almost afraid to show it to Madame de Mauriac. But she asked in a low clear voice:

"Is it finished?"

"Madame, I cannot add another stroke."

"Let me see it."

Already propped on the pillows, she raised herself still higher. He had never seen her move before.

"It is the face of a dying woman," she said.

"Madame"—

"Yes, it is.... The face of a woman horribly murdered.... But I shall live on in it.... He may destroy it, but once he has seen it he can never forget...."

She fell back with a gasp that was almost a cry. César thinking she had fainted returned the picture to its easel and flew to her side. She was perfectly conscious, and repeated the words 'never forget.' She was still smiling but the bitterness, the cruelty had gone out of her face, a faint colour had spread over it, her eyes had darkened with a strange tenderness. For a fleeting instant César saw her as she might once have been.

She asked him to call her nurse, and when the curious woman who had never seen the picture entered, he gathered up his materials and carried them to a small room assigned to him. This room was kept locked.

The next day he went early to look at the picture. He was told that Madame de Mauriac had taken a sudden turn for the worse. She could not see him, but he was handed a cheque for a much larger amount than he had asked for his work.

Curiously, the money meant nothing to him. He stuffed the cheque into his pocket, avoiding the eyes of the companion who brought it to him. He had a feeling that the entire household was seething with curiosity about the picture. All these dependents were conscious of the mystery surrounding it. He went into the room where it was and locked the door after him.

He stood before the picture and tried to put himself in the place of the husband who would see it only after his wife's death. What a shock it would be! Enough almost to unhinge a man's reason; that ghastly mask from which looked out those terrible eyes. Those eyes held him as so often the eyes from the bed had held him. That husband who had seen them glow up at him from her pillow where she lay flushed, adoring him.... Now these awful hollows, these shiny projections of bone almost through the parchment flesh! What thoughts for that man! What torture, the agony in those eyes, that crucified smile!

César pictured him standing before the picture bathed in an icy sweat of horror, remorse. He pictured him rising in the night unable to sleep because of the torture of it, standing before it in the stillness of the night, recalling the past. Even if he destroyed it, it was as she had said, he could never destroy the image of it, bitten into his soul by the acid of remorse.... It was not a sinister soul, César felt sure of that. He recalled certain incidents Madame de Mauriac had related to him. Even at the moment he had felt a kind of pity for de Mauriac. Now that pity rushed over him in a warm flood. What had the poor devil done that he should prepare such a torture for him? Besides he disliked Madame de Mauriac. She had the feminine qualities he found the most hateful — she was feline, relentless, self-centred, without imagination. He hated her.

The atmosphere in the room was dead. He flung open the window and let the fresh morning air sweep in. It was Autumn, and from a tree outside golden-tinted leaves were whirling on every gust. One of them blew in at the window and fluttered across the floor to his feet. He picked it up and laid it on his palm. A dead leaf, but beautiful in its death. Leaves... they were all leaves... soon to be blown away... an immense tenderness towards mankind possessed him... even towards that woman in the bedroom. He felt that the febrile terrors of his own imagination were in reality a form of pity....

He took up his palette and a brush. For a long time he stood motionless before the picture. Then, like one in a dream, he began to change, very delicately, the expression of the face. Across the brow he laid the smooth brush strokes like soothing fingers. The frozen eyes he softened into pools of yearning and love, and the horrible smile of complacent cruelty he changed to a smile of forgiveness and pity. The emaciation, the pallor were still there, it was still the face of a dying woman, but in place of terror it now inspired — ah, what feeling would it inspire in Paul de Mauriac?

As César gazed into the face he had re-created, at the heavy locks framing the emaciated head, at the hands lying like withered flowers on the embroidered counterpane, he felt that he should never again paint anything so beautiful, so disturbing. He would return to painting portraits that repelled rather than attracted patrons. But this time, gentleness, pity for de Mauriac like Autumn rain, had quenched the fever of his fancy.

Two days later Madame de Mauriac died. But to César she did not seem dead at all. For him she lived in the little locked room on his canvas. His mind dwelt constantly there brooding on the picture that changed from its second phase back to its first, and back again, with torturing rapidity. Not only that, it developed new phases. It was never still. It had a hundred moods like a perverse and wilful woman. It ogled him, it cajoled him, it glared at him with horror and with hate. He came to wish that he had never heard of Madame de Mauriac.

One day he was called over the telephone by de Mauriac himself.

"I am told by my wife's executors," said the voice of the man for whom César had endured so much, "that I have been left a portrait painted by you. I have permission to go and get it. I wish very much that you would accompany me. I should like to ask you some questions."

They arranged to go to the picture together that evening before dinner. In the car with which de Mauriac had called for César, the young painter tried to make out the features of the other. He saw only a slender figure, a pointed face, a sensitive compressed mouth. The eyes were hidden, shadowed by a drooping hat brim.

"I wish you would tell me something about this portrait of my wife," said de Mauriac. "How did you come to do it?"

"Madame de Mauriac had heard certain criticisms of my work, after an exhibition, which interested her."

"I see. And she sent for you?"

"She was very ill then, wasn't she?"

"Very ill, indeed."

"Yet she was determined to have this picture of herself before — the end?"

"Yes."

"Monsieur Barbet, how did you find her as a subject? A woman, would you say who had suffered much in her life?"

"Yes," said César, cautiously. "But we all suffer, is it not so?"

"True, we all suffer," returned de Mauriac and he added with apparent effort — "Do you know, Monsieur, I find the idea of looking at this portrait very difficult... almost unbearable. My wife and I could not get on. We had been apart for more than two years. It is with the greatest dread that I think of looking on this picture, painted just before she died. I dread to think what it may show me."

"You need not dread looking at it," said César. "It is a very beautiful picture."

De Mauriac cast a strange beseeching look at him from under the drooping brim. "I could not come alone to look at it," he said, with a shiver. "I wanted you who had painted it to be with me. Thank you for coming."

They scarcely spoke again till they reached the house. As they passed the door of the bedroom de Mauriac said —

"In there she died?"

César nodded. He took the key of the room which he for some reason had not wished to relinquish and unlocked the door.

"Ah, you have a key also," said de Mauriac, surprised. "The executors gave me this," and he drew a second key from his pocket.

"They probably had forgotten the existence of this one," returned César, his eyes already fixed on the portrait.

Slanting rays of sunshine touched the face into a divine radiance. The deep eyes seemed to glow with love, the dying lips to smile forgiveness, the pale flower hands to have fallen helpless after giving all. Only the strong rich hair, tossed over the embroidered pillow seemed to breathe perfumed sensuous recollections of bygone hours.

De Mauriac stood transfixed.

César thought: "Thank God I saved him from the horror of what he might have seen."

But, even as he was thinking this, he saw de Mauriac's cheeks bleach, and he felt a sinking in his own heart. A sense of foreboding crept over him, as though an unseen presence had glided into the room, a presence powerful for evil, animated by hate. A weakness came over him. He clutched de Mauriac's arm, and they stood like two children trembling before the picture.

Stronger than his pity for de Mauriac was her hatred for him. Had César absorbed it into his being during those long hours of the sittings, and now in spite of himself, irradiated it, as a kind of luminosity, that transfigured the portrait to its original horror, or had she indeed returned in spirit and looking through the painted eyes, leering through the painted lips, registered finally and terribly her loathing for her husband?

It was there, the cruel face, the very throne of hate, as César had seen it day after day, not to be denied. It was there but with something new — triumph at having overcome the laws of death.

De Mauriac turned a frozen face to César. "What an abomination to put on canvas," he said.

"You see it that way, too?" groaned the artist.

"What way?"

"This new way — no, the old — oh, I cannot explain! But has it changed since you came into the room?"

"Changed?"

"Yes, I tried... I did my best, but... she was stronger... even in death."

"You are mad," said de Mauriac. "Only a madman could have painted such a picture. For Christ's sake, let me away from here before I too lose my reason!"

Without daring to look again on the portrait, he turned and fled through the house. César heard his footsteps echoing through the dismantled halls, and then he heard the hollow clang of the heavy front door.

He turned his eyes fearfully towards the picture. In the last dark flush of the sunset the illumined features faintly smiled at him in the expression of tender forgiveness which he had imposed on them.

[1928]

The Cure

He was washed and combed and scented, and set up in his easy chair by the sunny window — just like an old doll, he thought. Ada, his wife, had been very much like a little girl, washing and dressing her doll, and propping it up in a chair, just under the canary's cage. Very much like a little girl, she had backed away from him to admire the effect, when all was done. She had made him a sprightly little bow, her hands clasped against her breast, her small grey eyes twinkling in that secretive way they had, as though she had just been plotting against him.... And so she had, often and often, plotted to buy finery for her body; or extravagant gewgaws for the house, like that set of Japanese birds painted on silk; or to give fanciful entertainments, like that Spring fête, when all the old chestnut trees in the garden had been strung with innumerable Chinese lanterns, and the summer-house suffocated in paper flowers, and a band rigged out like Hungarian gypsies. She had provided the costumes, and the whole affair, only one of many, had cost the devil of a lot of money. Why, the old silver punch bowls had never been allowed to be emptied. Even the band had had punch. Good stuff, too. Not like the disgusting fruit punches they gave you nowadays.... Well, people had talked a lot about that fête. Twenty-five years ago it look less to amuse people. They'd talk over any fun they'd had for days afterward. Now they'd have forgotten it by the next day. They'd be off after something else. He'd like to see the garden fête that would excite his nephews, Gordon and Fred!

The canary hopped down to the bottom perch and peered at him over the little brass fence that enclosed its cage. It cocked its blond head at him. He hoped it wasn't going to sing, for its noise hurt his head, but before he could stop himself, he had said — "tweet! tweet!" to it, and that was all the encouragement it needed. It burst into a cascade of shrill notes; then it turned to a piercing chatter from which, he thought, it would never desist. He lay back in his chair staring at it. He longed to have the bit of yellow fluff between his fingers. He would tweak its neck for it, by God — squeeze the senseless chatter out of it. Each note seemed like a tiny hammer on his brain. His forehead broke out in a sweat. He raised his voice and called, huskily:

"Ada! Ada!"

At the sound of his voice the canary sang more loudly than ever, completely drowning him out. He sat up and shook his fist at it and cursed it. Convulsed with joy it threw its head back on its ruffled throat and strained every nerve to excel all previous outbursts.

He sank back once more, and shut his eyes. Two tears pressed between the lids and trickled down his cheeks.

He lay quietly now, letting the sharp notes beat upon his brain, beat down his angry thoughts. He felt broken.... A heavy lorrie rumbled down the street. The noise of it shook the summer air and rattled the window pane. When it had passed, the canary had ceased singing.

He weakly opened his eyes and looked up at it. It was eating a seed. It dropped the shell to the bottom of the cage and wiped its beak sharply on the perch. Then it hopped to the bottom perch and began to drink. There fell a delicious silence everywhere. Not a sound in the house, on the street. The full rich perfume of chestnut blossoms came in at the open window. He rolled his head towards the sweetness of it, and through the brightness of his tears saw the great tree standing in glory, its white plumes upright like perfumed candles.

Quietness in the street and through the house. Quietness now in his own spirit. He would soon be himself again if only the damned bird would let him be. It was an awful thing for a man to have a wife — to have been tied up to her for thirty-five years — who always wanted a canary singing or a music box jigging in the house.

There she was coming now, up the stairs. Always that same tripping, high-heeled walk. Walk the same if her back was breaking. Great old girl, Ada. Lively for her age. Showed her clothes off. A good looker.

He tried to look even weaker than he was as she came into the room. He let his chin sink into his breast, his hands lie feebly on the arms of the chair. She had been humming a little, in forced gaiety as she came into the room, but when she saw the sunlight playing over his bowed head, and the way the silky white hair that curled like a child's, was gently stirred by the breeze, she hesitated, a look of mingled anxiety and compassion softening her features.

"Was he sleeping, then?" she asked, in a cooing voice.

"Hm — might ha' been if the damn canary hadn't screeched his head off. Nice bird to leave a helplesh man alone with." It was hard for him to speak distinctly. His tongue was thick and his throat husky.

His wife gave a trill of metallic laughter and made a little dart towards the canary.

"Oh, naughty, naughty, naughty," she said. "Tweenty-weenty! Tweenty-weenty! Did he hurt his dear master's head with him's 'ittle song?"

The canary, recognizing her, began to twitter petulantly. Her black, curled "transformation" made her look top-heavy. Her small grey eyes twinkled in her pale, powdered face.

Dick Boone regarded both her and the bird with equal disfavour.

"The matter with you both is," he said, "that you think too much about yourselvesh. Always prinking and twittering and hopping from one perch to another. That's what'sh the matter with you and the bird, Ada mine."

With a fluttering movement she came from the canary to him, and bent her face towards his, smiling into his eyes.

"And I pleased him once, didn't I?" she breathed. "There wasn't a girl could match Ada, for elegance, for style!"

"Get away," he said, crossly, turning his face away. "Suffocatin' me. I don' wan' to be bothered."

But she pressed closer, her thin lips folded in a smile. One of her long earrings was sharp against his cheek. The large sleeves of her pale blue silk tea-gown of the period enveloped him. The smell of her powder, and some scent that she always used on her "transformation", made him feel choky and helpless.

"Going to be good?" she whispered, looking commandingly into his eyes.

"Hm — hm," he grunted, playing with her beads.

"And take your egg-nog?"

"Hm — hm."

"And nothing else — now look at me — nothing else, to make you naughty and sick?"

"No — o."

She kissed him briskly and went into the bathroom.

In some ways the bathroom was like the little room behind a small chemist's shop. Phials, measuring glasses, miscellaneous appliances for the sick room and the toilette were everywhere in hopeless disorder. Almost empty bottles, grey with dust, their sticky labels quite illegible, crowded the stained shelves. It was like a small, untidy kitchen, too, for there were a gas ring, several saucepans, several bottles of milk — from the full bottle of morning's milk through sour degrees to the one whose curdled contents was crowned by a miniature forest of fuzzy green mould. Boxes of biscuits, cartons of eggs, tins of "foods", glasses of jelly overflowed to the top of the wicker soiled clothes basket. No servant was ever allowed in here to tidy up. This was Ada Boone's own secret room, where, filled with apprehensions, often sick at heart, though humming gaily so that Dick might not guess it, she administered to his needs in his bad times. And when he was "himself", it was from this room that they emerged in turn, fresh, scented, combed, shaved, curled, a still dashing, still to-be-stared-after couple. A strange, pathetic, vain, wayward couple, the Boones. Childless, they quarrelled and made it up like children themselves. Though each disliked the other's ways, they were deeply attached, very dependent on each other.

Presently, after the prolonged swishing of an eggbeater, she emerged, carrying an egg-nog.

"Nice 'ittle egg-nog for 'ittle boy," she said.

"Not hungry," he said, turning his head towards the window. "Rather look at the chestnut tree."

"Ah, but he must eat and drink to get well again."

He looked at her now, with a malicious grin.

"Drink?" he repeated.

"Not naughty stuff. Just milk to make him strong."

He took the glass and sipped.

"Pf," he said. "Insipid stuff."

"More sugar? A wee dash of nutmeg?"

He raised his childlike blue eyes imploringly to her face.

"Just a drop of rum, old girl, to take away that sickly taste, give some body to it."

All her softness was gone now. Her eyes struck compellingly into his. She said, harshly:

"Listen. Not one drop. Not if you went on your knees. Don't I know what's good for you? Am I not going to follow the doctor's orders?"

"Very well." He set the glass on the table beside him. "Shan't drink it then, and that'sh flat."

She went into one of her sudden passions. "You dare defy me?" she screamed. "I, who have not had my proper sleep in a fortnight because of you! You dare defy me!"

"I guessh I'm master in my own house."

She gave a loud, bitter laugh. "A fine master, you are, aren't you? Drinking yourself to death as fast as you can? I'd like to know where we'd be if it weren't for the boys. As loyal to you as if they were your own sons."

"You never gave me a son to go into the business," he sneered.

Her face became crimson.

"No. And I'm thankful I didn't, for he'd certainly have inherited your tastes. A man can't be like you and not affect his children."

Her voice beat him down, but he reiterated sullenly — "Shan't drink the beastly stuff."

"Not drink it? You'll do as I command — I am the major-general. You are the private. I am the Sultana. You are a — a —"

"Eunuch," he suggested, with a feeble laugh.

The canary, inspired by the hubbub, joined his hysteria to hers, rocking on his perch, his throat vibrating with madness.

Beads of sweat stood on Dick Boone's forehead. He reached submissively for the glass. He was broken. It rattled pathetically against his teeth as he gulped the sweet mixture. Seeing him so, Ada's anger melted as a tropical tempest into sunshine.

She took the empty glass from him, patted him encouragingly on the shoulder, and brought him the morning paper. But the egg-nog had not agreed with him. He hiccoughed, and was glad that he did so, since it showed that all was not well. But she only flitted about the room, smiling at him as she passed, touching the canary's cage into dizzy jigging on its spiral holder.

"Another day or two," she remarked, at last, "and he will be quite himself again. Go down to business like a nice little gentleman."

She was called to the telephone.... As soon as her loud, animated voice came from below he rose slowly from his chair, steadying himself by its arms, and grunting weakly. He took the empty glass in one hand and shuffled in his leather slippers to the tall old wardrobe. He fumbled with the key, opened the door cautiously, and thrust one hand into the back corner behind the coats, waistcoats and trousers.

He fumbled, and even put his head in among the clothes and peered into the dusk, but the bottle of Scotch he always kept there to be handy was there no longer. He made certain that this was so, then, baffled and resentful, he turned away. Someone had taken the bottle away. Ada, or one of the boys. If Gordon or Fred had done it, they'd hear from him. He'd not stand any damned interference from them. He'd make them eat humble pie! His sister Lizzie's sons daring to interfere with him! Well, Lizzie had been an interfering piece in her day, and her sons took after her.

The canary had put its beak between the wires of its cage to watch his proceedings before the wardrobe. Now it burst into jeering song. He knew it was jeering at him by the way it cocked one beady eye in his direction.

"Stop it, you little devil," he growled. "Whole world's againsht me — even canary."

It ceased its singing but began to utter ear-splitting "tweets!"

"I'll tweet you," he said, savagely, and struck the cage with his hand.

He had only intended to jar it, to vent some of his impotent anger in frightening the bird, but the blow must have been sharper than he knew, for one corner of the bottom of the cage was loosened and, like a golden flash, the canary shot forth, alighting with a wild flutter on the tall head of the bed.

He was horrified, contrite. What had he done? What would Ada say? There was the open window — Oh, dear! oh, dear!

"Pretty — pretty —" he coaxed, shuffling towards it, all his fine white hair standing on end, his delicate, aquiline face, flushed by concern. "Come down to Daddy, then — little rascal." Ada often called them Mammy and Daddy to the bird, and he unconsciously did so now in his anxiety to propitiate and capture it.

But it sped past his groping hand like a comet, floated on outstretched wings a second before the window, then struck itself against the mirror of the dressing-table.

Ada was coming. Humming as she came. He could not bear another scene. He would get into bed.

With sudden agility he clambered on to the high bed, and drew the rose pink satin quilt over him. Only his crest of white hair showed above the edge. He breathed heavily.

Ada entered with a sharp tapping of high-heeled shoes. There was a moment's silence, then she, in turn, exclaimed — "Oh, dear — Oh, dear —" And ran to the window and closed it. Now there were stealthy movements about the room. Deep sighs of aggravation. Then a "ha!" of blessed relief. She had caught him. He was in the cage.

Deeply, serenely, Dick breathed against the satin quilt. Ada leaned over him and looked into the smooth mask of his face. She drew the quilt down a little so he would get more air, lowered the blind, covered the canary's cage, and tiptoed from the room.

II

When he awoke he felt very much better. He got up without assistance, and, when the gaunt man-servant brought him his lunch, he spoke to him in a clearer, steadier voice than he had been able to produce since the last drinking bout.

He enjoyed his lunch. He had the fellow open the window and went and sat by it, breathing deeply of the warm, ambient air, scented with chestnut blossoms. A hose was playing on the greensward below, and a pair of robins were running in and out of the spray as if they loved it. New life beat in his blood like music. His hand, with its thick veins, that rested on the sunny window sill, was steady.

Ada came in, dressed to go somewhere in a flowered organdie, with enormous sleeves, and trailing skirt. She told him how the canary's cage had come apart, and what a time she had had to catch him without making a noise. She was going out but would not be gone long. She smelled like a flower bed.

He leaned out of the window as she sailed down the walk. She looked up and blew him a kiss. He threw kisses back.

"Romeo, ah, Romeo!" she called.

"Ha, ha, Juliet! Good old girl!"

She was a very emotional woman. Emotions, real or pretended, filled her life. And he had always had the good sense, or the weakness perhaps, to play up to them.

He watched her out of sight. He watched a watering cart lumber heavily by, drawn by two sweating black horses. He was willing to bet they had belonged to an undertaker once. He watched young Mrs. Cowan ride gaily by on her new red bicycle, a small sailor hat topping her golden pompadour. A pretty piece, plump as a partridge.

He began to think about his business. He would telephone the office at once and see how things were going on. He had telephoned several times every day since he had been under the weather, but the boys spoke so indistinctly, there was such a buzzing in the phone, that there was not much satisfaction in it.

He took down the receiver and asked for the office number, that number about which hung an unfailing charm, for he was deeply proud of the wholesale tobacco and cigar business, that had been carried on by the Boones under the same roof for three generations, founded by his grandfather, a well connected Carolinian.

"Main 3344."

He waited with almost pathetic eagerness in the dim hallway, a tousled-haired little man in a maroon dressing-gown.

"Hello," came in Gordon's deep, even tones.

"Oh, hello, Gordon. How's things?"

"Everything's fine. That is, Fred and I are working hard. How are you to-day, Uncle?"

"Oh — h, so, so. Anything new?"

"A big order from Martin Brothers. We don't know whether to fill it or not. I hear they're kind of shaky."

"Don't fill it!" His voice shook with excitement. "D — don't fill it till I look into things. Hear me, Gordon? Don't fill it!"

"All right, Uncle. All right. Just as you say. Good-bye."

"Now mind, Gordon — wait — better send Fred to the phone — tell Fred —?"

But Gordon was gone.

He hung up the receiver and climbed the three steps from the landing, shuffling back to his room.... The exhilaration of business stirred his blood. Why had that fool Gordon left the telephone so quickly? Those boys were getting above themselves and no mistake. Needed calling down. And they'd get it!

The man brought him a cup of tea.

He felt refreshed by it, and hastened weakly to the telephone again. He cleared his throat and demanded in a firm voice.

"Main 3344."

"Hello." This time it was the stenographer's thin voice.

"Miss Wayling. It's Mr. Boone speaking. Is Mr. Fred Mitchell there?"

"Just a minute, please, Mr. Boone. Mr. Mitchell's in the outer office."

He waited several minutes, then Fred's sharp, nasal voice enquired curtly, "That you, Uncle?"

"Oh, hello Fred? H — how'sh things?"

He had intended to be stern, the heavy uncle, but Fred's hard, crisp tones made him feel suddenly confused. He forgot what he had in mind when he came to the telephone.

"H — how'sh things," he repeated.

"Good as can be expected in times like these. Don't you worry. The new cigar is fine. Got a swell box. Screaming beauty of a Spanish girl on the lid. I'll tell you what you can do. Think up a name for it. We've got to have a striking name. Good-bye."

Before Dick could reply he was gone.

However, he spent the rest of the afternoon quite cheerfully, between playing Patience, and thinking of a name for the new cigar. At last he hit on Adabella, a fine sonorous name, and a compliment to his wife, Adabella, Ada beautiful.

He could hardly wait for her to come home so he could tell her. And when she did come and he told her, she was really charmed. She was especially tender with him that evening, and, when the boys came in after dinner, they were especially nice. All three stood about him, smiling down at him, and looking, somehow, rather anxious about him; Ada in her flowered dress with a dash of rouge on her lips; Gordon with his built out shoulders, and, already, the smug, aggressive look of the successful business man; Fred, sharp as a whip.

It was Fred who came in later, with a small glass in his hand, and approached his chair, smiling.

"I guess a little drink wouldn't do you any harm, to-night, Uncle," he remarked, casually.

Something steely in his voice, penetrating in his cold eyes, arrested Dick's attention.

"When I want a drink, I'll ask for it," he said, sulkily.

Fred showed astonishment, chagrin.

"Well, from what I have heard you wanted one pretty badly to-day," he observed.

Anger flamed into Dick's eyes. So they talked him over among them, did they?

"You can mind your own business," he retorted. "I'll not stand any interference from you."

Gordon came in from the hall. He must have been listening, for he said, with nervous cheerfulness.

"Well, if you won't have one with Fred, Uncle, have it with me. You've reached the stage where it'll do you good. Brace you up."

Dick turned on the two young men with sudden vehemence. "What's the matter with you two, anyway? What are you trying to do? Make me drink so you can have the run of things a bit longer?" Suspicion crept into his eyes. "Get out. Do you hear? Get out! I won't have it!"

His wife's voice came from the downstairs hall, sharp with anxiety.

"What's the matter, boys?"

He started toward the door to go to her, but Fred laid his hand on his arm, his steely eyes looked into his. He held the glass to his lips.

"Look here, Uncle, you've got to drink it. There's no use objecting."

Gordon was on his other side, gripping his other arm. Still both were smiling. He felt suddenly weak and confused. If they were set on his taking a drink, he'd better do it. He wasn't strong enough to resist those two smiling, staring, bright-eyed nephews. Shaking, he gulped the whiskey down.... Well, it was good. Nothing wrong about it, but they shouldn't have persisted that way. It wasn't respectful.

The room seemed to float around them, as though they were all under water. Above, the great globes of the gasolier shone like distant moons, through leagues of shimmering, green sea. The two nephews were white-faced and goggle-eyed, like strange fish. A booming, as of distant surf, made other sounds indistinct but he faintly heard Gordon say:

"Pretty dopey, what?"

He had his coat on. His silk hat was over one eye. Strange to wear a frock coat and silk hat at the bottom of the sea. Ada was there, too, a long-tailed mermaid. Adabella. She was kissing him. Shedding salt, salt tears. Adabella, Ada mine....

Lights flashed by. Wheels rumbled. He slept.

He had slept for several hours when he opened his eyes, refreshed, but with a sort of buzzing in his ears. There was a soft light in the room, shaded from the bed by a screen. It was several minutes before the shapes of the furniture in the room resolved themselves from unfamiliar shadows, and he perceived that all about him was strange. He turned to look for Ada's head, divested of its "transformation", on the other pillow but it bulged, smooth and white beside him.... A tremor of fear shook him. He raised himself on his elbow and stared wildly about the room. It was comfortable, with plain cretonne coverings on the chairs, in perfect neatness, very different from the luxurious disorder that he and Ada loved. He had never seen the room before.

With an exclamation of dismay, he would have sprung from the bed, but at the sound of his movements, a short thick-set man appeared from behind the screen and laid a restraining hand on his arm.

"Just lie down, Mr. Boone," he said, soothingly, in a muffled, heavy voice. "You haven't been very well. Dr. Searle will soon be in to see you."

Dr. Searle! The name struck his brain like a blow, and yet he could not dislodge from the murk of his bewilderment the sinister significance attached to it... Searle — White — Tom White — his friend, dead now, old Tom had been in Searle's Institute twice. The first time came out "cured", the second, died — after months — or was it years? — of it. Searle's Institute! A cure! He knew what their methods were. Disgusting.

And Ada had let him in for this. The boys he had generously taken into his business — the business of Boone and Son — had done this filthy trick to him — had persuaded Ada it was for the best. A cure! Searle's cure! A month of it would kill him. Kill him! And they'd be glad. Have the business to themselves. The miserable, ungrateful cubs. Lizzie's cubs. She'd been an ungrateful sister and now — her cubs!

The attendant regarded him speculatively. Was the old fellow going to be troublesome?

"Is there anything I can do for you, sir?" he asked. "Would you like a cup of cocoa?"

"No, no." His face was a pale mask. No sign in it of the turmoil of his thoughts. "Except my nightshirt. I'd like that. Why am I just in my underclothes?"

"Well, you see, sir, you wasn't very bright when they brought you in, and they thought the less fussing over you the better."

"Good boys," murmured Dick. "Kind, thoughtful boys. My nephews."

"Yes, sir. I'll help you on with your nightshirt now."

The man went to a clothes closet, and Dick had a glimpse of his clothes hanging there, limp and expressionless, like a dead man's clothes.

He was so weak, it appeared, that the attendant had to support him while the nightshirt was put on. He sank back on the pillow with a deep sigh of contentment.

"Let me be now," he muttered. "Want to shleep. Must get lots o' sleep."

The attendant lowered the gas. "If you want me, I'm right in the next room," he said. The only answer was a snuffling snore.

Dick heard him moving about in the next room. He heard footsteps coming along the passage, and another man's voice from the doorway asking:

"What's he like?"

"Quiet as a lamb. Sound asleep. I'm going to have a snooze myself. Goodness knows I need it after the time I had with Mr. Gidding last night. I'm going to make a big kick against all this night duty, you'll see."

III

His heart was hammering against his ribs as it hadn't done since he was a boy up to mischief, as, an hour later, he stood, fully dressed, in the doorway of the next room. It was a small sitting-room with a door leading into the passage. It stood open but when he had tried the outer door of the bedroom he had found it locked. He must pass through this room.

Carrying his top hat in one hand and his shoes in the other, he glided past the sleeping form of the attendant, huddled uncomfortably on a narrow sofa. The passage was dark, save for the moonlight that fell through a grated window at the end, but he could make out the dark cavern of the stairway, and, as he cautiously descended, the thick carpet deadened all sound, and his light weight caused no creaking of the steps. From a room above came a steady, dismal groaning that made his blood freeze. If he hadn't been wide awake, alert, resourceful, he might have stayed there to add his groans to the night.

The hall below was lighted by a gas jet burning under a coloured globe. Through an open double doorway, he saw the dim shape of a dining-table, and the faint glimmer of silver on a sideboard. He entered and examined the three windows. They were large, and locked securely by some patent device he could not discover. A cold sweat of fear bathed his body. Despair was about to seize him when he felt a cool draught on his back, and found that it came from the opening into a serving pantry. He thought:

"If I can only squeeze my body through there, I'm a free man."

Carefully he put his shoes and top hat through first, then, mounting a chair, he placed one knee on the projecting shelf.

"What a blessing, I am small," he thought, "for this hole is not much bigger than a rabbit's burrow."

Strained, bruised, shaking in every limb, he stood, at last, in the serving pantry. A fresh breeze gushed in through the wide open window.

With a sob of joy, he threw his hat and shoes out on to the grass, and clambered after them.

He was safe from that nightmare house! He was free beneath the velvet sky where the warm moon hung like a gilded lamp and the little stars trembled in the treetops.

He sat down on the grass and put on his shoes, fumbling over the lacing of them; he had already put his hat on one side of his head. No one saw him, a dishevelled little man, creep through the side gate into the street.

He paused a moment to cast a look of mingled triumph and abhorrence at the dark shape of the house towering above him, then moved like a shadow down the quiet street towards a small park that surrounded an old church, where he remembered a bench on which he could rest a while and think.

The City Hall clock struck four as he turned into the park. Already there was a faint luminous light in the east. He sank to the bench feeling weak, but filled with an odd exhilaration. He removed his hat and let the sweet air run like caressing fingers through his thick white hair. He emitted a great "whew" of relief and satisfaction. It was years since he had been out on the street at this hour alone. He recalled some of the nocturnal adventures of his young manhood and grinned audaciously at the dawn. Why, it must have been through this very park, at this hour, forty years ago, that he and that girl in the pink domino had run, with the others in pursuit. What a lovely, long white neck she had had! He thought of Fred and Gordon and their pleasures, and the thought made him sick. Gordon, and his built out shoulders — Fred, with his tight, sallow face.... He chuckled as he savoured the surprise he had in store for them.

He dozed, and when he opened his eyes it was daylight. Milk carts were rattling down the street, empty street-cars jolting past. He boarded one and rode to the station. In the station restaurant he had a chop and a cup of coffee. In the station barber shop he had a shave, a haircut, and his clothes brushed, remarking to the man that travelling all night made one look very seedy.

From the station, he took a cab to the warehouse. The gilt sign — John Boone and Son — glittered in the morning sunlight. Well, there was life in Son yet — he'd show them. As he passed through the office, there were looks of surprise at his early arrival — perhaps surprise that he should arrive at all — but there were smiles, real smiles of pleasure, and he glowed in return.

Old Parsons, the book-keeper, took his coat and hat, and he sat down behind his desk to await his nephews. While he waited he dozed a little but he was sitting upright when they came in together. Fred was saying:

"Well, I wonder how old 3344 feels this morning. He won't be calling us up anyway. Thank goodness."

"Old 3344 feels very well, thank you," answered Dick, leaning over the desk to glare at them. "Yes, he'll be calling up this office quite often but you won't be here to answer."

"Why, Uncle —" stammered the young men.

"Yes — 'Why, Uncle' " — growled their uncle. "You thought you'd put me in a 'Cure', didn't you? Well, it worked faster than you expected. Now, you may put your hats on your swelled heads and go. Never let me see your faces again."

"Oh, Uncle," pleaded Gordon, "I think that for Mother's sake —"

"Yes, I've borne with you for your mother's sake, and I bore with her for her mother's sake. Now, I'm through. Go."

* * *

He paid the cabman at his own door, opened the low wrought-iron gate, and walked up the gravelled path with an almost bride-groom feeling of nervousness and elation. What would Ada be doing? He attached no blame to her in this affair. It was all the nephews' doing.

The chesnut tree held its white plumes towards the sun, the lawn unrolled its dewy greenness, the tones of the largest music-box tinkled from within. It was playing "The Blue Danube".

It did seem a little callous of Ada to have set it going this morning. But, when, panting from the exertion, he reached the door of their bedroom, the sight that met his eyes would have melted any heart. Ada was lying face downward on the bed sobbing bitterly, her pink silk peignoir rumpled, her "transformation" askew.

"Oh, Dick," she was sobbing, and again — "Oh, Dick."

He hurried to her and raised her. "It's all right, Ada mine. I'm here. Safe and sound. I'm here — I'm here —"

As she turned towards him with amazement and relief, he added, with his face twisted like a child's that is about to cry — "I'm going to be good, Ada," and sank into her arms.

[1928]

Quartet

Behrens hesitated at the corner of the Via Parthenope and the Via Santa Lucia, wondering whether or not he should take a carriage to his destination. The moment his hesitation was noticed by the drivers who stood laughing and talking together on the seaward side of the street, the group broke up and the members of it hurried toward him, beseeching and commanding him to ride in the particular carriage of each.

He looked from one healthy, sunburned face to another, not understanding a word they said. He wished he had not hesitated, for it was a fine January morning, exhilarating for a long walk. He shook his head doubtfully, and half turned away, but two of the drivers followed him, one on either side, inviting him to take various expeditions.

He found himself beside the carriage of one of them, who, with a wide gesture, implored him to enter, shook out and displayed proudly a ragged, woolly rug for covering his knees.

Behrens had just put a foot on the step when his eye fell on the horse, its drooping head, its wretched side through which the bones seemed ready to protrude. Seeing his expression, the other driver caught him by the arm and pointed triumphantly to his own horse farther along the street.

"Very fine horse!" he exclaimed, unexpectedly in English. "Very fine. Fat. Round. Go very fast. The very best horse in Napoli!" He drew Behrens toward his carriage. "Very fine carriage, too. Very beautiful. *Molto bello!*"

There was no doubt about it, this horse, of a bright chestnut, was sleek and well cared for, able to work; while the other poor beast had little endurance left in him. Behrens chose the chestnut.

When Behrens had seated himself, a bitter altercation began between the two drivers. The first seemed to have half a mind to carry Behrens by force to his carriage. The second sought to climb to his seat, but the other pressed his body between, waving his whip and letting loose all his Neapolitan vitality in curses.

Behrens, rather anxiously, awaited an exchange of blows. Seeing the flash of their eyes and teeth, he felt that even a thrust from a knife would not be surprising. He had a mind to alight from the other side of the carriage, but miraculously, the dispute ended, the second driver gave the first a halfhearted push on the chest, got onto the seat, and cracked his whip. The first strolled back to his companions, his rage apparently subsiding into tolerance. A moment later he was again laughing and talking in the sunshine.

Above the blueness of the bay was the blue arch of the sky. From Vesuvius rose a golden feather that spread and hung plume-like against the sky. Capri lifted a bronze shoulder from the sea. From behind the Castello dell'Ovo a racing skiff rowed by eight youths darted into the open, their bare arms shining in the sun. They uttered a rhythmic musical singsong as they pulled. It was all delightful, Behrens thought.

He planted his stick between his feet, clasped his hands on it, his eyes obediently following the pointed whip of the driver, but his mind not taking in the descriptions in broken English of the buildings. He was thinking: "All of this is perfectly natural to Alice. By now none of these things looks strange to her. This is her home, and she's absolutely used to it. Loves it, I suppose."

Everything he saw he tried to see not as a tourist, a stranger, but as Alice, who was now accustomed to its foreignness. A little band of blind musicians was playing by the roadside. Extraordinarily sweet, wistful music, Behrens thought. He fished out a coin and threw it on the small tin plate one of them held out. The blind man bowed, smiled, but at that instant a bicyclist, passing between, knocked the dish from his hand and the coin to the road. Behrens gave a "Tck!" of compassion and craned his neck as the carriage rolled on to see whether the man had recovered the coin. He could see him on hands and knees groping for it. His comrades had begun a fresh tune. Behrens sighed.

His eye was now caught by a friar of some sort, whose bare red heels showed at every step beneath his rough habit. His tonsured head gleamed; his face had an expression of inscrutable patience. Meeting him were two tiny children in white fur coats unbelievably short above slender bare legs. Their nurse, wheeling a perambulator, wore a black velvet skirt, a yellow lace-trimmed apron, and a fringed scarlet shawl. Her gleaming black hair was massed beneath a tortoise-shell comb. The friar passed them without seeming to see them. "And all this strangeness," thought Behrens, "is as natural to Alice now as Massachusetts once was."

They turned into the shadowed intricacies of the side streets. The driver continued to point out objects of interest, and Behrens suddenly remembered that he had never told the man where he wanted to go. He leaned forward and touched him on the arm.

"Please drive," he said in his slow, rather heavy voice, "to the villa of Count Rombarra."

Even as he heard his own voice saying the name, it seemed unbelievable that he should be going to see Alice. Six years since he had seen her, and that on the day of her marriage to Rombarra. How exquisite she had looked that day! Beautiful, with the pride and happiness of a freshly opened flower. And it was Rombarra who had brought that happiness, not he! He had never been able to stir her to anything warmer than a feeling of placid friendship for him. He was an old story. A great disadvantage it was to be neighbors and all that, if you suddenly fell in love with a girl and wanted to impress her. He had been able to make no impression in that way; it had taken Rombarra with his Latin fire to do that. Well, he was going to see her now, after six years, and, thank goodness, he had got over it and would be able to make a friendly call without any humiliating embarrassment on his side.

A young woman was letting down a basket by a rope from a balcony, and a man was waiting with silvery little fish to put into it. In a doorway an old woman was cooking apples over a charcoal fire. The air was full of unfamiliar sounds. It was all strange and exhilarating to Behrens. After all these years of hard work and colorless surroundings, he felt as though he were experiencing a new birth. In this ancient place he felt his own newness as ludicrous, even pathetic.

If only he had someone, as naïvely impressed as himself, as companion! Supposing that he and Alice were making this trip together for the first time. On the voyage over and in the hotel he had met several couples abroad for the first time, laughing together, getting mixed over the foreign money together, experiencing this new birth together. But, he remembered, it would not have been new to Alice, after all, for she had been to Europe twice as a young girl. Strange that he should have forgotten, when it had been on one of those trips that she had met Rombarra.

A street rose on his right, ascending in a flight of sunswept stone steps. One above another were the stands of the flower sellers, mingling the colors of carnations, roses, violets, and heliotrope. A small boy ran from the nearest stand, holding a bunch of violets toward Behrens.

Behrens shook his head. No, he could not take violets to Alice. Rombarra might not like it. He felt sure that Rombarra of the sloe eyes and chiseled features would not like it. But the boy thrust the nosegay onto Behrens' knees, running alongside and holding up his little brown paw for money. Behrens could not resist him. He found a five-lire piece and put it into the hand.

They were on the heights, the old city spread out below. It looked immense, crowding about that blue bay. A great, rather frightening foreign city for a young girl like Alice to have come to. The driver had alighted and was awaiting his fare. Behrens paid him and entered the gate, glancing curiously about the terraced garden with its urns, its statues and trickling fountain. Apparently without reason his heart began to pound heavily; his lips became dry; and he found no moisture on his tongue to moisten them. He rang the bell, wishing very much that he was not carrying the little nosegay of flowers. Still, if Alice were alone, if, perhaps, Rombarra were busy with his own affairs somewhere, it would be all right. Alice might like to have the flowers, for the sake of old times, her old life.

He was shown into a vast, high-ceilinged room, furnished with quite wonderful antique pieces, Behrens supposed. But he thought, standing there, his heart still thumping, that he should have hated to live with them. One would have the feeling always that they would look exactly the same five hundred years hence, when one's bones were only a handful of dust.

And the penetrating chill of the room! He shivered in his handsome gray tweed coat. He heard steps, voices. Alice and her husband and her little girl of four (Behrens had forgotten about the child) came into the room. They shook hands. Rombarra's long, cool finger touched Behrens's without enthusiasm. Alice's hand was hot and dry, Behrens noticed, and her fingers seemed to curl almost feverishly about his. Her eyes smiled up at him beautiful as ever, more beautiful — or perhaps he had forgotten just how lovely she was.

Behrens thought, with a sudden pang, that Rombarra was a much more suitable mate for her physically than he would have been. Rombarra was wearing the romantically dashing uniform of an officer of the cavalry. Alice explained, in her voice that had exactly the same soft, precise quality as of old, that they had just returned from the Horse Show, where her husband had been riding. He was very fond of horses and had done remarkably well in the show. Behrens congratulated him, and the Italian smiled, showing a rim of perfect teeth.

Behrens wondered, with sudden misgiving, if Rombarra understood English. But, surely, after six years of marriage with Alice, he would have learned to speak her native tongue. Behrens knew that he himself, slow though he was, would have learned to speak Arabic, had it been the language of Alice. He said, in halting French, to Rombarra:

"I was congratulating you on your success in the Horse Show."

It was as though he had touched an electric button. Rombarra's face became brilliant. He began to talk swiftly and eagerly in French. Behrens could not understand a word, and murmured so, apologetically, to Alice.

"Oh, it does not matter," she said. "I want you to come and sit down by me. It's so wonderful seeing you again after all these years."

Behrens sat down near her. He felt intensely embarrassed, for Rombarra's intelligent eyes were fixed on his face, not with the look of suspicion that Behrens had half anticipated, but with a look which seemed to say: "Come, now! Let us talk about horses. I can see that you are fond of them and so am I. Let us talk about them."

Behrens said to Alice:

"Please explain to your husband how stupid I am. I knew my French was very bad, but I didn't realize how little I have of it."

"It does not matter," she repeated. "And he understood quite well that you were congratulating him."

"But what was he saying to me?"

"Really, I did not notice. I was thinking only of you — how strange and wonderful to see you here." She was sitting on the edge of the sofa, poised in an attitude that suggested recklessness — Behrens thought that she looked like a bird just about to fly upward. Behind her stood a tall bureau, inlaid with ivory, on the top of which was a nude female figure in alabaster in an attitude of gentle resignation. The contrast between this figure and Alice was so great that Behrens's eyes and mind were held by it for a space and he missed what Alice next said.

She had drawn her little girl beside her, and he now heard her say:

"You knew I had a child? Her name is Félicité. She was born in the first year of our marriage or, you may be sure, I should never have called her that."

Behrens was startled and bewildered. Why had Alice spoken so? And in front of her husband, even though he understood little English? Was it possible that Alice was not happy?

He covered his discomfort by picking up the little girl and putting her on his knee. He placed the nosegay of violets in her hands, glad to be rid of it.

"Flowers," he said emphatically, hoping that in this case he would be understood. "I brought them for you."

The child took them, laughed, and held them to her face. She jigged her little body happily on his knee.

"Children always loved you," Alice said; then spoke to the child in Italian.

"Grazie, signor," murmured Félicité. She threw herself back against Behrens, laughing roguishly. She had never lain against such an enormous, comfortable body before, and was delighted by its proportions.

Behrens, looking down at her, felt a deep and tender thrill pass through him. Alice's child! And he had once hoped that Alice's child would be his also. He bent his head and pressed his lips against her hair.

"You little darling!" he murmured. He had never known anything so delicious as the feel of this supple, exquisite little body in his arms. He wondered if Rombarra loved her as he would have done.

When he raised his eyes, they looked straight into those of Rombarra, who was leaning forward, an expression of gratification on his handsome face. They smiled across the child.

"Bellissima bambina!" cried Behrens, reckless of what a few words of Italian might bring forth.

Again the Neapolitan's face was illuminated, but this time there was added to its brightness a tender pride that touched Behrens. Rombarra broke into a flood of musical Italian which ended in a pointed question.

Behrens turned ruefully to Alice. "Whatever does he say?" he implored.

"He is asking you if you have any children of your own."

Behrens shook his head. *"Non, non,"* he said. *"Je n'en ai pas."*

At once Rombarra obligingly turned to French.

"But," exclaimed Behrens desperately, "how can I talk to him? The moment I say a word or two in Italian or French, he says so much that he frightens me! Doesn't he know any English at all, after — after all these years?"

"No," returned Alice in a cool, clear voice. "He is far too narrow-minded, too stupid, to learn English."

Behrens could scarcely credit his senses. Alice, sitting there poised on that sofa, with the reckless air of a bird about to fly straight upward, calling her husband narrow-minded and stupid before his face, to Behrens, whom she had not seen for six years!

"For God's sake, be careful!" he said.

"Oh, there's no danger. He doesn't know a word of English. He probably thinks we are saying how well he looks in his uniform." She smiled serenely at her husband. He put another question to Behrens, who, following Alice's remark, had glanced involuntarily at the uniform.

"What does he say?" asked Behrens miserably, knotting his forehead.

"He wants to know if you, too, are in the army."

"No, I am not," replied Behrens firmly and distinctly. "I am a stockbroker." He gazed into Rombarra's eyes, beseeching him to understand. He was trying to tell Rombarra not only that he was a stockbroker, but that he was an unwilling participant in this dreadful situation. For surely, though the count could not understand English, he must feel the impact of those appalling words beating about him. Behrens was afraid of Alice, afraid of what she would say or do next. She seemed capable of anything.

She said: "He looks clever, doesn't he? With those intense eyes and that smile. But he's only clever at lovemaking. He's jealous of me. He wouldn't let me have you here without his being present, but he's absolutely unmoral himself. Before we had been married two years I found out that he had been unfaithful to me time and again!"

She spoke composedly, her eyes, with a pleasant, friendly light in them, on Behrens' face. She had leaned back, and her graceful arms were extended along the back of the sofa. To Behrens their curve seemed like the outline of half-spread wings. His forehead was flushed crimson. He stared straight at Rombarra, striving, with that stare, to build a wall around him, to protect him.

The little girl struggled to her feet and ran to her father, holding up the nosegay for him to smell. Rombarra began to talk rapidly and caressingly to her.

Behrens got out, in a muffled tone: "For the love of God, Alice! Don't talk like that. I simply can't bear it. I'll have to get out. Isn't it possible for me to see you alone?"

"No, no! It would be too dangerous. Besides, what would be the good? He appears to be friendly to you, but you don't understand him. He is sly, and he can be violent."

Behrens had an odd sensation of floating; there was a singing sound in his ears. He wondered if he might be going to have a stroke. He experienced, too, a feeling of deep self-pity. How cruel of Alice to create such a ghastly situation as this! He had suffered so much because of her in the past. He had come here feeling that that was all over. He had been reasonably sure of himself, prepared for a meeting that might revive a little the old pain, but that would establish a new picture of Alice in his memory — an Alice dignified, happy in her husband and child, with perhaps an affectionate backward glance for the old life in which he had had a part. His hands trembled. He tried to speak, but even his English seemed to desert him now. He turned a troubled gaze on her.

Her voice went out, not cool and even now, but staccato, with little gasps, as though at any moment she might lose control of herself:

"Of course, you were the only one I ever really loved, David. It was just that I was carried off my feet by Gaetano. You seemed so commonplace, so terribly uninteresting beside him. I thought that life with you would be intolerably dull, and now — if you only knew — how beautiful you look to me, sitting there! If you knew how I am longing to put my arms around you, and kiss you and kiss you!"

If Rombarra felt nothing strange in the atmosphere of the room, the child certainly did. She got from her father's knee, with a strange look of excitement, and began to run round and about the three, tearing the nosegay into pieces and scattering the violets over the marble floor. Rombarra laughed at her, clapping his hands together.

Alice bent and picked up the violets that had fallen at her feet. "I shall always keep these," she said. "The nosegay was really intended for me, wasn't it, David? Do you remember how we used to hunt for the first violets together, under last year's dead leaves? Do you remember, David?"

He nodded, gulping. "I'm not likely to forget, Alice."

At the sound of his wife's name Rombarra turned his head sharply toward them with an intense and significant gesture.

The child began to run about over the flowers, trampling them with her little feet. When she passed Behrens she threw back her head and looked up at him with a defiant and challenging gaze.

Behrens muttered: "Why do you stay with him? Why do you bear it?"

"There's the child. He would never give her up. You see what he is like with her."

"You will endure it, then? After — this meeting? All you have said today?"

"Yes — I will endure it. And I'm sorry for having made you suffer, David. But I wanted you to know. And I wanted to be unfaithful to him — he's been so unfaithful to me. And I have been unfaithful — before his very eyes. Can you understand?"

The little girl ran suddenly to her mother's knee. Alice took her up and held her close. "I must not fail Félicité," she said.

Félicité stared across at Behrens as though suddenly resentful of his presence. Rombarra regarded his wife and child with satisfaction, then turned toward Behrens with a questioning smile. Behrens rose to go.

He thought he would take advantage of the foreign custom and touch Alice's hand with his lips. It would be their last kiss. As their flesh touched he had the feeling that he was kissing the hand of a stranger. This was not the Alice he had known. He was afraid of her, and he longed to be away.

As the two men shook hands, Behrens said in his broken French: "It has been very pleasant meeting you."

This time the Italian made no attempt to respond, but he gave Behrens's hand a quick, almost sympathetic grip, and his eyes still held that look of questioning.

Behrens passed the columns and urns of the sunlit garden, and, as he reached the gate, he turned and looked back at the villa. He had felt that he was being observed. Now he saw that the three had come out on a small iron balcony. They were watching his departure, the child linking Alice and Rombarra together.

Behrens raised his hat. They waved to him. With a great sigh of relief, he strode swiftly down the street, hidden from their view now by a row of tall palms.

[1930]

Old Reynard in Springtime

It was a pity to leave the garden on this March day, for it was springing with a new, a varied life. All the little spring flowers were singing together, some with their faces just visible above the spears of grass, others swaying on such delicate stems that they seemed at any moment ready to fly skyward.

Their song must surely have been audible to the goldfish in the pond, for they showed a new vivacity in their movements and the largest leapt clear of the water, with a flourish of his spear-shaped tail. There are seven goldfish, and my children have named them for the days of the week. The one which had just leapt is called "Sunday," and so they are graduated down to little "Saturday Pence," for Saturday cannot be separated from the thought of the weekly allowance of tuppence apiece.

It needed no sensitive ear of a goldfish to hear the song of the birds. The missel thrush, perched among the glistening buds of the magnolia tree, poured out his heavenly chatter, and the blackbird whistled richly. In the deep shadow of the trees the ringdove gave forth the sulky sweetness of his call.

How beautiful the trees were in their fine new leafage! Even the pines had a new shine on their needles. The weeping beech trees, which send long trailers drooping to the ground, were forming their thin, satiny leaves. "Like the leaves of my new prayer book," said my little girl, and she could pay them no higher compliment.

Ours is rather a grim-looking house, despite the ivy that enfolds it, but it stands on a lovely slope which rises to the mystery of a wood. Up this slope the daffodils were uncovering their golden heads in a brave procession, and in the wood the stalks of the bluebells swelled as they drew up moisture from the deep, rich earth.

Halfway up the slope there is a thatched summerhouse, and an old sundial bearing the words: "Make the passing shadow work thy will." They seemed stern words to me on this blowy soft March morning. How could I make a shadow work my will? And I but another shadow! The motto was better suited to that noted engineer who once lived here. He built the Jubilee Drive that climbs the hills to the Herefordshire Beacon, in commemoration of Queen Victoria's Golden Jubilee. Just beside the sundial a large, thrice-circling hoop of iron hangs from the spreading branch of an oak. In those days the engineer's servants used to beat on this to summon him from across the valley to his forgotten meals.

I had a fancy to hear its voice speak again. I picked up a stone and struck the hoops sharply. I made them sound their heavy note again and again. Then silence came, and regret. I had frightened the birds. Silence lay thick among the trees. A bloom like the bloom on grapes lay there — silence made palpable.

Then a new sound, as though an echo of the gong, rose from a neighboring wood. Our two puppies came running along the mossy path and looked eagerly up into my face. The Scottie's tail was a tense question mark above his muscular haunches, the Cairn's eyes were luminous under a fringe of mouse-colored hair. "The hounds!" tail and eyes said to me, as plain as words could speak. "The hounds are baying and we want to go to the Hunt!"

I had their leads looped over my arm, and before they could run off again I fastened the Scottie's plaid collar round his neck and slipped on the Cairn's green harness. The Scottie lay prostrate, grinning up at me. Little shivers ran over the Cairn. When we set off they trotted so close together that their sides touched — the one jogging like a pony, the other moving with smooth slinky grace.

A rabbit darted across the path and there were two simultaneous tugs at the leads. The rabbit disappeared into the rhododendrons and again that sad sweet music of the hounds came on the breeze. We trotted along the path to the iron gate that stands at the back of the grounds. We followed another path to the public road and climbed the steep hill toward the Wyche, with far ahead the Worcestershire Beacon hunched against the blue sky.

We were not the only ones who had heard the baying of the hounds. When we neared the top of the hill, where there is a scattering of small houses, I saw that out of each women and children had come and were standing fascinated, their eyes fixed on a copse on the steep above. Two youths on bicycles had dismounted; two more had clambered down from the seat of a lorry; a farmer had drawn up his pony and sat looking on from the seat of his gig. A man raking in a garden, a laborer digging a drain, threw down their tools and joined us others who had gathered by a low stone wall on which we could rest our arms. I lifted the Scottie and the Cairn on to it and all stared at the copse from where the sound of a horn now rose.

Yet, while we fixed our eyes on this small space, a spacious panorama was spread before us, hill upon hill, fold upon fold, embracing the lovely valleys, encircling the fields where flocks of black-faced sheep grazed. And in the distance the sunlight silvered the black mountains of Wales.

"There he is!" cried one of the youths, and "Yon's the fox!" called a woman, holding up her child to see.

Across a pale-green field he flashed — a bronze arrow of fear. The hounds came tumbling out of the copse after him, in a stream of liver and white, their bellies close to the ground, their throats swelling with the bell-like notes. And after the hounds the horses with flying manes and streaming tails, their riders in pink or brown or gray, stretched their powerful legs across the tender grass.

" 'This is the last day of the huntin', " observed an old man at my side. "If he gets away to-day he's safe till autumn." The man's voice expressed neither hope that the fox would escape nor desire that he should be caught. It expressed, in its rich Herefordshire accent, only complete satisfaction in the spectacle before him and complete acquiescence in its finish — whatever that might be.

Suddenly the hounds showed bewilderment; they became silent and scattered themselves across the field. The horses slackened to a trot. The fox had disappeared into some undergrowth that fringed a little stream. A bird began to sing timidly. The Scottie and the Cairn became restive; they looked questioningly into my face. The old man gave it as his opinion that the fox had gone to earth. A gentle spring sweetness rose from the land over which the ancestors of this same fox and these hounds had raced for many generations.

Then a hound raised up his voice and all the pack joined in the clamor. The horn sounded. The Whip shouted. The scent was again strong.

"Look! Look! There he is! By gum, he's coming straight this way!" Excited voices rose all about me. Then I saw the fox.

He came down the hillside toward us, clearly seen by us but still invisible to the Hunt. He came at an easy trot, not spending himself, his head turning warily from left to right as he sought for escape. He showed no fear at the sight of all these people, but drew nearer in his soft, loping trot, his pointed muzzle turning this way and that.

For a moment he disappeared, but again we saw him, now poised on the top of the wall surrounding a cottage garden. A woman stood in the doorway, staring at him open-mouthed. She had been feeding her fowls, which were pecking at the corn, oblivious of the nearness of their enemy.

He hesitated, turning his bright gaze on them, as though he had a mind to pick one up on his way, but the baying of the hounds rose from the other side of the wall and he moved delicately across the vegetable garden. The gate stood open and he trotted through it, like an accustomed visitor, on to the road where we stood.

I have seen foxes in captivity, foxes stuffed, and many skins of foxes, but he was the handsomest I have ever seen. He was large, in beautiful condition, sleek and graceful. His fur was a lovely red russet, and strength and experienced maturity were in every movement.

He gave us a glance, half sneering, wholly self-contained, and crossed the road. I felt the bodies of the terriers rigid against my side. Their hackles rose. The Scottie gave a loud yell of fury as the fox clambered over the wall near us, and struggled to be after him. The Cairn lifted his lip and turned his pretty little face into a mask of hate.

Now through a farm gate the Hunt poured, in a confusion of hounds, horses, and pink coats, into the road. The sides of the horses were heaving; foam flecked their bright coats. I knew some of the riders, but they passed, seeing nothing outside the chase, excepting one, an elderly man who came last and shut the gate after them. He recognized me and touched his cap with his crop. "He's a tough old rascal," he exclaimed. "He's been hunted a dozen times this season." He himself looked tough-sinewed and wiry. The skin of his thin aquiline face was weatherbeaten and red. The sleeves of his coat were too short — his red wrists protruded; and he had evidently had a fall, for his back was plastered with mud.

Now old Reynard stretched his supple length in desperate need. He flew down the green slope with the hounds baying closer to the red plume of his tail. Their voices had become hysterical, half mad with the lust to tear him to pieces. The horses thundered after the hounds, rising to jump a thorn hedge under which he had slipped. The hounds pressed, whimpering at the delay, through a thorny gap. A young boy was thrown from his pony, but he captured it, remounted, and went boldly after the others.

We, at the top, looked down on the scene, not with godlike impartiality, but heart and soul for the escape of the fox. There had been something in the way he had looked at us. He had taken us into his confidence. "See me!" he had seemed to say. "Watch how I will diddle them!"

We could see his russet body flying across a smooth meadow — too smooth, for it meant that the hounds gained on him. But ahead was a wood, and if he could win that he might have a chance.

"Ah, I do hope he gets away!" cried the woman whose garden he had passed through. "He came that near me I could have touched him and he'd such bright eyes!"

Now the fox did a strange thing. He turned aside and glided into the sparse undergrowth by the edge of the stream. He seemed to be throwing away his one chance of escape. The hounds ran here and there, muzzles snuffling, tails waving. Then one raised his voice, the others jostled him, and again they were off. They disappeared into the wood.

" 'T was a master stroke," said the man at my side. "He came on the scent of another fox and crossed it to save his own skin! He's thrown the hounds off the scent. I warrant they'll never get him now."

It was true. Up the hill side to the right we saw the old fox gliding. There was no mistaking his unusual color, his size, the almost studied grace of his movements. But he moved slowly now. He was very tired.

In the valley the tumult went on. It came mysteriously out of the wood, invisible to us except for the occasional gleam of a polished flank, the flash of a pink coat. The silent hills unrolled themselves, fold upon fold, dark green upon pale green, blue upon purple, purple on the azure horizon.

At last beyond the wood we saw the Hunt flash out and stream across the fields. We saw the hounds slither across the stepping stones of a stream, the horses arched above it for a spectacular moment. The horn sounded faintly, the bright colors dissolved into the colors of hedge and mead.

"My goodness!" exclaimed the cottage woman. "I thought he was for snatching one of my hens! But just the same I'm glad he got away!"

"Him's a noble-looking feller," said the old man. " 'T is to be hoped he breeds more of his kind this year."

More of his kind to be hunted! More of his kind to strain with breaking hearts to reach the haven of their burrows or be torn to pieces! Little cubs, playing at their mother's side through the summer days — reared for this tragic culmination of their strength and speed!

Was it better, I wondered, to be torn for this than never to be born at all? For certainly it is the Hunt which preserves the fox. If it were not for the Hunt the farmers would soon demand his extermination, as he increased in boldness and numbers. I thought of old Reynard, now stretched at ease, his breathing gradually becoming tranquil, the baying of the hounds no more than the faint ringing of a distant bell; his woods, his meadows, safe for the summer. Yes, it was better to be born to suffer in the beauty of this world than not to be born at all.

I had lifted the puppies from the wall. The Scottie was already engaged in digging a hole. The Cairn was submitting coyly to the advances of a woman in a burberry coat. The little group of people was already dispersed. Bicycle, lorry, and cart were continuing their way.

As we went toward home my mind turned to the first meet of the season on a day last November. The meet had been at Barton Court and we had gone, packed in our car. The children's kindergarten class had been given a holiday; so had the boys of the near-by preparatory school. It was a chill morning, but there was rich color on the countryside. The beech mast lay thick beneath the great smooth-boled trees, the russet oak leaves clung sparsely to the wide branches. Sheep grazed close together on the rimy green pastures. A roan pony drew wisps of hay from a shapely new rick.

When we had arrived most of the Hunt was already gathered at the Court. Plates of sandwiches and plum cake, glasses of cherry brandy, were being passed to those who rode and those who came as onlookers. The children ran to join their little friends. Indoors our host was talking to villagers who were enjoying the unusual treat of plum cake and coffee in mid-morning.

The cobbles of the yard were wet and slippery; the horses sidled on them impatiently, while their riders cajoled or shouted at them. The dappled hounds stood shoulder to shoulder, gently surging, like a gathering wave. A deep undertone of excitement stirred through all.

Now the hunting season was over. There was peace for the hunted.

[1937]

The Ninth Life

"Harriet! Harriet! Harriet!" Her name echoed through the pine woods. It echoed across the water to the next island, was flung back from its precipitous shore in a mournful echo. Still she did not come.

The launch stood waiting at the wharf, laden with the luggage attendant on the breaking up of the holiday season. Summer was past, October almost gone, wild geese were mirrored in the lake in their flight southward. Now, for eight months, the Indians and the wild deer would have the islands to themselves.

The Boyds were the last of the summer people to go. They enjoyed the month of freedom at the end of the season, when tourists were gone. They were country people themselves, bred in the district. When they were not living on their island they lived in a small town at the foot of the lake, thirty miles away. The year was marked for them by their migration to the island in the middle of June and their return to winter habitation in October.

They were well-to-do. They owned their launch which now stood waiting at the wharf with the Indian, John Nanabush, at the wheel. He stood, dark and imperturbable, while Mrs. Boyd, her daughter and her cook raised their voices for Harriet. Mr. Boyd prowled about at the back of the cottage peering into the workshop, the ice-house, behind the wood-pile where freshly cut birch logs lay waiting for next year's fires. Now and again he gave a stentorian shout for Harriet.

They had delayed their departure for hours because of her. Now they must go without her. Mrs. Boyd came to the wide verandah where the canoe lay covered by canvas. She lifted the edge of the canvas and peered under it.

"Why, mother, what a place to look!" said her husband. "The cat wouldn't be in there."

"I know," said Mrs. Boyd. "But I just feel so desperate!"

"Well, we've got to go without her."

"And it's getting so cold!"

On the wharf the girls wailed, "Oh, father, we can't leave Harriet on the island!"

"Find her, Pat! Find Harriet!" said Mr. Boyd to the Irish terrier.

Pat leaped from the launch, where he was investigating the hamper of eatables, and raced up the rocky shore. In his own fashion he shouted for the cat. A chipmunk darted from the trunk of a jack pine, sped across a large flat rock, ran halfway up a flaming red maple and paused, upside down, to stare at the group on the wharf.

John Nanabush raised his soft, thick, Indian voice. "You folks go along home. I'll find Harriet. I'll keep her for you."

"That's a good idea," said Mr. Boyd.

"Harriet would never stay with John," said Mrs. Boyd. "She's devoted to us."

"Guess she'd rather stay with me than freeze," said the Indian.

"Will you promise to come back to the island to-morrow and search till you find her?"

"Oh, I'll find her," said Nanabush, in his comforting, sly voice. "We ought to be gettin' on now if you folks want to be home before dark."

"Pat! Pat! Oh, where is Pat gone?" cried the young girls.

Pat came bouding out of the woods, rushed at the launch, scrambled on board and sat there grinning.

"He's got some sense, anyhow," said the Indian.

"Sound the whistle, John," said Mrs. Boyd. "That might fetch her."

"What if she's dead!" cried the younger girl.

"You can't kill a cat," said Nanabush. He stretched out his dark hand and blew the whistle.

All eyes were turned to the woods.

The cook said, "I left a bowl of bread-and-milk for her by the back door."

"Come, mother," said Mr. Boyd, "it's no use. We can't wait any longer."

The launch looked like a toy boat as it moved among the islands. The reflection of the islands lay on the dark blue lake, more perfect than the reality. They were deserted.

It was only an hour later when Harriet came back. She was tired and hungry for she had been on a more strenuous hunt than usual. She had cut one of her feet and the hunt had been unsuccessful. She had curled up in the hollow of a tree and slept long, on the far side of the island. She had heard faint shouts for her but feline perversity had made her curl herself closer.

Now she circled the cottage, meowed outside the doors, leaped to the window-sills and peered into the rooms. There was a desolate air about it. She went to the wharf and saw that the launch was not there. The family would return in the launch.

She glided back to the cottage and found the bowl of bread-and-milk. She attacked it greedily but after a few mouthfuls her appetite left her. She began to wash her face, then to lick her coat to cleanliness and lustre. Her coat was a pleasing combination of tawny yellow and brown. She had a hard, shrewd face but there was affection in her.

The October sun sank in spectacular grandeur among the islands. There was no twilight. A blue, cold evening took swift possession. A few glittering stars were reflected in the lake. The air became bitterly cold and a white furry frost rimed the grass. Harriet crept into the canoe where Mrs. Boyd had lifted the canvas. There was a cushion in it. She curled herself up and slept.

At sunrise she leaped from the canoe and ran to the kitchen window. From its ledge she peered into the room. There was no fire. There was no cook. Harriet gave a faint meow of disappointment. She bent her acute sense of hearing to catch a sound of life in the cottage. All she heard was the whisper of little waves against the shore. Pointed leaves from the silver birches drifted in the golden air. It was very cold.

Harriet went to the bowl of bread-and-milk and began to eat it. She discovered that she was ravenous. But there was so much of it that she had to take breath before she could finish it. Even in her repletion she uttered a meow of longing. She was four years old and she had never been separated from the Boyds before. Her mother and her grandmother had belonged to the Boyds. She knew their movements and their life as she knew the pads of her own paw.

The bowl was emptied. As empty and hollow as the world in which she now found herself. Mechanically she began to wash her face, groom the fine hair behind her ears till it was erect as the pile of fine velvet. She stretched out her hind leg and swiftly licked the fur on the rim of her thigh. In this attitude it could be seen that she was with young. Her little teats showed rosy and fresh.

She heard a rustle in the fallen leaves and turned her green eyes defensively, fearfully, in that direction. A pair of porcupines stood staring at her, side by side, their quills upright, their yellow teeth showing in their trepidation. They had come to investigate the empty cottage.

Harriet gave a hissing scream at them, making her face as horrifying as she could. She stared, with her back to the kitchen door, screaming and making faces. The porcupines turned and ambled away, pushing into a dense growth of junipers.

An acorn clattered across the roof of the cottage and fell close to Harriet. She stood up, wondering what was coming next. The chipmunk that had watched the departure yesterday now looked over the eave at her. He knew she could not get at him where he was, but he longed to retrieve his acorn. His neat striped head darted from side to side, his eyes questioned her. Her tail lashed its implacable answer. He put his little paw against the side of his face and settled down to watch her.

With a sudden leap she sprang toward the acorn, curved her paw about it, toyed with it. Beneath her fur her muscles flowed as she bent low over the acorn as though loving it, leaped back from it in disdain.

Paw to cheek, the chipmunk watched her.

Then, from all the empty world about her, her misery came to taunt her. She was alone, except for the helpless kittens that stirred inside her. She sank to her belly and gave a plaintive meow.

For a long while she lay with closed eyes. The chipmunk longed for his acorn. No other acorn could take its place. He kept elongating his neck to see into Harriet's face. She seemed oblivious of everything but he was not deceived. Still he could not resist. He darted down the wall of the cottage, made a dash for the acorn, snatched it.

He almost succeeded. But his nearness electrified her. In a flowing curve she sprang at him. He dropped the acorn and turned himself into wind and blew back against the wall of the cottage. From the eave he chattered at her. She stared out across the lake, ignoring him.

As the sun neared the tops of the pines she heard the delicate approach of a canoe. She ran to a point of rock and crouched there, among the junipers, watching.

It was John Nanabush come to look for her. The lake was very still and the reflection of canoe and Indian lay on the glassy water in silent companionship. He dipped and raised his paddle as though caressing the lake. He gave glittering diamonds to it from the tip of his paddle. He called, in his indifferent Indian voice: "Horriet! Horriet! You there?"

She crouched, staring at him. She watched him with acute but contemptuous interest.

"Horriet! Horriet!" The canoe moved on out of sight behind a tumble of rocks but the Indian's voice still echoed dreamily.

She would not go with him! She would not go. Surely there was a mistake! If she ran very fast to the house she would find the family there. The cook would be there, frying fish for supper. Harriet ran in swift undulations up the rocky, shaggy steep to the cottage.

The chipmunk watched her approach from the eave, his little paws pressed together as though in prayer. But he reviled her shrilly.

She ran along the verandah and sprang to the sill of the kitchen window. Inside it was almost dark. There was no cook. The frying-pan hung against the wall. She heard the chipmunk scampering across the roof, in haste to get a good view of her. She sat down on the sill and opened her mouth but no sound came.

The chipmunk peered down at her, turning his striped head this way and that, quivering in his excitement. She lashed her tail but she would not look up at him. She began to lick her sore paw.

The red of the sky turned to a clear lemon colour. There was an exquisite stillness, as the trees awaited the first hard frost. An icy fear, a terrible loneliness descended on Harriet. She would not spend another night on the island.

As she ran to the water's edge she meowed without ceasing, as in protest against what she must do. A wedge-shaped flock of wild geese flew strong and sure against the yellow sky.

Before her the lake stretched dark blue, crisping in its coldness, lapping icily at her paws. She cried loudly in her protest as she walked into it. A few steps and she was out of her depth.

She had never swum before but she could do it. She moved her paws knowingly, treading the icy water in fear and hate. A loon skimming the lake was startled by her stark cat's head rising out of the water and swung away, uttering his loud, wild laugh.

The next island was half a mile away. The last sunlight was held in the topmost branches of its pines. It seemed almost unattainable to Harriet, swimming in bitter stubbornness toward it. Sometimes she felt that she was sinking. The chill all but reached her heart, still she struggled toward the blackness of the rocks.

At last the island loomed above her. She smelled the scents of the land. All her hate of the water and her longing for home tautened her muscles. She swam fiercely and, before she was quite exhausted, clambered up on the rocks.

Once there, she was done. She lay flattened, a bit of wet draggled fur. But her heaving sides and gasping mouth showed that life was in her. The wet hairs of her fur began to crisp whitely in the frost. Her tail began to look stiff and brittle. She felt the spirit going out of her and the bitter cold coming in. The red afterglow on the black horizon was fading. It would soon be dark.

Harriet had a curious feeling of life somewhere near. Not stirring, just sending its prickling essence in a thin current toward her. Her eyes flew open in horror of being attacked in her weak state. She looked straight into the eyes of a wild goose, spread on the rock near her.

One of his wings had been injured and he had been left behind by the flock, to die. He was large and strong but young. This had been his first flight southward. His injured wing lay spread on the rock like a fan. He rested his glossy head on it.

They stared at each other fascinated, while the current of his fear pricked her to life. She tightened the muscles of her belly and pressed her claws against the rock. Their eyes communed, each to each, like instruments in tune. She drew her chin against her frosty breast while her eyes became balls of fire, glaring into his.

He raised himself above his broken wing and reared his strong other wing, as though to fly. But she held him with her eyes. He opened his long beak but the cry died in his throat. He got on to his webbed feet and stood with trailing wing, facing her. He moved a step nearer.

So, they stared and stared, till he wanted her to take him. He had no will but hers. Now her blood was moving quickly. She felt strong and fierce. His long neck, his big downy breast, were defence-less. She sprang, sunk her teeth in his neck, tore his breast with her hind claws, clung to him. His strong wing beat the air, even after he knew himself dying.

It was dark when she had finished her meal. She sat on the rock washing her face, attending to her sore paw. The air had grown even colder and snowflakes drifted on the darkness. The water in pools and shallows began to freeze. Harriet crept close to the body of the goose, snuggling warmly in its down. She pressed under its wing, which spread above her as though in protection.

She meowed plaintively as she prowled about the island next morning. The people who owned it had gone to their home, in a distant American city, many weeks ago. The windows of the cottage were boarded up. The flagstaff, where the big American flag had floated, was bare. Harriet prowled about the island, looking longingly at the mainland, filled with loathing of the icy water.

As she crept to its frozen rim she lifted her lip in loathing. A bit of down from the goose clung to her cheek. She crept on to the thin ice and, as it crackled beneath her, she meowed as in pain. At last, with a despairing lash of her tail, she went into the lake and set her face toward the mainland. It was three quarters of a mile away.

This ordeal was worse than last night's. The lake was more cruelly cold. But it was smooth, stretched like cold steel beneath the drifting snowflakes. Harriet's four paws went up and down as though the lake were a great barrier of ice she was mounting. Her head looked small and sleek as a rat's. Her green eyes were unwinking. Like a lodestone, the house at the foot of the lake drew her. Her spirit drew courage from the fire of its hearth.

A snake also was swimming to the mainland. Its cold blood felt no chill. Its ebony head arched above the steel of the lake. A delicate flourish on the steely surface followed it. The two swimmers were acutely conscious of each other but their cold eyes ignored.

Harriet scrambled on to the crackling ice at the shore and lay prone. The life was all but gone from her. She remembered neither food nor fire nor shelter. The snake glided over the stones near her, slippery and secure. She tried to rise but could not.

The flurry of snow passed. A wind from the south-west made a scatteration among the clouds. They moved north and east, settling in grey and purple on the horizon. The sun shone out strongly, turning the October foliage to a blaze of scarlet and gold. The sunlight lay warm on Harriet's sagging sides.

She felt new life creeping into her. She raised her head and began to lick her sore paw. Then she ran her tongue in long eager strokes across her flanks. Her fur stood upright. Her flesh grew warm and supple.

She crept out on a rock, from whose crevices hardy ferns and huckleberry bushes grew. A few huckleberries glimmered frostily blue among the russet leaves. Harriet peered into the pool below the rock. She saw some small bass resting there in the watered sunshine.

She crouched, watching them intently. Her colours mingled with the frost-browned fern and bronzed leaves. She settled herself on her breast as though to rest, then her paw shot into the pool, her claws like fish-hooks drove into the bright scales. The bass lay on the rock, its golden eye staring up at her.

Now she felt refreshed and strong. She found the sandy track through the woods and trotted along it toward the foot of the lake. All day she pressed forward, meeting no one. She stopped only to catch a little mouse and eat it and rest after the meal.

At sundown a deer stepped out of a thicket and stood before her, his antlers arching like the branches of a tree, his great eyes glowing. He looked at her then bent his antlers, listening. He raised a shapely hoof and stood poised. Harriet saw something shining among the leaves. There was a sharp noise. The shock of it lifted Harriet from her feet, made every hair of her tail vibrant.

The tall deer sank to his knees. He laid the side of his head on the ground and his great eyes were raised imploringly to the face of the hunter who came out of the wood. The hunter knelt by him as though in compassion. Then a stream of red gushed from the deer's throat. A dog came and sniffed his flank. Harriet peered down from a tree where she had hid. It was long before she dared go on.

She had gone only a short way when she saw a doe and a fawn, standing as though waiting. The doe lowered her head at Harriet but the fawn looked proudly aloof, holding its head, with the face innocent as a little child's, high on its strong neck. Harriet glided away, her paws brushing the snow from the dead leaves. She curled herself in a hollow in a tree and lay licking her sore paw. She thought of the dead deer's great body and the large pieces of flesh she had seen cut from it.

In the morning she was very hungry but there was nothing to eat. The sky was dark, the snow had turned to a rain that dripped from the trees and soaked her fur till it clung to her. But she ran steadily along the track, always drawn by the lodestone of the house at the foot of the lake. Passing toward it, she sometimes gave a meow as faint and thin as the fall of a pine needle. She ate a few blueberries from the dried bushes. She came to a space carpeted by glossy wintergreen leaves. She even ate some of the scarlet berries, eating them with distaste and curling lip but she was so hungry because of the kittens she carried. There seemed nothing living abroad except her.

The path crossed a swamp dense with a growth of cranberries. Beyond this she came to a settler's cottage, clean and neat, with poultry in a wire run. There was a hen turkey in the yard, followed by three daintily moving poults. A girl was milking a cow in an open shed. Harriet stood staring, lonely, hungry. She felt weighed down, almost too tired to go on.

A man came out of the house with a bucket. He saw her, and a piercing whistle brought two hounds. He picked up a stone and threw it. It struck her side.

Harriet turned into a fury, an elongated, arched, fiery-eyed, sneering fury. The hounds hesitated before her claws that reached for their eyes. She whirled and flew down the path. They came after her baying, sending up the volume of their voices in the rain. They urged each other on with loud cries. With her last strength she clambered into a tree and sat sneering down at them, her sides palpitating.

The hounds stood with their paws against the trunk of the tree, baying up at her. They changed places, as though that would help them. They flung themselves down panting beneath the tree, then sprang up again, baying. But when the shrill whistle sounded again they ran without hesitating back to their master.

On and on Harriet limped over the rough track. Sometimes she had a glimpse of the lake between trees but she scarcely looked to right or left. The homeward cord drew her ever more strongly. One would scarcely have recognised the sleek pet in this draggled tramp, this limping, heavy-eyed, slinking cat.

She could see the twinkling lights of the town across the bay when her pain came on. It was so piercing, so sudden that she turned with a savage cry, to face what seemed to be attacking her in the rear. But then she knew that the pain was inside her.

She lay writhing on the ground and before long gave birth to a kitten. She began to lick it, then realised that it was dead. She ran on toward the town as fast as she could.

She was still two miles from it when she had two more kittens. She lay beside them for a while, feeling weak and peaceful. Now the lights of the town were out. Harriet picked up one of the kittens and limped on. With it in her mouth she went along the paved street. She gave a meow of delight as she reached the back door of her own home.

She laid the kitten on the doorstep and herself began limping back and forth, the length of the step, rubbing her sides against the door. For the first time since she had been left on the island she purred. The purr bubbled in her throat, vibrating through her nerves in an ecstasy of home-coming. She caressed the back door with every bit of her. She stood on her hind legs and caressed the door handle with a loving paw. Only the weak cry of her kitten made her desist.

She carried it to the tool-shed and laid it on the mat where the terrier slept in warm weather. She laid herself down beside it, trilling to it in love. It buried its sightless face against her lank belly. She lay flat on her side, weary to the bone.

But the shape of the kitten she had abandoned on the road now crept into her mind. It crept on silken paws with its tail pointed like a rat's and its eyelids glued together. Round and round it crept in its agony of abandonment, tearing her mind as its birth had torn her body. She flung herself on her other side, trying to forget it but she could not.

With a piteous meow of protest against the instinct that hounded her, she left the kitten's side and went out into the dawn. The rain had stopped and there was a sharp clear wind that drove the dead leaves scurrying across the frozen ruts.

The pain of her sore paw on the ice ruts was like fire but she hurried on, draggled, hard-faced, with the thought of the bereft kitten prodding her.

The dreadful road unrolled itself before her in an endless scroll of horrible hieroglyphics. She meowed in hate of it, at every yard. She covered it, mile after mile, till she reached the spot where she had littered. There, in the coarse wet grass, she found the kitten. She turned it over with her nose, sniffing it to see if it were worth taking home. She decided that it was.

Along and along the road she limped, the kitten dangling from her unloving mouth, the dead leaves whirling about her as though they would bury her, the icy ruts biting her paw.

But the clouds had broken and the Indian-summer sun was leaping out. As she hobbled into her own yard her fur was warm and dry on her back. She laid the kitten beside the other and gave herself up to suckling them. And as they drew life from her, her love went out to them. She made soft trilling noises to them, threw her forelegs about them, lashed her tail about them, binding them close. She licked their fat bodies and their blunt heads till they shone.

Then suddenly a noise in the kitchen galvanised her. She leaped up, scattering the sucklings from her nipples. It was the rattle of a stove lid she had heard. She ran up the steps and meowed at the back door. It opened and the cook let out a scream of joy.

"Harriet! Harriet! Harriet's here!"

Pat ran to meet her, putting his paw on her back. She arched herself at him, giving a three-cornered smile. The cook ran to room after room, telling the news. The Boyds came from room after room to welcome Harriet, to marvel at her return.

"She must have come early last night," said the cook, "for she's had kittens in the tool shed."

"Well, they'll have to be drowned," said Mr. Boyd.

[1937]

The Sacred Bullock

"Hoi! Hoi!" Young Davey shouted, as he and the dog which was a mixture of several breeds and combined the intelligence of all of them, drove the little bullocks along the rocky path toward the pasture where they were to be fattened for market.

"Hoi! Hoi!" he shouted, even when it was not necessary, for he liked the sound of his own voice in the desolate place, and his brain was so empty that a single word like "hoi" meant much to it.

The great barren hills, in the heart of Wales, that seemed to have upheaved themselves from the bowels of the earth, might have been expected to have dwarfed the figure of a man driving a dozen bullocks before him, with a dog at his heels, but they did not. He, in his heavy boots, thick corduroys, with his broad shoulders and plunging walk, looked massive, towering above the little beasts he drove like some powerful prehistoric man. On their part they looked soft and weak, their sturdy legs not yet accustomed to the rough paths, their eyes timid, as they looked over their shoulders at the dog.

Beyond and beyond, the hills reared their rocky heads, their shoulders shaggy with bracken. Beyond and beyond, they crouched and sank like receding waves. There was always the endless variety and endless monotony of the hills. Up and up the morning sun showed its face among them, lifting their veils of mist, casting their dim shadows into the valleys. In the most fertile of the valleys was the farm where young Davey worked. From this height you could see its stone walls and its two chimneys. He looked down at it and, for a moment, the faces of the two who lived there came into his mind. Then it was empty again and he shouted "hoi, hoi!" to the bullocks and drove them along the path.

The two who lived there were a farmer named Owen and his daughter Glennys. Twenty years ago Owen had come home from the War, blinded. He had married the girl who had been waiting for him and, two years later, she had died in giving birth to his daughter. All these years he had been worked for, waited on by a married couple but last summer the husband had strained his back. It was little he would be able to do for a long while, so young Davey came from a distant farm to help. He was so strapping, so willing that Owen liked the sound of him about the place. He asked Glennys to tell him what the boy looked like.

"I wish you could see him," said Glennys, laughing, "he's a funny-looking boy!"

"Ugly to look at?"

"Well, not exactly but he has a thick neck and a high head and he has tow-coloured hair in curls on the top of his head and his eyelashes are almost white."

"He sounds ugly and not a bit like a Welshman."

"Oh, he's Welsh!" laughed Glennys. "He can't speak a word of English."

"I like his voice," said Owen. "I wish he spoke oftener. And I like the sound of his step."

Young Davey slept in an attic room under a roof that sloped to the floor. There was nothing but a bed in the room and an old iron-bound chest for his clothes. He owned a quite good coat which he wore when he went to church but the heels were always out of his socks. He owned a Bible in very fine print but he could not read. He washed himself in a shed at the back of the house. All his life he had washed with coarse yellow soap but now Glennys gave him a piece of pink soap with a scent to it. It had only cost tuppence but to him it seemed luxurious and he was careful not to be extravagant with it.

He was happy as he drove the little bullocks along the track. He shouted "hoi, hoi!" loudly and felt the strength of his power over them as they ran and stumbled, not knowing what they were expected to do. Far below he saw the farm-house, looking very grey and small. Then his mind returned to the bullocks which were to be fattened for the market and he called to the dog to harry them up the path to the pasture.

The pasture lay on a plateau against the side of a ruined Abbey. Owen had had the piece of sheltered rich land fenced in and the grass grew thick and strong here. A protecting hill rose on the north and the walls of the Abbey kept off the cold east wind. It was said that in olden times the monks had their garden here and that a richness had been left in the soil that would for ever nourish what grew there.

"Hoi! Hoi!" Davey shouted at the little beasts and they crowded in at the gate, looking with frightened eyes at the dog who just touched their legs with his teeth.

There was one bullock that was not so obedient as the others. He turned and faced Davey with a wondering look and lowered his head, with its little coral pink bumps of horn, toward the dog. Davey had noticed him before and now he had a good look at him.

He was white, with a peculiar milky whiteness above his pink skin. The others were red, or red with a patch of white. But he was white all over and it gave him a look of purity and innocent power. There was a bunch of white curls on his crown, rather like Davey's. His tail ended in a white ringlet. Only his great liquid eyes that seemed to see but a short way, were of a midnight blue.

"Hoi!" shouted Davey. "Hoi!" and waved his staff.

The dog barked sharp orders at the bullock. It wheeled and went after the others.

Davey could not keep his eyes off it. As it bent its massive little head to graze he stood staring at it, admiring it. It was shy but not timid. He filled his hand with its curly topknot, ran his hands over its silky sides, appraised it for the good beef it would put on to its sturdy frame. It stretched its neck, its wet pink nose following his fingers, its under-lip thrust out in its instinct for sucking.

The bullocks had been bought by Owen for fattening. Twice a week he asked Davey how they were getting on.

"They're putting on the fat wonderful," said Davey. "There's a white one."

"Oh. Is he a good one?"

Davey laughed. "He's the best. He looks like a regular little —" He could not talk for laughing because Glennys was in the room and the sight of her filled him with confusion.

Christmas was past. It was January and a misty sunlight, not without warmth in it, slanted across the hills. Owen said:

"I think I'll go up the path and see the beasts."

"He can't see them," thought Davey. "He means feel them." And he chuckled to himself.

"All right, Father," said Glennys. "Shall we go now? Davey could come with us, couldn't you, Davey?"

She looked so beautiful to him, standing in the dim room, with the fairness of her skin and the darkness of her hair and her large grey eyes, that his legs felt heavy and his head light. He twisted his fingers together and looked at her from under his white lashes, not able to speak.

Owen was on his feet, groping for the peg where his cap hung. He did not like being helped, so the boy and girl watched while he found it and put it on his head. He led the way through the door and along the cobbled path. At the end of it he stopped and threw up his head.

"What's that I smell?" he asked.

"Snowdrops," said Glennys. "It's wonderful how you can smell them, Father. Their scent is so faint."

Owen smiled proudly. It filled him with pride to do some things better than other people could. Glennys picked a few of the flowers and put them into his hand. He laid his other hand on her arm.

Davey led the way up the steep rough path, up and up, his strong legs springing before them, the rags dangling from his coat, the dog pressing close after him. He was so eager to show off the bullocks that he could scarcely endure to wait for Owen's slower steps. The sheep grazing on the hillside moved closer to each other, for they seldom saw so many people. A faint baa came from their midst. It came from the first lamb of the season who stood, peering between the bodies of the sheep, that were a woolly barrier between him and the world.

" 'Tis a new lamb," said Davey. "The ewe dropped it yesterday. There'll be more before sundown."

The lamb cried out again, his close curled wool shaking with the strength of his baa. Suddenly he dived under his mother and bunted the milk from her udder with his curly head. His cry had gone through Owen with the piercing sweetness of the first voices of spring.

"I wish I could see the lamb," he said.

Glennys led him on up the path. The ruin of the Abbey rose before them, the broken arch of grey stone, the crumbling tower solid against the fragility of the wintry blue sky. Through the windows Glennys saw the little bullocks grazing in what had been the chapel.

The bullocks raised their heads and stared meditatively through the windows at the group approaching. Then, as though with calculated design, they passed through the narrow door of the chancel into the open pasture — all but one.

This was the white bullock and he stood motionless on the delicately carved altar-stone that had fallen and now lay sunk in the grass.

"Oh, lovely!" cried Glennys. "Doesn't he look lovely there?"

"Who? Where?" demanded Owen, turning his face impatiently from side to side.

"The white bullock. He's like the sacred bull of pagan times. The sacrificial bull."

"Is he getting fat?" asked Owen.

"He's best of them all," said Davey. He was smiling in pride because of the girl's surprise. He strode to the bullock and grasped him by the curly topknot and drew him toward Owen. He came docilely, stepping daintily over the grass, but his eyes were two luminous globes turning in courage and pride.

Owen passed his hands over him. "What a silky hide!" he said. "Yes, he's putting on the flesh."

"What a pity he has to be killed!" said Glennys. "He looks so lovely here. I'd like to keep him.... He looks sacred."

"You're a foolish girl," said Owen, pressing her arm against his side.

"The beast should be saved for breeding," muttered Davey in Owen's ear.

"Hmph, well, he just came with the lot I bought. Take me to the others."

They passed through the door and found the little herd in a russet clump among the bracken. The white bullock followed them. Even when they were far down the path he stood staring after them. He watched their movements contemplatively till they were out of his sight. Then he returned to his companions but never seemed entirely to belong to them.

The remembrance of the visit Glennys had paid to the ruin was always coming into Davey's mind. "She got a surprise, she did!" he would chuckle, and he would wonder if ever she would come to see the bullock again. He would pull and push him till he got him on the altar stone, then he would stand gazing at him in wonder and admiration.

The bullock soon learned that he was singled out for attention but he scarcely had to learn it, for he was not timid like the others.

He watched for Davey's comings and pressed forward to get the hay he spread on the ground or to thrust his nose first into the bucket of meal. Davey would lead him into the chancel and strew his share on the altar because that was where he had stood on the day Glennys had praised him.

One day she showed Davey a picture in an old book of a sacred bull. His horns rose out of a chaplet of flowers and young girls and youths, in Greek dress that showed their lovely limbs, danced in procession after him. They had musical instruments in their hands and vine leaves in their hair. Davey had never seen a book like this before. He took it reverently and, as he looked from the picture to her face and back again, a smile lighted his face and a tremor ran through him. He asked, in his Welsh tongue:

"Was there really times like that — in the world once?"

"Of course there were!"

"I wish I'd lived then."

"Oh, Davey, you would have looked funny among the Greeks!" Then her eyes swept him appraisingly and she added: "Well, from the neck down, you'd have looked all right. Yes, the Greek tunic would have suited you."

He did not understand but he stared at the picture, trying to draw sense from it. He was ashamed of the fervour of feeling that swept over him. A rich colour rose from his neck and flooded his boyish cheeks.

"I'm going to sew a patch on your coat," said Glennys, "and darn your socks."

He looked at her, startled by the fervour in him. He pushed the book into her hands and clattered up the stairs to his attic. From the chest he took his clean pair of socks that had both heels worn through, and hid them under the mattress of his bed. He found pins and pinned up the tear on his sleeve. "She'll not mend for me whatever," he said, the tears filling his eyes.

But, when he hung the coat on a peg in the kitchen while he cleaned out the stable, she took it down and mended the tear and when he next looked in the chest there were the socks folded together, with neat darns on the heels. He held the socks to his breast and his heart throbbed like an engine against them.

He could not thank her but, when they met in the passage, he said:

"You'd ought to come and see the white bullock, how he's growing."

"So I should," she answered, her face bright in the dim passage. "I'll come to-day."

"Do you think your father will come too?" he asked timidly.

"No. He's tired. He's been out all the morning. I shall come alone."

She saw the muscles about his mouth quiver and his eyes turn away, as though he was afraid to let her see into them. She had a sudden feeling of power. Yet the power was tremulous with something strange. Ought I to go alone with Davey? she wondered. It may seem too familiar. Yet surely I can go to look at my father's beasts when he can't see them himself!

As they passed through the garden he said:

"You ought to bring some flowers to make the bullock one of them things — what you said — for his head."

Glennys laughed. "Davey, you are romantic!"

"What's that?"

"Oh, having pretty ideas about flowers and oldtime customs and all that."

"We could take some daffydils."

"We shall do no such thing."

She spoke a little sharply and there was silence between them as they mounted the steep path. But the March wind was so sportive and so scented with new growth, the clouds were so white and so flowing that, before they reached the plateau, they were laughing into each other's eyes for joy in the little lambs that played all about them.

The lambs were strewn over the hillside, white and weak and gay. They broke into sudden sidewise darts. They flung out their woolly legs in an abandon of play. Forehead to forehead they tried their infant strength against each other. The sheep watched them with no maternal pride, no responsive gaiety. Their cold eyes and flat pale cheeks were bent toward the grass and they forgot that they ever had been lambs.

The white bullock was not with the others that came to meet Davey.

"Where is the white bullock?" Glennys asked.

"You wait and see."

He led her into the Abbey and there, standing on the altar-stone, was the massive little beast, his eyes luminous for the feed that would be strewn there, his hoof gently pawing the stone.

"I've never seen anything like it!" cried Glennys. "It's wonderful! Have you bewitched him, Davey, or has he bewitched you?"

"Hoi! Hoi!" shouted Davey to the bullock, and he strewed a little meal on the altar-stone.

"How clean and white he is!" she said.

"I brush him. He's like that beast in the picture you showed me. He's sacred."

"But he's for the market."

"Don't tell your father how he thrives, will you? I'd like to keep him a little longer."

Glennys felt troubled as she looked at Davey standing there in his strength and his ignorance. He was like the white bullock. He was aloof and belonged to another age. They were like the lonely hills and the wind-swept stones of the Abbey. She went to the beast's side and laid her hand on his shoulder. He swung his head on his thick neck to touch her with his tongue. She saw how his little horns were growing so that they arched above his curly pate, smooth and sharp and threatening. But his eyes were gentle, she thought. As she looked into their blue-black depths, she saw no intelligence there, just an overwhelming instinct.

"Isn't it strange," she said, "how the monks once lived here? Do you ever think of them, Davey, and imagine what their life was like?"

"Monks!" he said. "Who where they?"

"Don't tell me that you haven't heard of the monks who built the Abbey?"

"I haven't heard." He looked at her dumbly, his hands clasping the smooth sickle of the bullock's horn, and she noticed how luminous his eyes were and the pulse that beat in his strong neck.

"The monks built the Abbey seven hundred years ago. They built it for worship."

"Worship?"

"Yes. Worship of God and prayer. That part out there, where the other bullocks are grazing, was the cloister."

"Did the monks live alone here? Without women?"

"Yes. They were holy men."

"Touch me," he said, moving closer to her. "Lay your hand on me — like on the bullock."

She spoke to him in a high clear voice:

"How did you think the Abbey came to be here?"

"I thought it had always been."

"But it had to be *built*!"

"Put your hand on me." He came still closer. "Like on the bullock." She could see the white glimmer of his skin under his shirt.

She turned pale and moved quickly away from him. "I made a mistake, coming up here with you," she said.

The bullock moved through the space between them and pressed through the narrow priests' door into the cloisters among the others. Glennys turned her back, trembling with fear, and walked swiftly out of the ruin. But Davey did not follow her. He stood looking after her through the broken arch of a window, till she was only a midget descending into the valley. Then he followed the bullock and laid his mouth against the place where her hand had lain on the animal's side. Tears fell from his eyes and he sought to make something clear, that he might understand, out of the confusion in his mind.

Spring had come too soon. Now, in the middle of March, winter came back for a space. The hills turned savage and bleak. The snow came down in thick flakes and was blown in drifts against the iron of the hills. When the young lambs saw it falling they knew it for their enemy and ran out bravely to meet it, stamping on it with their little hoofs, flattening the flakes into the ground. But the lambs were weak. They could not stamp all day long and, after a while, they crept under the warmth of their mothers' wool and huddled there.

The ewes watched the snow coming down for two days, standing close together, their cold eyes without apprehension or compassion for their lambs. Then they sank to their knees and the drifts began to bury them. Davey worked all day shovelling them out of the snow, dragging them up to their feet. The sweat poured from him and he took a slab of bread and cheese from his pocket and ate it, leaning on his spade.

That night the snow came down harder than ever. Davey did not wait for daylight but was out of bed in the bitter cold dawn, staring through the leaded panes of the attic into the terrible white fortifications of the hills.

Glennys had not spoken to him since the scene in the ruin but now he clumped in his hobnailed boots to her door and rapped.

"If the sheep are to be saved," he said, "you must come and help me."

"I'll come at once," she answered.

"What is the matter?" shouted Owen from his room.

"It's the snow!" she called back. "I must go with Davey to help with the sheep."

"Oh, curse this sciatica of mine!" cried Owen. "I should be going too!"

"Don't worry, Father. We shall save them."

With a scarf wrapped round her head and neck she plodded up the hill after Davey, placing her feet in the holes his feet had made in the snow. He carried the two spades and she a basket with sandwiches in it and a thermos of cocoa. He felt a fire of strength in him as he struggled upward, knowing she was close behind. He leaped through the drifts, eager to show off his strength.

A great mound marked where the sheep huddled. Davey and Glennys ran to it and began frantically to dig. The sheep were uncovered, stretched on their sides, their pale tongues lolling, their white eyelashes motionless over their pale eyes. Sometimes they lay heaped on top of each other. Then the ones at the bottom were dead. Most of the lambs lay dead, some with noses close to the ewes' udders. There had been more than thirty lambs. Now there were just three. Davey dragged the living sheep to their feet and supported them but they gave him no look of gratitude, or pleasure at the lambs that lived, or pity for the ones that were dead. They stood humbly, gently, waiting for the life to come back into them.

"Don't cry so," said Davey.

"I can't help it," answered Glennys. "The lambs were so sweet." She was holding the weakest of the three living ones in her arms. He was the only black one and his little black face lay on her breast. She was so hot that she had thrown back the scarf and her fine hair clung to her head in a dark mass.

Davey looked at her kneeling there in the snow and his mind was clouded and dark, like the sky overhead. His speech came thickly.

"Stop your crying and pull your scarf on your head. You'll take cold."

She smiled a little at the authority of his words. She dried her eyes on the corner of her scarf but she did not cover her head.

"I'm so hot," she said, "I should die if I covered my head."

Davey threw down his spade and strode to her. Before she could stop him he took her scarf in his hands and drew it close over her head.

"You shall keep your hair covered!" he said thickly. As he returned to his digging, he kept on saying: "You shall keep it covered. You shall...."

They worked in silence then, digging out the sheep. The black lamb's dam was dead and no living ewe would suckle it. Perhaps it was because of its colour but, weak as they were, they gave pale hatred to it out of their eyes and would not let down their milk.

At last Glennys was so tired that the spade fell from her hands. The sweat trickled down her face.

"You stop digging and drink some cocoa," said Davey. "I can finish the job. Look at the sun. There's a change coming."

A mildness was in the air. In one place, like a tunnel in the clouds, the pale sun peered through. A breeze stole up from the south. The black lamb's fleece began to curl closely.

"Yes, I must rest for a bit," she said. "My back aches. Look! The sun is really coming out."

"Rest in the stable," Davey said. "It's nice in there."

"The stable?"

He pointed with his spade, to the ruin. "I call that the stable."

She laughed. It was the first time she had laughed that day and, when he saw her white teeth and her lips parted and the escaped black lock on her forehead, he felt the joy of her nearness almost unbearable.

She thought: "If he follows me into the Abbey I will go out at the other side. I will not be alone with him in there." With the lamb in her arms she went through the snow which was not so deep on the plateau, into the Abbey. Here it was sheltered and the sun poured between the delicate stone arches and filled the ruin with an ethereal beauty.

Glennys laid the lamb on her skirt. She unwrapped the scarf from her head and covered the lamb with it. She had found a corner with clean straw in it and she laid her food on the carved top of a fallen column. She did not let her mind dwell on the sheep and lambs that had died but on those that had been saved. She wet her finger in the cocoa and the lamb beside her sucked it.

Then she saw the bullock appear in the narrow doorway that opened into the chancel. He stood looking in at her, the crescents of his horns bent above his curly poll, his forelegs thick and short beneath the bulk of his strong breast.

He stood staring at her in surprise. She could hear the breath blowing in his wide nostrils. He pressed through the door and she wondered if she ought to be afraid of him. There was the lamb's little head, showing above the scarf. Perhaps the bullock had it in his mind to harm the lamb.

He came closer. His glowing yet senseless eyes moved insolently in their sockets. His coat glistened, the long hair silky like fur. He stared at her and at the lamb. Now she gave a loud clear scream and struck at him with her fist.

Davey came leaping through the snow. He shouted:

"Don't be afraid! He means no harm. Look now, he does just what I tell him!"

But the bullock pushed Davey aside with his shoulder and thrust his wet nostrils against the girl's breast. "He means no harm!" shouted Davey and caught him by the horns and swung him away.

Glennys watched the two of them wrestling together. Whether there was anger or just mischief in the bullock, she could not tell. Now he swung Davey from side to side, as though he would hurl him off. Now Davey bent the beast's proud neck and pushed him closer to the door. Now he had the upper hand. The bullock was thrust outside the Abbey. A heavy wooden bar closed the entrance.

Davey was laughing but his breath came in harsh gasps. He dropped to his knees beside Glennys. "It's a pity he frightened ye," he said, "for he means no harm."

"I wasn't frightened," she answered, "except for the lamb. That was why I screamed for you."

His love poured from his eyes and she began to rise but he put out his hand and held her by the skirt. "Hold me," he said, "like you did the lamb. Hold me in your arms."

Glennys tore herself from him and ran out of the Abbey. She ran through the deep snow down the hillside, putting her feet into the holes made by his. "How dared he! I hate him! I hate him!" she said over and over again. Yet her anger was so mixed with love that she could not tell one from the other.

After a while Davey carried the lamb into the kitchen. He said gruffly:

"Is the lamb to die, or will you feed it?"

"I have warm milk in a bottle, waiting for it," she answered gently.

She took the lamb from him and laid it on the warm hearth. "Oh, pretty, pretty, pretty!" she whispered to it, and it sucked from the bottle with all its might.

Its body warm, its stomach full of warm milk, it soon began to totter about the kitchen, putting its pert face into every corner and, as it felt its strength return, gambolling as it would in a meadow.

Before long Owen sent for a cattle buyer to look at the bullocks. He needed money for his season's work. But, on the morning, Davey told him that one of the bullocks, the white one it was, should be held back for a little. It had been struck by a stone falling from the tower of the Abbey and hadn't thrived for a bit, but it would be all right.

Owen told the drover to have a look at it, in any case. But it was not with the others and Davey said that it was shut in the stable.

"What stable?" asked the drover.

"Oh, a stable," answered Davey, vaguely. "He isn't ready for killing yet."

When the eleven red bullocks had been herded away, Davey let down the bar and the white bullock stepped out of the chancel, in his pride and his beauty. He raised his head toward the April sky and the round white clouds that drifted across it were not whiter than he.

Now Davey had him all to himself. The hills stretched, wave upon wave, hump upon hump, to the horizon and, on this hill, he and the white bullock alone together. Davey did not ask himself why he loved the beast, why the thought of him being butchered was more than he could bear. He did not ask himself why he doted on his beauty and fed him delicately and kept fresh straw for him to lie on. In some mysterious way the beast now bore the burden of Davey's love for Glennys. Davey would put both arms about him and press his forehead to the place where her hand had lain.

But, since their bout of wrestling, the bullock was not so docile as he had been. Now, when Davey approached, he swung his tail and pawed the tender grass. There was a challenge in his eyes, even while he did what he was bid. He was restless, always moving in and out of the Abbey, throwing up his head and distending his nostrils against the wind. He seemed to be always expecting some fresh service from Davey. He did not move sedately, as the other bullocks had, but with force and arrogance.

Owen kept asking about him and Davey always said: "He's better, but not fit for killing."

Davey had grown sullen and scarcely looked at Glennys. But she looked at him more and more often.

The farm labourer whose back had been strained was now well and able to work. Owen paid off Davey and told him he could go.

"This is the end of it all," thought Davey, in the chaos of his mind. From the garden he stole spring flowers and carried them to the ruin of the Abbey. With his thick hands he made them into a wreath and placed it on the bullock's head.

"Now," he said, "you are like the sacred bull in the picture...."

Davey was to leave the farm that day but when evening came he had not returned to the house for his box, which stood packed, waiting on the doorstep.

"Wherever can the boy be?" asked Owen, again and again.

Suddenly Glennys said she would go and look for him.

"Let the man go," said Owen.

"No, Father, I shall go myself!"

She climbed the hill, in the golden evening light. In the Abbey, on the altar-stone, she found Davey lying dead. Near by the white bullock was quietly grazing. The crescents of his horns rose above a chaplet of spring flowers and the points of his horns were red with blood.

[1938]

Come Fly With Me

He had his eye on her for some time. Each time he looked at her something deep inside him thrilled in sudden joy. There was that about her which made her unlike all other young females. An observer might have discovered nothing different in her. Nothing to cause that vibration through his nerves. But even in the far South, where they had wintered, she had had an attraction for him and in some subtle way he had been able to communicate this to her. So now after the long flight northward, during which he had had only occasional glimpses of her, he awaited her coming with confidence. He and a group of other swallows had sought out the breeding place of last year, a country home in the southern part of Ontario.

He had been hatched in one of the tall chimneys of this stone house on the hill and he now circled with unerring instinct about it. If any of the other swallows were his kin, he was unaware of the fact. His vibrant little being was held by only one bond, the bond between him and the one whom he awaited. For three days he awaited her.

Then suddenly he saw her.

There was no mistaking her! The instinct that had guided him to this home of his desire had guided her to him. Between them there passed a joyous tremor of recognition.

But she did not fly to his side. Instead she alighted on a gable of the house. She was tired after her long and hazardous journey, during which she had encountered gales and driving rain. Now in the warm spring sunshine she shook out her plumage and sank contentedly to her breast. She left the next move in their courtship to him.

He had but one thought, to delight her by the marvel of his flight and by his beauty. Back and forth he darted in front of her, his forked tail, his long, pointed wings etched in myriad gestures against the sky. He circled, he wheeled, he soared, he turned from side to side so that she might be dazzled by the beauty of his throat and the underside of his wings. She did not move. She looked almost indifferent and began to preen the feathers of her breast which she had neglected on the journey.

His new spring plumage, glittering with health, shone in the sunshine. Now he swam close above her. He picked up an imaginary straw and flew into the chimney with it, in a symbolic gesture of nest-building. When at last he alighted not far from her she remained motionless, accepting his nearness.

Other birds were circling skyward, delighting in the warmth and the ardour of the mating season. The gardener was digging in the perennial border and several full-breasted robins were drawing sleek worms from the freshly turned soil. Beyond a lattice fence the lawn fell steeply down to a stream. On this lower level there was a great elm tree where a pair of orioles were already building their nest. Like a small flame miraculously detached from a heavenly conflagration, the male darted in and out of the elm's foliage, beating the air with his bright wings in the haste of construction.

The two on the gable of the house sat motionless, held by the fragile but exquisite bond of this new experience. They were so young, yet nature's ritual lay open before them. Another male swallow approached them. In graceful swoops and glides he displayed his power and beauty. She looked not ill-pleased but presently, as though to show her unconcern, she spread her own wings and flew over the roof and beyond, into the wood. The newcomer was disconcerted but he who had awaited her coming flew close behind her, and, when she alighted on the branch of a wild cherry tree, he dropped there beside her.

In the small wood they spent the night perched quite near each other. At sunrise he again wooed her with all the ardour that was in him.

Away she flew and he after her! But in her flight she uttered a sharp, clear note. They sped above the dark pines, above the housetop and, when she sank to the lawn, the mating rite took place.

In wild delight he now led, now pursued her, through the sunny air, but always his flight drew them toward the chimney. He would dart into it, making the symbolic gestures of nest-building, then up again to her side, fluttering about her, urging her to the descent. At last she flew down into the chimney with him.

Together they perched on the very smoke-blackened ledge where he had been hatched. Remnants of the nest still clung to it though the chimney had been cleaned. She looked about her and was satisfied.

Now began their joyful work of building a home. In and out of the chimney they sped carrying morsels of clay or strands of dry grass in their beaks. Squatting in it they smoothed and rounded it with their breasts. She was the more expert at this. Indeed she now became the leader. Like the wind she sped from field or stream's edge to nest, never tiring of her task. But at times he led her to fly with him for the mere pleasure of flying. Then, in an abandon of delight they soared upward till they were no more than two shimmering specks against the blue, or skimmed low to the stream and without resting sipped to quench their thirst, or even ruffled the surface of the water with their wings and sped on, bathed and refreshed.

Then she would bethink herself of her unlaid eggs and how she must conserve her vitality for them. More than once the marital rite had been accomplished while in full flight.

The nest was lined with feathers and down and there rested finally in it seven white eggs flecked with brown.

All this had not been completed without interference. During the time of nest-building her other suitor had followed them enviously, sometimes darting between them. The mated birds had borne this tolerantly but, when another female had approached and even entered the chimney, she had been driven off in a frenzy of anger by the little wife. Beneath the eave the sparrows were already feeding their young.

Now the oriole's nest was complete and hung with its hidden treasures high in the elm. All day the oriole sent forth his challenging song. At eventide his voice was the last to be heard, in a great sweet cadence. The stream rustled on among its reeds. The dim shape of an owl drifted across the fields. In the nest in the chimney the little wife felt the eggs quicken beneath her breast.

2

At the bottom of the chimney there was a deep fireplace in a long, dark-panelled study. This room was cool, though outdoors the weather was very hot. The little girl came in quietly, not quite knowing what to do with herself. She came softly in her sandals, making no noise.

Then she saw that she was not alone. A young bird, fully fledged but still not able to fly, sat on the hearth. When he saw her he spread his pointed wings and hopped toward her. He did not seem to be afraid but came as though he sought her help.

She gave a little cry of delight and caught him up in her hands. She ran with him to her aunt who was dying rose petals for *potpourri*.

"Look!" she cried. "A fledgling! He has fallen from the nest in the chimney."

They had known from the twittering of the young that there was a nest in the chimney. For that reason they had not been able to have a fire in the study all that summer.

"Poor little thing," said the aunt, dropping a handful of rose petals. "If only we could put him back!"

Now the child's mother appeared and, holding the fledgling to her breast, mourned over him. She ran with him to the fireplace crouching in the aperture, held him as far up as she could, urging his parents to notice him. But they were intent on feeding those which were left in the nest. Excited twitterings came from the young ones and when the one in her hands heard this he strained upward with his beak wide open.

"There is nothing for it," said the child's mother, "but to bring him up by hand."

"We have tried that before," said the aunt, laying some bright blue larkspur flowerettes among the rose petals, "and failed."

"But they were miserable little fledglings!" cried the mother. "See how strong and beautiful he is! See how long his wings and his forked tail! He's sure to live if we feed him properly."

"He is a pet," said the little girl. "Shall we name him Arthur?"

"Why Arthur?"

"Oh, I don't know, but it seems to suit him."

Arthur very much wanted to live. Whatever they brought him he eagerly swallowed. But now came the difficulty. Of a sudden flies and moths had almost disappeared from the scene. There had been a long drought. The dry earth refused to give up more than an occasional worm. The little girl had to abandon her play, the mother her work, the aunt her *pot-pourri,* in order to find food for Arthur.

He knew no fear. He fluttered to them with little cries of joy when they came to him. The next day he was stronger. He spread his long pointed wings and sought to raise himself from the floor. He looked from face to face without fear. The great thing was to find food for him. He was always hungry. They searched the lawn, the shrubbery, the orchard, and whenever they found insect or worm they flew with it to Arthur.

On the third day they went out to lunch, though with misgivings.

"I should not go," said the mother. "I should stay at home and feed Arthur."

"We must give him a good meal before we leave," said the aunt, "and come home early."

The little girl, all in white and wearing her best gloves, hung over Arthur in his nest of cotton wool, promised to return soon. But they went off with anxious hearts.

They could scarcely enjoy the luncheon party for their anxiety over Arthur, and hastened home. They hurried out of the car and into the house.

A change had come over the fledgling. He was ravenous but he was weak. He no longer fluttered or tried to fly but sat quite still.

"There now!" cried the mother. "What did I tell you? I should not have gone out to lunch. I have killed him."

"No, no," said the aunt. "He is just hungry. We must give him warm milk." She hurried to inspect her rose petals which she had left in a copper kettle on the terrace to dry. "Oh, my *pot-pourri!*" she said distractedly. "The wind has blown half of it away."

The child and she set about picking up the innumerable petals while the mother warmed milk.

Arthur took it eagerly. They began then to search for food for him. But no insects were to be found. They heaved up heavy stones to see what might be beneath but those wriggling hairy worms were too repulsive to offer Arthur.

"At the bottom of the ravine," said the little girl, "the earth is damp. We might find worms."

They scrambled through the undergrowth down beneath the bridge. They had brought a trowel but the earth, though damp, was hard. They had a time of it to dig up half a dozen thin worms. Arthur ate them as though famished. Then, with his tiny crop distended he slept. They had not realized that, being a swallow, insects and not worms should be his only food. But there were no insects.

The next morning the little girl hurried to peep into Arthur's box. She saw at once that he was dead. She said nothing but ran to the swing and swung as hard as she could.

After a while she decided to give Arthur a beautiful funeral. She lined a small box with rose petals and gently laid him on them. Then she made a little coverlet of pansies. He looked sweet and peaceful in there.

She took a sheet of her best drawing paper, cut a square from it and carefully inscribed his memorial notice.

In Memory of
ARTHUR
A little fledgling which
fell down the Chimney
on
August the 7th, 1940

On the oak chest in the hall she set his bier with the notice above it. All day he lay in state. Everyone who passed through the hall stopped to look.

In the evening she buried him in the flower border. She placed forget-me-nots in a little jar on the grave and the memorial at its head. A gentle rain began to fall.

3

Now the nest was empty. The young birds had been taught to fly. Now in the evening they circled and swooped with their parents in search of insects. At night all perched in a row on a secluded branch of one of the pines. Once more the mates were free to care. Still they were held in the bond of their love. Sometimes they forgot the young ones and rode the summer breeze together as in the first rapture of their mating. They had seen the orchard bloom. Now they looked down on the golden fields of the harvest. The orioles too had reared their young and the song of the male rang out bold and free. The sparrows beneath the eave were rearing a second brood. As the swallows darted past they could hear the cheeping of the young ones.

Perhaps it was this that gave her the idea. Certainly it was no wish of his. When he peered down into the chimney and saw her on the nest he was astonished. When she uttered her sharp love cry and swept before him above the lawn he followed, almost reluctant. But she had her will.

The first time she had laid seven eggs. This time she laid five. She showed almost fierce absorption in the brooding over them. Storms came and the sparrows' fledglings were swept from their nest and washed in a torrent of rain down the verandah roof. Their naked blue bodies lay scattered in the morning sun. But her nest was safe. In due time she hatched out five lusty ones.

He did his share of the feeding without enthusiasm. Often he was restive and longed to fly, with her winging at his side. But he was loyal. The fledglings throve and began to grow their feathers. This was well because a chill was now in the air. At night they were thankful to snuggle beneath her comforting breast.

One morning when the reeds by the river were whispering and a golden mist hung on the horizon, he fed the young ones with no help from her. She did not come. He flew in wide circles above the housetop and the trees, looking for her.

Suddenly he saw her perched on the chimney. He flew joyfully to her side. She darted away and he after her. They flew for a space, then he sought to turn her back. In cajoling circles she led him on. But the thought of the fledglings held him. He pressed back to them with strong strokes of his wings. On the way he captured a plump moth and flew with it down to the nest. Five upward straining beaks greeted him. He thrust the moth into the throat of the nearest and flew up and looked anxiously about for his mate.

What he saw was his grown-up brood, perched with two score of other swallows on the telegraph wire. There they sat, like beads on a necklace, and she was fluttering above! She was urging him to join them!

He tried to drive her, to harry her back to the fledglings, but she would have none of them. The flock rose and moved swiftly southward, their forked tails etched against the sky. He hesitated, torn between love and fatherhood, then spread his wings and flew away with her.

[1944]

The Celebration

"Oh, I can't believe it! I can't believe it!" Mrs. Evans almost screamed in her hilarity. "Oh! it seems too good to be true." And she sat down and burst into tears.

Her son Robert looked down at her with mingled sympathy and grudging. It was all very well for her to be excited but there was no need to go on like this. Jimmy had had a wonderful piece of luck. Robert only wished it might have been himself.

"Do you really think he'll get the money?" Mrs. Evans quavered, raising her streaming eyes to his.

"Sure. Those Irish Sweepstakes always pay up. They're O.K."

His mother reached out and took his hand. "I hope he'll do something nice for you, Bob," she said. "You've had an awful lot to contend with."

"I'm not counting on that," he returned gruffly. "You're the one he ought to do something for."

"No, no, I don't want anything out of it. I just want to see my children get on. Sakes alive, won't your father be surprised?"

"You bet. And the girls. It'll all come out in the evening papers. The reporters are up at Jim's place already. They'll be photographing him and Lyla."

His mother gasped. "Photographing them for the papers! Oh, my goodness! Won't Lyla be conceited?"

"It's a pity Lyla isn't prettier. Now, if it was *my* wife she'd be worth taking a picture of."

His mother gave an embarrassed laugh and he remembered the unwieldy bulk of Lizzie, who was soon to have a child, her fourth. He said, in a grumpy tone, "Anyhow, she has a pretty face."

Mrs. Evans agreed. "Yes, and she's not ten years older than her husband — the way Lyla is. When I think of that boy of eighteen marrying a woman of twenty-eight, it makes me mad."

"They've been married a year now and she's got him just where she wants him —her and her parents."

"Jimmy's a real affectionate boy," cried his mother. "My, I wish he'd come and see me. I want to give him a big hug."

The words were scarcely out of her mouth when Jimmy walked into the room. He was flushed and excited.

"Hello, Ma," he stammered, in a voice that cracked, the way it did when it was changing. "Say — w-what d'you think of the Irish Sweepstakes now? Th-thirty thousand bucks! How d'you like havin' a millionaire for a son?"

She took him in her arms and almost hurt him with the strength of her hug. He was a fragile little fellow. She looked at her two boys, Bob stocky and reliable, a family man at twenty-six, finding it hard to make ends meet, what with doctors' bills and the high cost of living, Jimmy married far too young, to a woman far too old, and now the sudden possessor of such wealth as none of them had ever dreamed of. She thought of her two married daughters and their husbands, of her youngest girl who was only fifteen, and the baby of the family, a boy of nine. They all would be proud of Jimmy's good fortune. And their father — what would he say — he who felt himself so superior to his family?

"Say, Ma," said Jimmy. "I can't stay long. Lyla wants me to go out with her and buy some clothes."

"For you or her?"

"For both of us. Everybody will be looking at us."

"Oh, Jimmy, are you sure you'll get the money?"

"Course I shall. This thing's O.K. Look." He took the notification of his prize winning from his pocket and spread it before her.

"Get my glasses, dearie."

He brought them and she perused the document. Bob leaned over her, his blunt features rigid with envy.

"It's sure swell," he said. He rubbed his head against his mother's as though to remind her that he too was her son.

The little boy, Ronnie, came running in from school. He was told the news and stared at Jimmy, as though he were a marvel of perspicacity. Then he burst out — "Show us the money!"

"He left it at home — with Lyla," grinned Bob.

The telephone rang. Jimmy sprang to answer it. Bob exchanged a look with his mother. "I'll bet it's her," he said.

It was. "I'm to go right home," Jimmy got out breathlessly. "It's another reporter. Gosh, what a life!"

His mother caught him by the arm. "Listen, Jimmy. I'm going to have a celebration for you — and for Lyla, of course — tomorrow night. We'll have the whole family. Be here early for supper, will you? And Lyla's father and mother too, if they'd like to come."

"Lyla's ma don't go out at night and he won't go without her. But we'll come."

"Come early."

"Sure."

"Bring your appetites with you. I'll bake the things you like."

With difficulty he wrenched his mind from his own affairs. "Corn fritters, Ma?"

"All you can eat. And the lemon custard cake Lyla likes. Be sure and come early."

He promised, half dazed by excitement, kissed her, freed himself and left.

The Evanses lived in a flat above a small undertaking establishment. They acted as caretakers and, in return, had their quarters rent free. These rooms were the best they had ever lived in, fine hardwood floors, clean new decorating throughout, excellent plumbing. The undertaking business on the ground floor was Jewish and the funeral services held there were, at first, rather disturbing and strange to the Gentile family. Mr. Katz, the undertaker, was a kind man. He was interested in Henry Evans, whom he looked on as a man of superior intelligence and education. They had long talks together in the room where the coffins were stored. Henry Evans had a good deal of spare time.

Mrs. Evans had wanted to keep the great news till her husband returned from the printers, where he had a part-time job, so that she might have the thrill of telling it to him herself. But on the way home he bought a newspaper and the first thing his eye lighted on was the picture of his son Jimmy, taken with his wife and parents-in-law. He read the heading: NINETEEN-YEAR-OLD MILK-TRUCK DRIVER WINNER IN IRISH SWEEPSTAKES.

He did not know the man sitting next him but he showed him the picture, trying to keep the hand that held the paper steady.

Soon all the other passengers were looking at the same picture in their own papers. "He's always been a good boy," declared the father proudly, "except that he wouldn't go to college."

He felt that people looked at him with more respect after that. He almost believed that he could have afforded to send Jimmy to college. His step was light as he hurried along the street and turned in at the door above which hung the sign KATZ FUNERAL PARLORS. His wife met him at the top of the stairs. She saw at once that he had heard the news.

Her face fell. "Oh, Henry, who told you?" she cried. Then she saw the newspaper. "But you hardly ever buy one!"

The evening paper was delivered to them by their own son, Ronnie, as they were on his route.

"I guess some instinct told me to buy it." Evans spoke in rather precise accents. His education, his manner of speaking, set him apart from his family, made the humorous things he said seem more humorous, the sarcastic things more sarcastic. He was lightly built and carried himself very straight. Mrs. Evans was stocky and reliable. Bob took after her.

"Isn't it wonderful?" she quavered, her eyes full of happy tears. "Our Jimmy — thirty thousand dollars — just for the price of one ticket!"

"Have you seen him?"

"Yes. He was here and Bob too. Jimmy couldn't stay. I guess he hardly knows if he's standing on his head or his heels."

"We'll go to his place and see him after supper," said her husband. "I hope he'll do something nice for you out of the money."

The small boy put in, "Can I come too? Do you think he'll do something for me?"

"Certainly," answered his father. "He'll probably buy you a fine bicycle."

"Now don't go putting ideas in the child's head." But Mrs. Evans herself was quivering with ideas.

The fifteen-year-old daughter who was rather an objectionable teen-ager, came tearing in. She could not wait to be told details but flew to the telephone to spread the news among her friends. This prevented her two married sisters from getting on the line. After repeated attempts they gave up and, after eating a sketchy evening meal, hastened with their husbands to the flat.

Nothing could have pleased Mrs. Evans better. She wanted all her children about her in this hour of triumph. She looked on her two sons-in-law as her children also, for one of them was an orphan and the other came from the West and had no relations of his own in the city. She hugged all four and told them the amazing news over again, as if they did not already know it. She repeated it, right from the moment when Jimmy had told her he had bought a ticket for the Sweepstakes and she had said he was foolish to waste his money that way, to the coming of Bob with the announcement of the lucky draw.

"I guess Bob wishes it was him," said her son-in-law, Bill Clark, "with three kids and another on the way."

"There's nothing jealous about Bob," declared the mother. "He's just glad Jimmy's had such luck."

"That old wife of his will be more stuck-up than ever," put in the teen-ager.

The two elder sisters laughed, rather maliciously. The pretty one said, "You'll see Lyla with a fur coat and a diamond ring before long, mark my words."

The plain one added, *"And* a car. I bet they buy one inside of a week."

"I know of a good secondhand car for sale," said Bill Clark, "I can get a commission on it if I find a buyer. I'll phone Jim before someone else gets in ahead of me." He sprang to the telephone. There was silence in the room as the family, one and all, listened avidly to his end of the conversation. Jimmy and his wife, from being nobodies, had become of breath-taking importance.

"Hello," Bill was saying genially. "Is that Lyla?... Oh, hello, Lyla — congratulations. This sure is wonderful news.... Yeah, aren't you the lucky pair? And you certainly deserve it.... Yeah, everybody's saying how glad they are.... Huh-huh, we're all here. The whole damn family — wish you and Jim were here.... Say, could I speak to Jim? Got to congratulate him personally.... Oh — tired, is he? No wonder — all those newspaper guys.... Sure.... but I'll just keep him a minute... Too tired to talk? Well, I'll be darned. What's he doing?... *Gone to bed?* For the love of Mike! Well — I just wondered if he's thinking of buying a car. I know of a dandy secondhand one.... *What?* You've ordered a new one? *Already?* By golly, you haven't wasted much time. But I'm certainly glad. I just thought if you wanted a second-hand one — what make did you order? I'd just like to know so's I can tell the folks.... A new model Buick! Well — that sounds good. Everybody here'll be tickled when I tell them.... Sure, tickled pink....

Well, remember us poor relations to Jim. Be seeing you tomorrow night. Bye-bye, Lyla." He hung up the receiver.

A volley of questions met him when he rejoined the circle. Though they had heard every word he said and guessed pretty accurately what Lyla had said, they wanted it repeated. Bill, who was quite a mimic, imitated Lyla's drawling, nasal tones.

"They're not wasting any time spending the money," said Henry Evans. "Believe me, they'll run through it in no time."

"But a new *Buick*," cried his pretty daughter, pink with envy. "They must be crazy."

"I thought Lyla'd have more sense," the plain one added, "seeing that she's nine years older than Jimmy."

"She's a stuck-up old thing," declared the teen-ager.

"Why did Jimmy go to bed?"

"I guess the poor lad's tired out," said the mother.

Bill Clark gave a hoot. "I wish I was that kind of tired," he said.
The pretty sister gave herself a searching glance in the looking glass above the sideboard.

"It must be awful," she said, "to have photographers pushing right into your apartment to take your picture."

Everyone stared at her, thinking how she would have loved it.

"You'd certainly take a prettier picture than Lyla," said her father. He gave her an appreciative look, noting her resemblance to himself. He was, in fact, pleased with all his family at this moment. He looked forward to tomorrow morning at the printing office, when he would speak with nonchalance of his son's "bit of luck."

The quiet son-in-law, who had acquired a reputation for wisdom by almost never speaking, now opened his lips.

"I'm kind of thirsty," he said.

Mrs. Evans sprang up. "I'll make coffee for everybody."

"No, no, Mother." Bill Clark laid a restraining hand on her arm. "The kid can go to the corner and get some ginger ale." He drew silver from his pocket and gave it to Ronnie.

"I'd sooner have a coke," said the teen-ager.

"You'll drink what the rest do," said her father. In these days he disapproved of this girl. He disliked the way she dressed, the way she talked, the way she looked — almost ready to burst with health. Now she threw herself back in her chair, stretched out her legs, in their turned-up slacks and crumpled white socks, and sulked.

Her mother gave her a propitiatory look. "There's a coke in the icebox, Joanne."

The girl ignored this, for she wanted to continue with her sulking. The little boy had already run off.

"I wish Bob and Lizzie were here," remarked the plain sister. "I'd like to know what Bob thinks about it all."

"You'll see them tomorrow night," Mrs. Evans said happily. "I'm having a celebration. You've all got to be here early. There'll be lots to eat."

"And drink too," added Evans.

There was so much to say, so many speculations about Jimmy's future, that it was midnight before the married couples left, but as neither pair had any children, they had no need for anxiety on that score.

It was a restless night that Henry Evans and his wife spent. As they lay side by side in the dark, one of them would no sooner begin to get drowsy than the other would renew the talk about Jimmy and the prize money. By three o'clock they still hadn't closed their eyes. Jimmy's new situation in life was considered from every angle. They planned exactly what they themselves would have done had such a fortune come their way. Henry felt that his son should be equipped for such a responsibility and he told his wife how he was going to take the boy in hand, right from tomorrow, and guide him in the way of prudent investment and careful living. He enumerated the points in which he would give Jimmy counsel. It was then that Mrs. Evans grew sleepy. Soon he was left awake in the dark alone.

He scarcely realized that he had slept when the alarm went off at six-thirty. Yet when he set out for the printers he was brisker than usual. He bought a morning paper and, chuckling in a half-apologetic way, pointed out the picture of Jimmy and Lyla to the other passengers in the streetcar. There was an article in which Lyla was described as a slim blonde.

Mrs. Evans had a morning paper too and when she read that laughed out loud. "Slim blonde," she exclaimed. "She's no more a slim blonde than I am." She pictured Bill Clark greeting Lyla tonight with "Hello, slim blonde!" And she wondered how Lyla would take it. She hoped there'd be no unpleasantness.

It was hard to get on with her housework this morning, for her friends and relations kept ringing her up. Some dropped in to congratulate her. Added to this, her excitement made her less efficient. She kept letting things slip out of her hands. She broke her best cake plate. Ronnie developed a cold in the head and the teen-ager disappeared with her friends and did nothing to help. The lemon custard for the cake was inclined to run. At the fruit store she went quite wildly extravagant and bought four boxes of expensive strawberries. She bought ham and pressed veal and salad stuff. Everyone in the shop knew about Jimmy.

All day long she kept expecting Lyla or Jimmy to ring her up. She knew how busy they were, yet she still kept expecting it. Every time the telephone rang she was sure it was one of them on the line. She kept counting the hours till six o'clock. That was the time she had set for the celebration. Half an hour before that time she was dressed in her best and the teen-ager had, under pressure, consented to set the table. Everything looked inviting, Henry Evans thought when he came into the room. He gave an admiring glance at his wife, at her flushed cheeks and bright eyes. He himself wore his Sunday suit and the tie she had given him on his birthday. He looked spruce and dignified. He said, "I've been thinking we ought to have some flowers for Lyla. It'd show her we know how to do things in good style."

"A corsage, you mean," put in the teen-ager.

He stared at her. "*I* call it a bunch of flowers."

"Corsage," she repeated.

"Flowers cost a lot," said his wife. "I've spent enough on this supper as it is. Anyhow Lyla didn't do anything. It was Jimmy bought the ticket."

"This is no time for economy," laughed Henry.

He hurried out, down the stairs, through the undertakers and into the street which seemed to wear an air of gaiety that evening. He bought three orchids, tied with a bow of chiffon, at the florists. He bought something else too — when his wife saw it, she cried, "You shouldn't have brought that stuff home. I've got plenty of ginger ale and Bill's sent a case of beer."

"This is just for us old folks," he grinned.

"I won't touch it. You know that."

"I mean Lyla and me."

She had to laugh but she was annoyed at him, both because of the expense and because of her fear that he might take too much of the stuff. He was not a man who could carry liquor well.

He took the quart bottle of whiskey into the kitchen and uncorked it. The small boy knelt on a chair beside the table watching with interest.

"May I taste, Dad?" he asked.

"Sure."

Ronnie picked up the cork and gingerly licked it. He made a face. "I don't like it."

"Stay that way," advised his father.

"Do you like it?"

"Once in a while when I want to celebrate."

"Like tonight?"

"Yes, like tonight."

"Dad, now Jimmy's rich do you s'pose he'll help you and Mamma?"

"I hope so."

"If I was rich, I would."

"I'll bet you would."

The first to arrive were Bob and his wife. Lizzie looked tired but her pretty face was lighted by an excited smile. She was a favorite with her parents-in-law and was kissed by each of them in turn.

"I thought you'd have brought the kiddies," said Mrs. Evans. "I've set places for them at the table."

"Goodness' sakes," Lizzie gave a big sigh, "I get enough of their noise. We left them at my mother's."

She looked admiringly at the table, carefully set out with good things to eat and, laid by Lyla's plate, the three orchids. She picked them up and examined them.

"What do you think of that?" asked her mother-in-law.

"Well, I've certainly never had an orchid."

Evans spoke from the doorway. "I'll buy you one when your baby arrives, see if I don't."

"Don't worry," she returned, a little sharply. "I don't want any orchids."

She went into the bedroom to remove her things.

The married sisters and their husbands now arrived. They had brought all the newspaper clippings and pictures they had been able to collect. There was a great deal of laughter as these were compared to the ones Mrs. Evans already had. Everybody was excited. Envy was forgotten in happy expectation. Bob filled glasses for all but the younger ones. It was arranged by Henry Evans that, as soon as the door opened and Lyla and Jim appeared, a toast was to be made to them. Everyone was a little tremulous excepting the teenager, who looked completely unimpressed.

Lyla and Jim were already late. Mrs. Evans had taken the scalloped potatoes from the oven but now she wondered if she had not better put them back.

"I'm going to give Jim a ring," said the father, "and find out what is keeping them."

"Don't be fussy, Dad," said his plain daughter. "They're likely on their way."

"Well, I'll give them ten minutes, then I'll ring."

Before that time had passed the telephone rang.

"Somebody else to congratulate us," Mrs. Evans exclaimed. "I never saw the beat. You answer it this time, Bob."

Willingly Robert took up the receiver. The more congratulations the merrier.

"Hello." He smiled expectantly into the telephone.

He listened for a moment, then the smile left his face.

"Why, Lyla," he said, "you can't do that."

His sisters demanded, "Can't do what?"

"Sh-h," he ordered them, and again listened.

"But Mother's got everything ready," he said loudly. "We're all waiting."

"What's the matter?" cried his mother.

"O.K." he growled into the telephone and banged down the receiver.

They crowded anxiously about him.

"Is Jimmy sick?" Mrs. Evans demanded.

"No, Jimmy's not sick. But some of Lyla's folks are there and Jim and Lyla can't leave. She says they'll be over after supper."

Mrs. Evans flopped into a chair. Her face was blank with disappointment.

"Well, if that wouldn't make your blood boil," exclaimed the pretty sister.

"I knew it'd be like that," the plain one added. "Jim will be dragged just where she wants to go and he won't go anywhere else."

"But I've got the supper ready," wailed Mrs. Evans.

Her son-in-law Bill patted her shoulder. "Don't worry, Ma."

The quiet son-in-law remarked, "There'll be all the more for the rest of us."

"But I made all the things they like," she moaned.

"Let me at the phone," said her husband. "I'll tell that woman a thing or two."

"No, no, we mustn't have any words. Not at a time like this."

"But it's so *mean!*" cried Lizzie.

"Just like that old Lyla," put in the teen-ager.

"What's Lyla done?" demanded the small boy.

"Haven't you got ears?" Bob demanded.

"What time did Lyla say they'd come?" Mrs. Evans asked Bob.

"About nine o'clock. She said they were sorry."

"Sorry!" echoed his sisters scornfully. "They've spoilt everything."

"No, they haven't." Mrs. Evans forced herself to be cheerful. "We'll just enjoy our supper, as though nothing had happened and then, when they come, give them a hearty welcome."

Grumbling a little they obeyed her. They carried their beer to the table and drank it there. Bill told a funny story and the four wives laughed immoderately, as though forcibly to throw off the shadow that had fallen. Henry Evans began to show off a little, as he liked to do in front of his family. Mrs. Evans, who usually tried to repress him in this, now encouraged him. By the time the meal was finished they were in quite good spirits, even though the orchids at Lyla's place were a constant reminder of the absence of the guests of honor.

While the women cleared away the supper things and Bill had a sparring match with little Ronnie, Henry Evans brought out the bottle of whiskey and poured drinks for the men. The hands of the clock moved with, it seemed, added speed, and before they realized the lateness of the hour, ten o'clock was striking.

Bob said angrily, "What the dickens has happened to Jim and Lyla? Why don't they come?"

"Gosh, it's ten o'clock," added Bill.

The quiet son-in-law muttered under his breath, "They're not coming."

"Not coming!" Bob's voice was sharp with anger. "I'll see whether they're coming or not." He strode to the telephone and dialed Lyla's number. Every face turned expectantly toward him. The women came from the kitchen and gathered about him.

"Is that Lyla?" he demanded. "Oh, tell Jim I want to speak to him." He put his hand over the mouthpiece. "It's some friend of theirs. She's gone to fetch one of them. I can hear a lot of voices. Must be having a party there too. Say, I'll tell that boy a thing or two when I get him on the line." He removed his hand from the mouthpiece.

"Hello! That you, Lyla?" He spoke with false geniality. "Well, we're getting tired of waiting. When are you folks coming over?"

They could hear Lyla's voice, but he interrupted her. "Bring them along. Lots of room here. We'd like to meet them."

Now Lyla was speaking.

Bob's tone changed. He exclaimed roughly, "Send that kid to the phone. I want to tell him he's got to come!"

Again Bob listened, his face flushed and a frown darkening his forehead. Then he groaned — "Oh, my gosh — too tired to come?"

Lyla's voice rattled on. Henry Evans who already had had a little more to drink than was good for him, strode to Bob's side.

"Give me that receiver," he ordered. Bob put it into his hand.

"Now —" Henry rapped out in a staccato tone "— Explain yourself, Lyla. I want to know just why you and Jim haven't turned up tonight."

He listened attentively, standing very erect. His daughters were giggling. Bill was pouring himself another drink of rye. Lyla's voice rattled on and on in the telephone.

Mrs. Evans put in somewhat shakily, "If Jimmy's too tired, tell Lyla it'll be all right."

Her husband did not reply. His attitude was so rigid that everyone in the room became rigid, except the teen-ager, who lolled on the couch examining the soles of her flat-heeled shoes. Ronnie felt that someone was being unkind to his mother and he climbed onto her lap.

Would Lyla never stop talking! Would Henry go right on listening, with that terribly set expression! Presently he did speak.

"Listen," he said, in his most educated voice. "Listen, Lyla, for this is probably the last time I shall ever speak to you. I just want to tell you that, when Jim married you, we — every one of us — felt pretty sick. We thought you'd lead him round by the nose. Now we know it. We don't care what you do. You and he can drive to Banff or to hell for all we care and stay there. Send Jimmy to the phone. If he doesn't come I'll go to your house and tell him and your parents and your friends what I think of you. Tell him to come or he'll be sorry." The last words were almost shouted into the receiver. His family could see how he was trembling.

"Oh, Henry," implored Mrs. Evans, "do be careful what you say. Remember —"

He stopped her with a furious look. Then he said, "Is that you, Jim? Well, aren't you a mean dog — letting your mother get a fine supper for the celebration and never coming to it? If I had you here I'd mop the floor with you. What?"

He listened to Jimmy's mumbling at the other end and then broke out, "We don't want you here nor your wife either. If you came now you'd get a hot reception. You can go your own way, from now on — you sneaking, sniveling, henpecked little louse. As for that bitch Lyla —"

Mrs. Evans was coming toward him, calling out, "Henry — *stop it!*" He slammed the receiver on the hook, strode to the table and poured himself a drink. He stood swaying with it in his hand, glaring belligerently at his family.

Lizzie was unnerved. Tears were trickling down her cheeks. Bob sat scowling at the floor. "I don't like this kind of talk," he said, "in front of my wife."

"Shut up," said his father. "I don't want any lip from you." He drained his glass.

Mrs. Evans came to take the bottle away but he guarded it with his body. "No, you don't!" he said. "I'm going to have a little fun out of this — after all the expense I've been put to."

"What I can't get over," growled Bill, "is them two with a new Buick, starting out on a trip to Banff."

"Who cares what they do?" The pretty daughter made a grimace of disgust.

The plain daughter gave a snort. "Everybody'll be laughing at them. They look and act so silly together."

"I wish they'd take me with them to Banff," said Ronnie.

"You go to your bed," ordered his father, "and don't let me hear another word out of you."

He watched the little boy drag himself reluctantly from the room, then turned his tragic eyes on his wife.

"The trouble is," he said, "that you've spoilt all the children. You made a fool of Jimmy from the start because he was delicate. You've made fools of them all. You've made a fool of me. But I'm not going to put up with any more." He waved his arm derisively at the circle seated about the room. "Look at them!" he said. "What a stupid lot. Look at their faces. Look at the mates they've chosen. Not the kind of people I was brought up with. And more of them coming!" He gave a sardonic jerk of the head toward Lizzie. "More and more of them! Almighty God, I'm sick of everything." He took another drink and walked swaying but still light on his feet, up and down the room. Before he married he had knocked about the world a bit and picked up some choice profanity. This he now released as was his habit when he had too much to drink. Lizzie never had seen him like this before. She began to feel completely unnerved.

"Don't mind what he says," Mrs. Evans counseled her. "He doesn't mean a word of it."

"It's shameful the way he goes on." The pretty daughter used her lipstick, as though to fortify herself.

"What's that?" shouted Evans. "What's that about me going on?"

"I didn't say anything," she muttered, reddening.

"You'd better not. If there's any man in this city could keep his temper better than I have tonight, by God I'd like to meet him!" Another blast of profanity leaped from his trembling lips.

From the undertaker's rooms below there now rose a sound of wailing, as some mourners wept for their dead.

Lizzie got heavily to her feet. "I want to go home," she whimpered. "Ring for a taxi, Bob."

"You bet I will," he muttered, giving his father a resentful look. "And we'll not come back here in a hurry."

Mrs. Evans began to cry.

"Everybody's suffering," remarked the quiet son-in-law.

"It don't mean anything to me," said the teen-ager.

Bob had called a taxi. He now led Lizzie to the bedroom where her coat and hat were. Evans followed them to the door and, while she put on her things, treated them to some more bad language. Bob kept his back turned. As the young couple moved toward the head of the stairs Evans had an idea. He went to the disarranged supper table and found the orchids he had bought for Lyla.

"Here you are, Lizzie." He proffered the flowers with a leer. "Don't say I never gave you orchids."

"I don't want them," she screamed hysterically. "Take them away." She tottered at the head of the stairs.

Bob picked her up in his arms and carried her down. The taxi driver was waiting by the outer door. All was quiet now in the funeral parlor.

Evans followed after Bob and Lizzie, clutching the banisters with one hand, while in the other, at arm's length, he held the orchids.

"Lizzie, Lizzie," he supplicated, "do accept them, with my love and respect."

Lizzie went on crying as Bob, without a look at his father, carried her to the taxi. Evans stood in the doorway alone. The street was quiet and a fine rain was falling. The night air calmed his brain. He remembered he was caretaker of the funeral parlor. He closed the door softly and then went into the silent room, where the dead body of a woman lay in a coffin. Evans turned on the light and stood looking down on the aloof face which showed no sign of suffering. He could hear movement in the room above, and then the sound of his daughters' and their husbands' leaving.

He stood a little longer, then he noticed the orchids he still carried. He laid them on the folded hands of the dead woman. He put out the light and slowly climbed the stairs to his own apartment.

His wife was stacking the dishes in the kitchen sink. She did not look at him.

"Has everyone gone?" he asked.

"Yes."

"Kids in bed?"

"Yes."

He came close to her. "Let me help."

"I'm not going to wash dishes tonight. I'm too tired."

"I bet you are. Me too. Tired out."

She did not upbraid him. She put her large kind hand on his arm.

"Get to bed," she said, "or you won't be fit for work tomorrow."

He laid his head on her shoulder and began to cry.

[1952]

Bibliography

I

PRIMARY

NOVELS:

Possession. Toronto: Macmillan, 1923.
Delight. New York: Macmillan, 1926.
Jalna. Boston: Little Brown, 1927.
Whiteoaks of Jalna. Boston: Little Brown, 1929.
Finch's Fortune. London: Macmillan, 1931.
Lark Ascending. Boston: Little Brown, 1932.
The Thunder of New Wings. Boston: Little Brown, 1932.
The Master of Jalna. Toronto: Macmillan, 1933.
Young Renny. Toronto: Macmillan, 1935.
Whiteoak Harvest. Boston: Little Brown, 1936.
Growth of a Man. Boston: Little Brown, 1938.
Whiteoak Heritage. Boston: Little Brown, 1940.
Whiteoak Chronicles. London: Macmillan, 1940.
Wakefield's Course. Boston: Little Brown, 1941.
The Two Saplings. London: Macmillan, 1942.
The Building of Jalna. Boston: Little Brown, 1944.
Return to Jalna. Boston: Little Brown, 1946.
Mary Wakefield. Boston: Little Brown, 1949.
Renny's Daughter. Boston: Little Brown, 1951.
A Boy in the House. London: Macmillan, 1952.
Whiteoak Brothers (Jalna, 1923). Toronto: Macmillan, 1953.
Variable Winds at Jalna. Toronto: Macmillan, 1954.
Centenary at Jalna. Toronto: Macmillan, 1958.
Morning at Jalna. London: Macmillan, 1960.

PLAYS:

Low Life. A Comedy in One Act. Toronto: Macmillan, 1925.
Come True. Toronto: Macmillan, 1927.
Low Life and Other Plays. Boston: Little Brown, 1929.
The Return of the Emigrant. Boston: Little Brown, 1929.
Whiteoaks. Boston: Little Brown, 1936.

COLLECTIONS OF SHORT STORIES:

Explorers of the Dawn. New York: Alfred A. Knopf, 1922.
   Contents: "Buried Treasure," "The Jilt," "Explorers of the Dawn," "A Merry Interlude," "Freedom," "D' Ye Ken John Peel?," "Granfa," "Noblesse Oblige," "The Cobbler and His Wife," "The New Day".

The Sacred Bullock and Other Stories. Toronto: Macmillan, 1939. Illustrated by Stuart Tresilian.
   Contents: "The Sacred Bullock," "Electric Storm," "Tiny Tim," "Justice for an Aristocrat," "April Day," "The She-Gull," "The Pony That Would Not Be Ridden," "The Ninth Life," "Bob" (The manuscript of this story is entitled "The Virtues of Man Without His Vices"), "Cat's Cruise," "Peter—A Rock," "Reunion".

A Boy in the House and Other Stories. Boston: Little Brown, 1952.
   Contents: "Auntimay," "The Celebration," "Twa Kings," "The Submissive Wife," "The Broken Fan," "Patient Miss Peel," "A Word for Coffey," "The Widow Cruse," "Quartet," "A Boy in the House".

SHORT STORIES:

"The Thief of St. Loo," *Munsey's Magazine* (October, 1902), pp. 182-187.

"Son of a Miser," *Munsey's Magazine* (August, 1903), pp. 750-757.

"The Spirit of the Dance," *The Canadian Magazine* (May, 1910), pp. 39-48.

"The Years at the Spring," *MacFadden Fiction Lovers Magazine* (May, 1911), pp. 141-152.

"Canadian Ida and English Nell," *MacFadden Fiction Lovers Magazine* (June, 1911), pp. 279-289.

"Buried Treasure," *The Atlantic Monthly* (August, 1915), pp. 192-199.

"The Comrade," *The Canadian Magazine* (December, 1916), pp. 148-151.

"Romance," *The Canadian Magazine* (March, 1916), pp. 385-400. The manuscript of this story is entitled "The Cross Road."

"Explorers of the Dawn," *The Atlantic Monthly* (October, 1919), pp. 532-540.

"Freedom," *Women's Home Companion* (September, 1919), pp. 15-16.

"D'Ye Ken John Peel?," *Women's Home Companion* (November, 1919), pp. 14-15.

"Granfa," *Women's Home Companion* (February, 1922), pp. 11-12.

"A Word for Coffey," *Century* (April, 1926), pp. 746-751. Also in *Maclean's Magazine* (April, 1926), pp. 23-24, 59.

"Good Friday," *Maclean's Magazine* (October, 1927), pp. 2-5, 45, 47.

"Portrait of a Wife," *The Canadian Nation* (February, 1928), pp. 13-17, 24, 26, 28, 30. Also in *The Graphic* (December 3, 1927), pp. 426-427.

"The Cure", in Raymond Knister, ed., *Canadian Short Stories*. Toronto: Macmillan, 1928.

"She Went Abroad," *The Bystander* (April, 1930), pp. 24-29.

"Quartet," *Harper's Bazaar* (June, 1930), pp. 34-38.

"Dummy Love," *Harper's Bazaar* (April, 1932), pp. 105-106.

"Baby Girl," *London Mercury* (October, 1932), pp. 498-507.

"The Widow Cruse", *Maclean's Magazine* (December, 1932), pp. 7-9, 38-40.

"Love in the Highlands," *Harper's Bazaar* (August, 1933), pp. 30-31, 88, 94.

"The Sentimental Story of a Lady," *Good Housekeeping* (April, 1934), pp. 32-33, 35, 98.

"Tiny Tim," *Nash's Pall Mall* (June, 1934), pp. 22-25, 94-95.

"The She Gull," *The Tatler* (October, 1934).

"Peter: A Rock," *Pictorial Review* (February, 1935), pp. 12-13

"The Submissive Wife," *Harper's Bazaar* (August, 1935), pp. 28-30.

"Reunion", *Pictorial Review* (February, 1936), pp. 10-11.

"The Sale at Clough Manor," *Good Housekeeping* (August, 1936), pp. 6-9, 100-104.

"Cat's Cruise," *Nash's Pall Mall* (February, 1937), pp. 10-12. Also *Redbook* (November, 1936), pp. 11-13.

"Old Reynard in Springtime," *The Atlantic Monthly* (April, 1937), pp. 477-481.

"Pity Poor Me," *Redbook* (July, 1937). Also in *Good Housekeeping* (December, 1937).

"Ninth Life," *Ladies Home Journal* (August, 1937), pp. 26-27.

"Electric Storm," *The Atlantic Monthly* (October, 1937), pp. 440-441.

"Auntimay," *Good Housekeeping* (December, 1937), pp. 41-43.

"Mrs. Meade Savors Life," *Canadian Home Journal* (May, 1938), pp. 7-9, 38, 40-42.

"The Artists," *Good Housekeeping* (November, 1938), pp. 36-39.

"The Sacred Bullock," *London Mercury* (December, 1938), pp. 171-183. Also in *Redbook* (December, 1938), pp. 16-28.

"The Pony That Would Not Be Ridden," *Scholastic* (May, 1940), pp. 30-36.

"Pamela," *Canadian Home Journal* (December, 1940), pp. 8-9.

"Twa Kings," *Canadian Home Journal* (April, 1941), pp. 11-13, 27.

"Come Fly With Me," *The Atlantic Monthly* (March, 1944), pp. 97-100.

"Spring Song," *Canadian Home Journal* (April, 1944), pp. 5-6.

"Grandmother," in William Lyon Phelps, ed., *The Mother's Anthology*. New York: Doubleday, 1940.

"A Boy in the House," *Chatelaine* (November, 1952).

"A Fighting Chance," *Harper's Bazaar* (March, 1954).

AUTOBIOGRAPHY:

Ringing the Changes. London: Macmillan, 1957.

BIOGRAPHIES:

Portrait of a Dog. Boston: Little Brown, 1930.

Beside a Norman Tower. London: Macmillan, 1934.

The Very House. Toronto: Macmillan, 1937.

HISTORY:

Quebec: Historic Seaport. London: Macmillan, 1946.

BOOKS FOR CHILDREN:

The Song of Lambert. London: Macmillan, 1955.
Bill and Coo. Toronto: Macmillan, 1958.

POEMS:

"Hunger," *The Canadian Forum* (July, 1932), p. 382.
"Elm," *The Atlantic Monthly* (January, 1946), p. 136.

ARTICLES:

"My Scottie," *Good Housekeeping* (October, 1930), pp. 46-48.
"The Past Quarter Century," *Maclean's Magazine* (March 15, 1936), p. 38.
"My Home in the Cotsworlds," *Arts and Decoration* (January, 1937), pp. 23-27.
"All Their Sons are Heroes," *Toronto Daily Star* (February 1, 1941), p. 1.
"Guardian of Canada's Future," *Toronto Daily Star* (February 15, 1941), p. 5.
"Inside Jalna," *Wings* (November, 1944), pp. 4-7.
"My First Book," *Canadian Author and Bookman,* 28 (Spring, 1952), pp. 3-4.
"My Most Memorable Meal," *Maclean's Magazine* (October 27, 1956), p. 60.
"I Still Remember," *Maclean's Magazine,* 70 (April 27, 1957), pp. 15-17.
"My Most Memorable Christmas," *Chatelaine,* 29 (December, 1957), pp. 14-15.

OTHER PUBLISHED WORKS:

Review of Michael Sadleir's *Desolate Splendour* for *Canadian Bookman* (March, 1923), p. 70.

Introduction to George F. Nelson, ed., *Northern Lights.* New York: Doubleday, 1960.

UNPUBLISHED WORKS:

(a) PLAYS:

The Celebration (Three Acts).
Dabbling in the Dew (Three Acts).
Frontenac (Four Acts).
Lark Ascending (Four Acts).
Mary Wakefield (Four Acts).
The Mistress of Jalna. A Play based on *Mary Wakefield.*
Nothing Could be Fairer (Three Acts).
Snow in Saskatchewan (Three Acts).
The Submissive Wife (Three Acts).
Wonder Gas (One Act).

(b) SHORT STORIES:

In a Cathedral Town.
A Chariot and Four.

Chinese Checkers.
The Christmas Spirit.
A Day in the Life.
The Father.
The First Violin.
Fun With Waterai.
Guy and Gaetona.
Hermione and the Robber.
A Lover of Luxury.
The Marked Woman.
Nothing Could be Fairer.
The Parachutists.
The Regenerate.
A Slave to the Senses.
The Secret of the River.
Unwilling Patriots.
The Wheel Chair.
White Horses.

(c) POEMS:

Black Magic.
Conversation Between Two Cows.
The Drake (subtitled "Wakefield's Poem").
The Guinea Fowl.
The Lost Ewe.
The Pine Tree's Complaint.
Player of Reeds.
Queen of Mercies.
The Returned Soldier.
The Sky Was a Deep Bay.

(d) OTHER UNPUBLISHED WORKS:

Why I Like Montreal.

PAPERS AND MANUSCRIPTS:

The Atlantic Monthly Press, de la Roche Papers, Boston.

Macmillan of Canada, de la Roche Papers, Toronto.

Queen's University, Katherine Hale Papers. These papers include letters from de la Roche.

University of Toronto, de la Roche Papers. These include manuscripts, letters to and from de la Roche and the research material of Ronald Hambleton.

II

SECONDARY

"Biographical Note," *Scholastic*, 36 (May 13, 1940), p. 23.

BISSELL, Claude T. "Letters in Canada," *University of Toronto Quarterly*, XX (1951), pp. 262-272.

――――."Letters in Canada," *University of Toronto Quarterly*, XXII (1952), pp. 280-292.

――――. "Letters in Canada," *University of Toronto Quarterly*, XXIII (1953), pp. 263-270.

――――. "Letters in Canada," *University of Toronto Quarterly*, XXVIII (1958), pp. 365-368.

BREWSTER, Muriel. "Mazo de la Roche," *Toronto Star Weekly* (April 6, 1927), p. 7.

BROADUS, E. K., "Letters in Canada", *University of Toronto Quarterly*, V (1935), pp. 368-388.

BROWN, E. K. "The Whiteoaks Saga," *The Canadian Forum*, 12 (October, 1931), p. 23.

"Children As They Should Be," *Canadian Bookman* (March, 1922), p. 93.

"Civic Honors for Prize-Winning Author," *Canadian Bookman* (May, 1927), p. 151.

CORBETT, A. J. "A Farm with a Romance," *Canadian Countryman* (April 25, 1931), p. 13.

DAYMOND, D. "Tradition and Individual Freedom: The Life and Work of Mazo de la Roche, Unpublished Ph. D. thesis. Queen's University, 1972.

――――. "Mazo de la Roche's Forgotten Novel," *Journal of Canadian Fiction*, Volume III, Number 2, pp. 55-59.

――――. *"Possession:* Realism in Mazo de la Roche's First Novel," *Journal of Canadian Fiction*, Volume IV, Number 3, pp. 87-94.

――――. "Whiteoak Chronicles: A Reassessment," *Canadian Literature*, 66 (Autumn, 1975), pp. 48-62.

――――. "Nature, Culture and Love: Mazo de la Roche's *Explorers of the Dawn* and *The Thunder of New Wings," Studies in Canadian Literature*. Volume 1, Number 2, pp. 158-169.

DEACON, W. A. "Literature in Canada — In Its Centenary Year," in Bertram Brooker, ed., *Yearbook of the Arts in Canada*. Toronto: Macmillan, 1929, pp. 23-26.

――――. "The Canadian Novel Turns the Corner," *Canadian Magazine* (October, 1936), pp. 38-39.

DICKSON, Lovat. "A Fond Recollection of Mazo de la Roche," *Toronto Star* (January 15, 1972), p. 61.

DOBBS, Kildare. "Our Critic Enjoys Jalna Books...," *The Toronto Star* (January 15, 1972), p. 61.

EAYRS, Hugh. "Bookman Profiles: Mazo de la Roche," *The Canadian Bookman*, 20 (October-November, 1938), pp. 17-22.

EDGAR, Pelham. "The Cult of Primitivism," in Bertram Brooker, ed., *Yearbook of the Arts in Canada*. Toronto: Macmillan, 1929, pp. 39-42.

FELLOWS, Jo-Ann. "The 'British Connection' in the Jalna Novels of Mazo de la Roche: The Loyalist Myth Revisited," *Dalhousie Review*, 56 (Summer, 1976), pp. 283-290.

FULFORD, R. "Mazo de la Roche: Still a Mystery," *Toronto Star* (November 17, 1966), p. 42.

————. "Mazo de la Roche: A Strange Love," *Toronto Star* (April 23, 1966), p. 37.

HALE, Katherine. "Joan of the Barnyard — A Young Poetess Who Loves Chickens," *The Star Weekly* (February 7, 1914), p. 1.

————. *Toronto*. Toronto: Cassell, 1956.

HAMBLETON, Ronald. "A Portrait of Mazo de la Roche: Her Critics and Her Friends," Script for a program for the Canadian Broadcasting Company. University of Toronto, de la Roche Papers.

————. "In Memory of Mazo de la Roche," Script for the Canadian Broadcasting Company's memorial program. University of Toronto, de la Roche Papers, July 19, 1961.

————. *Mazo de la Roche of Jalna*. Toronto: General Publishing, 1966.

————. *The Secret of Jalna*. Toronto: General Publishing, 1972.

HENDRICK, George. *Mazo de la Roche*. New York: Twayne Publishers, 1970.

"The House in the Woods," *The Canadian Bookman* (August, 1923), p. 216.

KENYON, Sheila. "Jalna, Canada's Forsyte Saga," *Chatelaine* (December, 1971), pp. 26-27, 49-51.

KNISTER, Raymond. Review of *Possession* in *Border City Star* (April 14, 1923).

LAING, N. "Behind the Scenes in the Filming of Jalna," *Chatelaine* (September, 1935).

LAWRENCE, M., *The School of Femininity*. Toronto: T. Nelson, 1936.

LIVESAY, Dorothy. "The Making of Jalna: A Reminiscence," *Canadian Literature*, 23 (Winter, 1965), pp. 25-30.

————. "Exploring Jalna Country," *Globe and Mail* (December 3, 1965), p 43.

————. "Mazo de la Roche 1879-1961," in Mary Quayle Innis, ed., *The Clear Spirit*. Toronto: University of Toronto Press, 1966.

————. "Mazo Explored," *Canadian Literature*, 32 (Spring, 1967), pp. 57-59.

LOGAN, J. D. and D. G. FRENCH. *Highways of Canadian Literature*. Toronto: McClelland, 1924.

MACGILLIVRAY, J. R. "Letters in Canada," *University of Toronto Quarterly*, VI (1936), pp. 347-368.

————. "Letters in Canada," *University of Toronto Quarterly*, VIII (1938), pp. 301-312.

————. "Letters in Canada," *University of Toronto Quarterly*, IX (1939), pp. 289-301.

————. "Letters in Canada," *University of Toronto Quarterly*, X (1940), pp. 292-299.

————. "Letters in Canada," *University of Toronto Quarterly*, XI (1941), pp. 298-305.

————. "Letters in Canada," *University of Toronto Quarterly*, XII (1942), pp. 315-324.

————. "Letters in Canada," *University of Toronto Quarterly*, XIII (1944), pp. 267-274.

MACKLEM, John. "Who's Who in Canadian Literature: Mazo de la Roche," *The Canadian Bookman,* 9 (September, 1927), pp. 259-260.

MARSHALL, Douglas. "The Dread Canadian Whiteoak Disease," Review of *The Secret of Jalna* for *Books in Canada* (February, 1972), pp. 12-14.

"Mazo de la Roche," *Chatelaine* (June, 1932), p. 4.

"Mazo de la Roche at Home," *Chatelaine* (March, 1944), pp. 8-9.

McKENNA, Agnes. "CBC Plans Jalna Series," *Mississauga Times* (March 31, 1971), p. 29.

McPHERSON, Hugo. "Fiction 1940-1960," in C. F. Klinck, General Editor, *Literary History of Canada,* Volume II. Second Edition. Toronto: University of Toronto Press, 1976.

MOORE, Jocelyn. "Canadian Writers of Today: Mazo de la Roche," *The Canadian Forum,* 12 (July, 1932), pp. 380-381.

MOSS, John. *Sex and Violence in the Canadian Novel.* Toronto: McClelland and Stewart, 1977.

MUIR, Norma Phillips. "She Has Never Seen a Movie," *Toronto Star Weekly* (July 31, 1926).

NEELY, Mary Ann. "Sources of Energy in the Jalna Novels of Mazo de la Roche," Unpublished M.A. thesis. University of Western Ontario, 1970.

NORTH, Sterling. *The Writings of Mazo de la Roche.* Boston: Little Brown, 1938.

PACEY, D. *Creative Writing in Canada.* Toronto: Ryerson, (1961).

———. Introduction to New Canadian Library edition of *Delight.* Toronto: McClelland and Stewart, 1961.

———. "Fiction 1920-1940," in C. F. Klinck, General Editor, *Literary History of Canada.* Volume II. Second Edition. Toronto: University of Toronto Press, 1976.

PIERCE, Lorne. *An Outline of Canadian Literature.* Toronto: Ryerson Press, 1927.

PRINGLE, Gertrude. "Miss Mazo de la Roche: Canadian Novelist and Coming Playwright," *Saturday Night* (January 29, 1927), p. 21.

———. "World Fame to Canadian Author," *Canadian Magazine,* 67 (May, 1927), pp. 19, 31-32.

RHODENIZER, V. B. *A Handbook of Canadian Literature.* Ottawa: Graphic Publishers, 1930.

ROPER, G. S. ROSS BEHARIELL and Rupert SCHIEDER, "The Kinds of Fiction: 1880-1920," in C. F. Klinck, General Editor, *Literary History of Canada.* Volume I. Second Edition. Toronto: University of Toronto Press, 1976.

SADLEIR, Michael. Review of *Possession* for *The Canadian Bookman* (May, 1923), p. 129.

SANDWELL, B. K. "The Work of Mazo de la Roche," *Saturday Night,* 68 (November 8, 1952), p. 7.

"Silver Tea Service," *The Canadian Bookman* (June, 1927), pp. 186-187.

SNELL, J. G. "The United States at Jalna," *Canadian Literature,* 66 (Autumn, 1975), pp. 31-40.

THOMAS, Clara. *Canadian Novelists: 1920-1945.* Toronto: Longmans Green and Company, 1946, pp. 31-33.

WATTERS, R. E. "The Ever-Bearing Chronicle," *Canadian Literature,* 7 (Winter, 1961), pp. 74-76.

WEEKS, Edward. "Mazo de la Roche," *Sun Life Review* (April, 1952), pp. 3-5.

————. "My Memories of Mazo," *Varsity Graduate* (University of Toronto: Spring, 1963), pp. 46-49, 78, 80, 82, 84, 86, 88, 90, 92.

————. "Mazo de la Roche," *In Friendly Candour.* Boston: Little Brown (1959), pp. 84-97.

————. *Mazo de la Roche.* Undated pamphlet published by the Atlantic Monthly Press, Boston.

WHITE, J. F. "Mazo de la Roche," *The Canadian Forum,* VII (May, 1927), pp. 227-228.

"Wins $10,000 Prize," *The Canadian Bookman* (April, 1927), p. 115.

WUORIO, Eva-Lis. "Mazo of Jalna," *Maclean's Magazine,* 62 (February 1, 1949), pp. 19, 39-41.